ARTAGEM
GRAPHIC
LIBRARY

To Colin!
STAY IN THE LIGHT...

Max Drudge

DARKER
IN THE SUN

MAX
DOWDLE

DARKER IN THE SUN
Stories Of Daytime Horror

By Max Dowdle

Special Thanks
Morrow Dowdle
Danae Wulfe
Chad O'Brien
Mike & Jude Chewning

Published by
Artagem Graphic Library
Hillsborough, North Carolina
www.Artagem.com
First Edition, October 2018
Printed in the USA

Visit us online at **www.Artagem.com** to peruse our other offerings.

Keep Running

"Too much for you?"

Brandon sniffed, and increased his pace. "No, I'm fine," he huffed. The early morning fog spread out in wispy smears, wrapping the runners in an ethereal, springtime embrace. The sound of sneakers clapped upon the pavement, echoing down Flint Ridge Road, which resembled a slate thread weaving through the country hills. Woods and farmland dominated the landscape, and what homes that infrequently emerged from the fog were invariably dark at this hour.

"Gonna have to pick up the pace." Jess's back was straight, and she'd yet to break a sweat. She shot a smile at her fiancée. "Only three more weeks."

"Don't remind me," Brandon said with a grunt. Despite the cool air he wiped at his brow. His legs throbbed, and the final remnants of his once large belly still jiggled with every stride. "This was a mistake."

"You're the one that wanted to run Garnet River, silly." Jess still smiled.

"I just thought…would be a fun thing to do. A marathon. Together." Brandon snorted and ran harder to keep up with his lady's even pace.

"And it is. But training is a part of that. C'mon, you've come so far since November, huh?" Jess glanced back at Brandon's flushed face, still dark in the wan, pre-dawn light. "Oh, look. We've got a buddy."

Brandon turned his head and saw, at least a half-mile behind, the shape of another runner. There was nothing strange about this though, considering all the health nuts that lived out here. Two cyclists had passed them already. This was a well-known good route for exercise because so few cars drove it this early. Brandon didn't answer. It was difficult for him to talk while running. The duo took a left on Red Terry Road, completing the third mile of their run.

"Keep running, *boy-o*," Jess sang. Brandon appreciated that she took it easy on him, as they both knew she could easily leave him behind at any time.

"Wish we had…some music," Brandon grumbled and waited for the familiar retort.

"Clear head, clear mind. No electronics. Just us and the road." Jess's ponytail whipped to the side as she glanced back. "Well, and our pal back there."

Brandon looked over his shoulder again and saw that the runner had turned with them, and had gained a few dozen yards. He could just make out the slap of the runner's feet on the asphalt. With a second peek he noted that the man had a peculiar, stiff hitch to his gait. Brandon focused on his breath, and pushed on.

"I've been thinking: Brandon Goodrich has a nice ring to it, huh?" Jess said cheerily.

"What?" Brandon asked, a hint of exasperation in his voice. "I'm not taking…your last name."

"Make you a deal. You beat my time in the marathon and I become a Poirier. And if I beat you..."

"No…deal," Brandon panted.

A vehicle approached, its headlights twin glowing coronae in the fog. The sedan passed and Brandon eyed the runner behind them as the light momentarily washed over his pale form. In that brief glimpse Brandon noted that, given the chill air, the man seemed poorly dressed for a run this early, sporting no shirt, white shorts, and strangely garish socks and shoes. Were they bright red? It was hard to tell from this distance. Though warm days had already descended, the mornings were still cool, a remnant of the long, lingering winter. Unlike the mysterious shirtless runner, Brandon and Jess were wearing full windbreaker suits to guard against the occasional cold wind.

"How about we do the hyphen thing, huh?" Jess teased. "Goodrich-Poirier or Poirier-Goodrich. Alphabetic, or by age?"

Brandon frowned. "Jess…think something's weird with that guy?"

"Who? Behind us? It's a *maniac killer!*" Jess laughed, the sound clear and high in the quiet morning.

The clump-slap of the man's footwear grew louder, as he'd gained more ground behind them.

"Let's just take a break and let him…go past," Brandon said.

"Oh, no! You're not getting out of this so easy. Keep running. We'll just turn on Sheep Rock up ahead, 'kay?" Jess favored Brandon with a lilting smile. "High gear now. The boogeyman's after us!"

"Ugh, not Sheep Rock." The soles of Brandon's shoes smacked at the road as he trailed Jess, an irritating reminder of this ill-planned activity. Sheep Rock Road was the hilliest route, only reserved for the days when Jess wanted to really punish Brandon. "I don't like him back there."

"Stop being so self-conscious. We don't own the road." Jess winked at Brandon. "You're doing well. Breath in. Exhale. Keep running."

The street sign for Sheep Rock Road was fast approaching. The runners veered left and started up the first of many steep hills. The road curved westward here. At the top there was another sharp bend where it was important to look out for cars; but they knew they'd see headlights long before meeting any vehicles. Right now the road was a smooth black expanse, trees towering on either side. Brandon wheezed as he slogged up the incline behind Jess. He cast his eyes back to the crossroad and saw the figure follow them around the turn. "He's still there."

"Brandon, he's probably just using us as pacemakers. It's no big deal. Happens all the time. Good news is we just passed the four-mile mark, and I bet you didn't even notice. Do we need someone trailing us each morning to get you to run faster, boyo?" Jess rocked her head from side to side, working a kink out of her neck. "Race you to the top of the hill!" And with that, she sped up.

Brandon, beginning to feel winded, took one worried look back and saw that the runner had gained more ground on them. The pallor of the stranger's skin, and the stiffness of the man's posture, disturbed Brandon, though he still couldn't be sure why. What was even up with those ratty socks hiked up high on his calves? And they *were* red. He could see that clearly now. Brandon tried to catch a look at the runner's face, but it was still too far away to make out his features. Only the palest indigo pre-dawn was backlighting the sentinel rows of trees that flanked the road. Commanding his legs to piston harder, Brandon tore toward the top of the hill, catching up to Jess and cresting the apex alongside her.

"A tie!" Jess said, "Good job." She gave him a playful punch to the shoulder. "We should do that at Garnet River. Hold hands while crossing the finish line."

The regular clump-slap of foot on road hammered away behind the runners as they descended the hill. Sweat poured freely down Brandon's face and he wiped his forearm across his eyes. "Hnh. Jess, let's turn down Clark…at the bottom here."

"Sure. You okay?"

"Yeah…just want to turn." Brandon let the downslope do the hard work while he focused on his balance. Every muscle burned after the hill sprint and he was ready to quit. *But* there was still that runner behind them.

Clark Road appeared and the runners took another left. Clark was a darker road than Sheep Rock because of the low pine trees that speared alongside the cut creating a tunnel of needled foliage. The road reflectors picked up fragments of light, creating a trail of dotted lines that led off into the foggy haze. They were less than a quarter mile down the road when Brandon looked back and saw the pallid figure tear through the grass at the side of the road, shaving off some of the distance between them. "Dammit!" Brandon spat between breaths.

"Okay, you're right," Jess admitted. "It *is* a little weird. There's all this space out here and he's still so close?" Jess's brows momentarily knitted tight.

The mist had largely cleared as the morning started to warm up. Ahead of them the darkened shapes of a family of deer bounded across the road only to disappear into the trees. A deep rumble resonated behind the runners. Brandon looked beyond the stranger and saw a logging truck turn on to Clark Road. The high beams of the truck briefly silhouetted the erratic, bouncing form of the runner, and then the truck blazed by, leaving the runners in the dim foggy light once again as the crimson taillights vanished around a turn.

Brandon panted and clenched his fists. "Wish I had…my phone. But, no. No, electronics…"

"Don't put this on me." Jess's voice had gone sour. "You always do *that*."

The clump-slap grew louder. The runner was only a few hundred yards behind them now. "I'm going to yell something…at him," Brandon said.

"What?" Jess had finally broken a sweat. The smile she had worn earlier had left her face, yet she still showed no signs of tiring. "Don't. Don't say anything, Brandon."

"Just something…friendly." He tried a smile on of his own, but it didn't take. Before Jess could protest he wheeled around and casually yelled, "Nice morning for a run, man!"

The runner did not answer.

"Hey! I said…nice morning for a run!" Brandon's voice sounded hoarse and weak within the tunnel of trees. "Jess?" he said thinly.

"Maybe he's wearing headphones," said Jess, though the look in her eyes said she didn't really believe it. She pivoted at the waist, raised an arm to make a big wave, back and forth, back and forth. "How you doin' back there?"

Brandon watched the runner for some sign of acknowledgement. The runner's focused pace persisted, matching Jess and Brandon's own, but there was no reaction.

"I don't like this, Brandon." Jess chewed at her lip. Her hand grasped Brandon's upper-arm, throwing off his stride. "What do we do?"

The muscles in Brandon's legs hummed with pain. His lungs burned, and the beginning of a stitch stabbed at his side. Even his teeth ached as he ground them together. He shook his head.

Jess wrinkled her chin. "Clark ends right up here. We can make a left on Holman Mill and that takes us home. But it'll be almost two more miles."

"I…I can't make it." Brandon shook his head furiously, freeing a spray of sweat droplets to patter onto his shoulders. He tore the windbreaker off his sodden back and yanked the sleeves into a knot about his middle. The skin of his neck had turned to cold gooseflesh. The clump-slap echoed, closer. The runner was speeding up. "And I don't want to…lead him back…to our house."

"Then *where*?" Jess snatched glances backward with every other step. The runners were drawing up on the end of Clark Road.

"Go right." A harsh wheeze had worked its way into Brandon's breathing. "The gas station…up Holman Mill. Maybe…a farmhouse before then." He pulled at Jess's arm as they careened out onto the wider, but no more busy, Holman Mill Road. The unvarying beat of the stranger's feet followed them around the turn.

"More flat here. Think you can go faster?" The wrinkles caused by a frown had taken up permanent residence on Jess's forehead.

Brandon's mouth hung open as he gasped great mouthfuls of air. He nodded and commanded his legs to pump harder, every strike of shoe on asphalt a concussive hammer-blow propelling him forward. They began to pull away from the runner as the first overtures of pale pink light suffused the soft dome of the sky. Wind whipped at Brandon's face, sticking early spring gnats to his sweat-slicked skin. The ordered and quickened clump-slap had grown loud again as well. Despite their sprinting the man gained ground significantly on the flat road. A little red hatchback approached, swinging into the opposite lane to give the runners a wide berth. Brandon waved at the car; panic animating his furiously gesticulating arm. The car sped by without even a tap to the brakes. Brandon tracked the path of the headlights as they lit on the stranger behind them. Dread chilled his blood, leaving his skin numb. "Did you see that?"

"Oh, God! His face…what's wrong with it, Brandon?" Tears slipped from Jess's fear-round eyes and disappeared in the sweat beaded on her cheeks.

"I…I don't know." Brandon began to mumble to himself; unable to get the image of the tortured rictus he'd just seen out of his head. "Why…why? What the fuck?!"

"Keep running," Jess said, falling back into coaching mode. "Just keep running."

The gradually lightening masses of trees on either side of Holman Mill gave way to a freshly plowed, fecund field. Gently sloping hills swelled to the left all the way to the horizon. Atop one of these stood a Dutch Colonial style farmhouse with a gambrel roof. Lights burned in nearly every window. The orange glow stood out like a warm heart amongst the cool lavenders and blues of early dawn.

"There!" Jess yelled.

"I see it." Brandon was nearly breathless now. He knew there wasn't much run left in him.

At the top of the next hill a mailbox indicated the place where a little dirt driveway led off the road to wend its long way up to the farmhouse. Jess pulled ahead of Brandon and turned down the driveway, her feet kicking up small puffs of powder. "Come on!"

As Brandon followed his fiancée he allowed one last hopeful idea that they'd been absurdly paranoid this entire time, expecting that he'd look back and see the runner blaze by the driveway on his own way to who knew where. But all doubt was finally removed. The stranger turned with them as well, red shoes, coupled with red socks, pounding at the dusty earth. There could no longer be any doubt that this man was purposefully trailing them. The stitch in Brandon's side had become a deep throb, and he fought to keep himself on the drive. The meandering duel snake of wheel ruts, shored up in places with gravel, which crunched as the runners sped toward the farmhouse, was rapidly growing shorter. Brandon willfully let go of all pain and discomfort that he felt, running as fast as he could in order to keep up with Jess. They hurtled, thundering up the porch steps and beat at the heavy front door.

"Help! Let us in!" cried Brandon.

Jess was sobbing. "He's after us!"

Brandon hazarded a look back and saw that the runner was quickly closing the distance, already breezing past the blue pickup parked halfway down the long drive.

The handle of the front door jiggled and the door swung inward on a tall, broad-shouldered man in a bathrobe holding a half-filled bowl of cereal. His long face wore a look of puzzled annoyance. Brandon pushed at Jess, forcing the man aside and spilling his breakfast on the hardwood floor. Mid-protest the man looked down his driveway and saw the nearing figure. The peculiarity of gait and single-minded nature of the man's approach was enough to cause the homeowner to slam the door and bolt it. The rest of the family, a wife and three little girls, had joined Jess and Brandon in the foyer by now with a burble of questions.

"Who the hell are they?" his wife demanded, gesturing at the panting duo with her half-filled mug of coffee. Any answer that might have been forthcoming was quickly cut short by the first heavy footstep stabbing at the porch stairs, and a powerful *whump* against the front door.

The man lunged at the door and fumbled at the lock, some instinct instructing him to check the deadbolt latch.

The three little girls all wore matching nightgowns in varying shades of pink and purple. They stood behind their mother in bare feet, well away from the slash of milk on the floor. "Daddy, what's happening?" the oldest girl said. She looked to be six or seven, with her long corn silk hair gathered into an unruly ponytail.

"Nothing, honey." The man turned and regarded his wife as another heavy *thump* shook the paneled door. "Darla, get your phone. Call the police. He pointed a finger at Brandon and Jess as he bounded up the stairs leading off the foyer, and shouted, "You two, stay put!"

Darla shooed her daughters into a formal dining room to the side as she began digging in her purse on the hallway table. "Stay in there. Elsie, keep your sisters in there."

There was frantic shuffling on the front porch, feet stamping at the wooden boards outside, almost in *frustration*. The entire house fell silent, save for Brandon's labored breathing. Then came a full and concussive thump to the front door. This was followed by another, and another. The girls screamed in the dining room. Darla pawed through her purse. Her husband came down the stairs by twos, shotgun in hand.

"Whoever that is out there you can go on 'n fuck off right now!" Jess's fingers dug into Brandon's shoulder as they edged into the dining room, and shrank into the corner.

"I can't find it!" Darla shouted. The pounding on the door was sharp and insistent. Each blow threatened to splinter the wood at any moment.

One of the little girls approached the muslin curtain of a low window off the side of the dining room, reaching to draw it back and see the visitor on their porch.

"Stop! Don't touch it!" Brandon said in a harsh whisper.

The girl twitched the curtain aside.

Though it was still dim, the wan light described the form enough to make Brandon's blood grow cold. Through the warped farmhouse glass he could finally see what had confused him so much about the man's shoes and socks. His mind turned in on itself, not willing to acknowledge what his eyes lingered on.

There *were* no shoes.

Blood pooled on the worn floorboards of the porch, slick under the flexing, pulsing remnants of the man's toes. What had once been feet were now tattered shreds of road-bitten flesh, beaten to a pulp under the unrelenting slap against the punishing asphalt. Splinters of fractured bone poked through the tops of the feet, and great fissures of raw, weeping meat ran the lengths of the calves as the runner hurled himself at the door once again.

"Daddy!" the little girl shrieked as she released the curtain and began to cry. "Make him go away!"

Numbness slithered down Brandon's back. "Jess," he whispered. "Jess are you with me?"

Jess snuffled, and nodded into Brandon's neck, gripping his arm with her nails.

"Here! Here it is!" Darla yelled.

The hollow blows to the front door continued, punctuated by the sharp ratchet of a shotgun being racked. The screams of the little girls had merged and melded into a high warble.

Brandon put an arm around Jess and guided her into the kitchen at the back of the house. "Come on," he implored as he shuffled past the full breakfast table, and pressed the light switch to extinguish the kitchen lights.

"Where are we going?" Jess looked up with tear-rimmed eyes.

Darla frantically shouted their home address into her phone.

"Last warning!" her husband barked at the intruder.

"We have to go," Brandon whispered. He led Jess to the backdoor and turned the knob quietly.

"We can't just leave them, Brandon. *We led him here.*" She whipped around at the crack-snap of wood breaking.

A shotgun blast lit up the foyer.

Brandon pushed Jess roughly, knocking the screen door aside. "Go! Go!" He heard the sounds of a brawl, feet clomping on the wooden floor. The screams of the parents joined those of their children. Another explosive bang from the shotgun discharged as Brandon and Jess darted into the damp grass of the backyard. The sun hovered bright and full above the tree line. Brandon looked back at the house and briefly saw the oldest girl scrambling toward the screen door, hand feeling for the handle, before being wrenched into the dark interior of the house. There followed what sounded to Brandon's ears like bones breaking.

Then, silence.

That insistent *swish* of windbreaker material filled the air. The familiar rhythm of running took over, as the runners' feet thumped at the earth. Brandon took comfort in that sound, knowing that every step was a step away. He faced nowhere but forward as they fled across the rear field. "Keep running, Jess," he said through gritted teeth. "Keep running."

Come Away, O Human Child!

Amos lifted his nose to the breeze, catching the fetid waft from the overgrown path, which was something akin to spoiled meat. He knew the smell well, for every time the creature had visited, the sour reek had filled in its wake. Amos looked to the low space in the trees, carved out by the secret traffic of their kind; the muddied trail cut was stippled with a collection of busy hoof prints, only broken by the impressions left by Sadie's small feet, drawn as they'd been through the still soft mire.

These were the hinterlands of Lancaster county, woods that Amos had never ventured into, nor his father, nor his father's father. They were forbidden woods that held secrets never given over to the likes of man, not even to the Plain Folk.

Secret shames hidden here by God.

It was a humid evening, abuzz with cicada song in the tall grass of the field leading up to the forest. The sweat dripped freely from under Amos's straw hat, rolling down his grave cheeks to collect in the wiry ginger curls of his beard. His body was solid from years of his good work, but the chase was beginning to tell on him. It had been nearly a full day since he'd kissed his Sadie on the forehead and bid her goodnight. Nearly a full day since the moldering demon had shouldered his daughter and fled the Beiler homestead, leaving Amos's wife Hannah laid out on the kitchen floor with a twisted neck. He regretted he'd had no time to spare for her.

Though Amos knew he was right in the bosom of the Lord, the thoughts of Hannah still played at his emotion, and his voice quavered as he spoke to the forest before him. "Father, I pray for those who suffer violence and injustice. I pray—that Your righteousness will reign, and that You will lead me to my Sadie. I must also ask for the bounty of Your grace, to deliver he that did what he did to my Hannah." Amos wiped the sweat of his bare upper lip against his sleeve and ducked forward, fitting his large frame into the small gap in the trees. He patted the rasp knife at his hip, deriving some power from its walnut burl handle. "In Jesus's name, stay my hand, for it seeks the blood."

The darkening shelter of the forest was a measure cooler than the fields and dusty roads he'd traveled that day, and he paused to catch his breath. Always he'd kept an eye primed for the sight of the stabbed hoof marks, or any sign of where Sadie might have been dragged. What must the little one be thinking, crying for her father as the *cursed* hauled her back to its hidden home? Out of all the trials she'd undergone, the poking and prodding at the hands of the Englisher, Dr. Jameson, at the Center for Special Children in Bridgeport being the first that came to mind, none of that could have been as bad as what she was going through now. Amos had worried that this day would come, for Sadie had always been *touched*, and children who were touched were known to go missing from the village periphery. Many score times he'd caught sight of the creature, hunched in shadow over Sadie's bed in the years since she'd been born, only for the nightmare to evade him when approached with candlelight.

The hoof prints continued into the dark interior, green leaves overlaid on black, seething with every gust of wind. Amos willed himself on, drawing the armor of the Lord over his worry.

Fearless, certain, and hot-blooded.

These were the traits for which man and woman knew him, but there was a time he'd been branded a coward. Amos had been brought up in the usual manner, working alongside Father in the family butchery. Beiler and Sons was a storied establishment begun by his grandfather, and it was only natural for he and his older brother Samuel to continue the tradition. Those days were long ago, but Amos could still remember Father taking the time to teach him how to do his job right: stowing materials in their proper places, sharpening a knife without catching up its surface, and of course, mopping the floor clean of accumulated blood. Amos had taken to his chores with glee but it was Samuel, five years older and bristling with the responsibilities of a firstborn, who got all the attention. Amos was left as an afterthought, and he'd grown to despair because of it, knowing no way to gain Father's notice other than willful tantrums.

The boys sprouted taller and Samuel continued to shine in Father's eye as Amos was branded "difficult." Weightier tasks were heaped on Samuel, but no matter how many times Father insisted Samuel take up the slaughter, it was the one job that he never had the mettle for. This was a niche Amos found he could corner. When he was nine Father reluctantly handed him the knife, showed him just where to slice so the animal would suffer the least, and turned him loose. It was not in joy for killing that Amos found pleasure; it was for the attention of Father that he honed his craft. Guiltily he found he'd also taken delight in Samuel's relegation to second best in *something*.

As Amos matured, the tantrums peppering his childhood gave way to a writhing sea of adolescent waywardness. And so with this, Amos began to shirk the duties he'd grown so adept at. The blossoming radiance of teenage years spurred him, sparking his attention to the distracting blaze of temptations, and finally to question life inside the insular community. He would watch motorcycles pass on the highway, yearning to grip the handlebars of such a powerful machine himself. The simple toss of blond hair over the pale nape of a bare-shouldered Englisher girl on her way home from the high school nearly brought him to his knees on more than one occasion. He'd wanted to stay in school but after eighth grade Father had insisted he take up full time at Beiler and Sons. Ever after, defiance had become his only means of interaction with the family. There'd been a whole world to discover out there, a place he'd been denied, trapped by the circumstances of birth. And so he abandoned those circumstances by leaving home.

Those days belonged to the past, a time that no longer mattered. What had been so important at sixteen seemed childish when compared to what Amos wrestled with now. His only concern was for Sadie, who at this moment was likely suffering under the clutch of the pestilence that had breached their quiet home. He wheeled in the darkened interior of the forest, seeking the signs of passage. Softened voices, just beyond the threshold of understanding, whispered below the shift of the leaves. Amos felt surrounded, cut off from the simple life he knew so well. This was a place of severing, a place where the muzzling effect of nature could insulate one from the bustle of life. Sharp slants of sunlight broke the canopy above, reminding him that God's glory reached everywhere, even this dim heart of the wood. Amos blinked back a stinging droplet of sweat and spied a clutch of snapped twigs across the clearing. He pushed the branches aside and stepped into the closeness of the forest deep. The sounds, so akin to human voices, continued to whisper their nonsense around him. If he were truly entering the homeland of these contemptible creatures, they were still too intimidated by his presence to show themselves fully.

"Get thee away!" he boomed, cutting the horrid voices to silence.

The memories of his time away from home floated about his mind like gnats on a festering wound. The drinks, the cars, the women, the nights, all bit at him, reminding him that there were other worlds out there; worlds within worlds, and even all that he'd seen was nothing when compared to the reckoning of God. When Amos had returned to the butchery, poor and prodigal, Father had simply nodded, handed over the knife and sent him to slaughter, as if the year he'd been gone hadn't even happened. Once the cows were bled Father had set down beside him and said, "Fear God and love work." Amos had branded those words on his heart and taken great pleasure in doing both every day since; so it was with fury that he responded when God or work were trampled upon, even a little bit.

Once, prideful Ephram Hostetler had accused Amos of lightening his signature panhaus with too much cornmeal. Amos had burned and spat, his face red with indignation. It was not but the soothing hand of Hannah that kept Amos from bringing his anger to bear on Ephram's body that day. As it were, Amos had made a mess of his work that afternoon, his knife ruining a freshly opened sow without focus, burdened under frustration as he'd been. The badly carved pig was an offence to Amos's work ethic and after settling onto one knee to ask for guidance, he'd placed the carcass into his largest pot, and cooked it until nothing but a gelatinous soup remained. The entire pig had been rendered down into panhaus, with nary a grain of cornmeal in it. There was enough to serve slices to every customer for the rest of that week, a sufficient insurance against any ill mouthing from Hostetler.

The withered glow of the setting sun struggled to keep the forest lit. Amos brushed the clinging branches away from his face in frustration as he forged ahead with nothing but the faint, sickening odor as a guide. The chase was telling on him; the exertions knocking his heart around in his chest like a heifer in a squeeze chute. His ears were pricked for any cry from Sadie, but there was no sound in the forest, save for the leaves set to rustling in the wind. Twilight retreated quickly as if frightened by the very same creatures Amos hunted. Before long the night hastened upon the wood, bringing with it a full, bulbous moon casting its silver about. Amos sought out places to step amongst the twisting roots of trees and curls of bramble on the forest floor. He was just beginning to wonder if he'd lost the path when he heard the unmistakable sound of a brook beneath his footfalls.

Amos picked up his feet and sought out the beckoning song of the water, aware for the first time of just how thirsty he was. The shallow stream cut through a clearing, sparkling between its banks with all the wealth and invite of a bag of coins. Amos dropped to his knees and knocked his hat from his head before dipping his face into the cold ecstasy. Calmness was returning to him and he sat up, taking in great gulps of air. Before lowering his face again to drink he thought better and cupped his hands, bringing the water to his lips, rather than drinking "like an unclean beast," as Father had once said. The fire was cooling for the moment, leaving Amos clever-minded.

Hannah had ever been the only person that could tame Amos. Her soft hand resting on the back of his calloused knuckle had unerringly been a salve to quiet boiling temper or strident timbre. Brought together by God Himself, like water quenching fire, they committed to matrimony and took their place within the community. As was expected, Amos grew his beard and Hannah bore them a child, pink and plump and named Sadie for Amos's mother. It was not even a full day after she was born though that Amos first spied the shadow hunched over her crib, withered spine curving jaggedly downward as the creature inspected the sleeping child. The gloom of the close nursery, dark in the witching hour, had mostly hidden the face of the beast when it had turned, hackles raising at the creak beneath Amos's bare foot. The bulge and pucker of its face, a parody of human features rucked up into wrinkled nests surrounding boiled-egg eyes, could never be unseen. A swift clatter, and then scrape of claws and hooves, and it had disappeared over the open sill, fleeing in a disjointed, loping stride through the forest verge, leaving the stench of decaying meat in its place. Amos hadn't dared to tell Hannah, nor anyone else in the community. There were tales of the strange and ungodly, living their unholy lives out beyond the copse of wild Choke Cherry trees, and Amos did not wish to add to the stories. But the creature had returned. Several times within Sadie's first year Amos had smelt the telltale odor, pervasive enough as it was to cut through the rank cloud generated by their livestock. And several times Amos had chased it away.

That damned smell. It hovered around Amos's nostrils as he laid back, belly full of creek water. There was a hint of something metallic in the stream, like water left in the kettle too long, and it bothered the back of his throat. Amos wished to stand, to follow the tributary and rescue his Sadie but neither bone nor muscle would heed him. His heavy eyelids fell, drawing the darkness of the night closer over him.

The insistent dawn greeting of a Mourning Dove woke Amos. He started and shuffled backward, trying to gain his feet. The forest was unfamiliar, etched in soft-edged shades by his groggy eyes. Whip tendrils of mist floated above the creek and snaked between the trees. Amos, sore and stiff from his slumber on the uneven ground, wiped at the mud on his face, freeing clumps clinging to his beard. He knelt to take up his straw hat and stopped. Scores of distinctive hoof prints were corralled in a vague circle around the patch of ground he'd slept upon. Each was no bigger than a deer print, but there were hundreds of them. He experienced a peculiar emotion, like a plumb bob of dread in a pool of self-assurance. He was going the right way. He felt that the Lord had led him here to the creek, and that he would soon see his Sadie. Though caution was the better tack, for he did not know if the multitude of tracks spoke to simply one active creature, or a great many. He dusted the dirt from his trousers and set his hand on the knife handle. "Lord, see me through to the other side."

There was renewed vigor in Amos's step as he set off upstream, fretting, for he had no idea how much time he'd lost, though he felt close. The odor had not dissipated, for it gripped the creek banks tenaciously. If the Lord saw fit, Sadie would be intact and without a spell on her. Amos worried at his lip with his teeth, remembering the first time little Sadie had fallen prey to one of her fits, five years old and sinking to the floor of the butchery. Her legs kicked out in spasm, overturning the slop bucket and spilling the offal across the bricks. Amos had taken her small body, taut like a wooden doll, and rolled her on her side. The closest object at hand was a scimitar knife, the handle of which he pressed to her lips, gently forcing it between her baby teeth as her blue eyes rolled back into her skull. Amos had soothed her in between frantic shouts for Hannah, bracing her against the floor with his knee as the shudders subsided.

Touched.

The creature had touched her. That was Amos's first thought when Sadie had begun to shake and shiver. Thereafter Amos's heart had twisted every time he'd seen Sadie slide off the edge of a chair or stumble into a bale of hay in the barn, for she was Amos and Hannah's only child.

While Samuel had managed to coax quite a brood from his fine-boned wife, hale Hannah had been barren after Sadie's birth, and this only depressed Amos further. The old cloud of Samuel's superiority began to spread once again, despite his distant location on the other side of the community, where he had involved himself in a prosperous dairy business, and a lucrative hobby of bridle making.

Samuel was not only successful in the ways of man, but he was favored in the eyes of God, for about the time of his fifth born he had ascended to the rank of district Bishop.

It was down to Bishop Sam to decide which issues to put to vote in the church, and what shape *Ordnung*, the guidelines for community living, would take. Outside of church Amos ignored his brother and his newly found station, and the brothers grew further apart than ever. There were never two different men made by the hands of the Lord. Bishop Sam was short and gaunt, grown gray like a withered hay reed, and in contrast Amos was a great bull of a man, iron with muscle through every inch of his six and a half foot frame. But it was Sam who wielded the power, sitting quiet in the corner of church every other Sunday, tucked into the hard pew like a forgotten handkerchief, until the moment he saw fit to address the gathered. Sam not only helped fashion *Ordnung*, discussing with the other elders everything from the proper width of hatbands to the particular shade of gray their horse-drawn buggies should be painted, he also meted out *Meidung*, the practice of excommunication. Whether you were an accused murderer or you were allowing the wicked snake of electric wiring into your home, you were the same in the eyes of Bishop Sam. Those who broke *Ordnung*, no matter how petty the offense, had the potential to be shunned, lest they repent and beg the mercy of the church. Amos knew too well that Bishop Sam looked upon all men the same, even those tied to him by blood.

A full year after Sadie's first spell, Amos's neighbor Jesse Stoltzfus had first suggested Amos take her to the Center for Special Children in Bridgeport. Bishop Sam had appeared on Amos's porch that rainy morning of departure with two elders flanking him. Sam stroked his thin beard and cast his hard eyes up at Amos in disdain, as if to level indictment on his younger brother's true nature: that bothersome tendency to seek answers outside the community when problems arose. Amos had stepped around the Bishop's retinue, Sadie's small hand in his, and begun hitching his horse for journey all the same.

Though Dr. Jameson had been recommended, he was an outsider, and Amos had been wary. His brow had nearly worried a hole in his own hat on the long trek to the clinic, but in the end what Amos believed was best for his daughter had won out over brother, and over community. They'd sat long in the brightly painted waiting room where the garish clowns on the walls had reminded Amos of the time he'd visited a carnival during his year of waywardness. Sadie had played with toys in the corner, something Amos shouldn't have allowed her to do, but his will to discipline had been worn down by the little girl's plight. Eventually she'd tired of the toys and brought Amos a stack of books to be read to her.

When they were finally admitted, Amos's fears turned out to be unfounded, as Dr. Jameson was kindly with Sadie. He was seemingly familiar with her affliction, which he'd labeled a seizure disorder. Amos had wondered how many other touched children had been brought to the Englisher, and had it made a difference? Dr. Jameson had prescribed medication, another thing Amos should have refused on account of its prohibition by *Ordnung*, but they'd already stepped out of bounds so much, why not go the whole hog?

Since the initial visit they had returned on every six-month mark for checkups. Sadie had bounced giddily in the seat of the buggy, actually looking forward to the trips with her father. But it wasn't the doctor visit that made her happy, it was the waiting room. Amos could see that his daughter had inherited all of his truculence, and that his lack of correction with the Englisher books might be a problem in the future; just the same he could not deny her something that brought her so much happiness.

There was one large book of children's poetry that had quickly become her favorite; the rhyming verses a refrain on every visit. Mother Goose, Lewis Carroll and W. B. Yeats. Amos had recited the lines so often he remembered some of the latter by heart. "*In pools among the rushes, that scarce could bathe a star, we seek for slumbering trout and whispering in their ears. Give them unquiet dreams; leaning softly out from ferns that drop their tears over the young streams. Come away, O human child! To the waters and the wild with a faery, hand in hand, for the worlds' more full of weeping than you can understand.*"

Whether it was sweat or tears that wet his cheek Amos no longer knew. He realized he'd been speaking aloud, and when he drew quiet he became aware of the soft voices of the creatures speaking their damned tongue into the winds around him. The metallic odor of the creek, combined with the reek of the creatures, had grown suffocating after the fog had burned off. Amos stared at the water, which was now slow and syrupy with rust-colored runoff, bringing to mind the sluicing wash of blood on the slaughter floor. The creek was narrowing and the vegetation becoming sporadic on either side. Stumpy, decrepit plants vied for nutrients in the ashen soil, twisted out of their natural shape by weathered perseverance. Amos clutched his handkerchief to his face, breathing hotly into it as he began to note the makeshift structures erected under the trees to either side of the fetid creek. The one closest to him was comprised of scavenged corrugated siding resting atop an arrangement of rust-eaten car doors. He squinted in the day's growing brightness, inspecting the shadowed hovels for any movement, but he was alone. His eyes returned to the path ahead and the tracks beneath his booted feet. The prints continued north, bending with the kink in the befouled creek.

Though there was no overt presence in evidence, Amos could feel the eyes all around him, intent to follow his every movement. Here, Amos was the outsider, and he knew it keenly. Ever since Bishop Sam had handed the shunning down for the disobedience of seeking outside aid, binding it about his own brother like the finely crafted bridles he was known for, Amos and his family had been turned to outsiders by friend and neighbor alike. But amongst the ruins of this deformed society, Amos was now truly an alien.

The fresh scar of the rust-caked creek wormed its way between three of the pitiful huts. Rotted trees parted on either side as he followed the stream and then, all at once he saw her. Sadie was standing there with her back to Amos, white and pure in her nightgown, lit by the ever-loving sunlight of God Himself. The little girl raised her head and swayed, reaching out to steady herself on a large mottled rock next to her.

"Sadie! My darling Sadie," Amos shouted as he ran forward. He was familiar with the slow, hypnotic movement that was a precursor to her seizures. Sadie did not react to the sound of her father's voice; instead the object that Amos had mistaken for a rock *unfolded itself and turned*. It was the creature, bare and complete in the sunlit Creation around it. Amos stopped a few paces away, searching himself for understanding. His eyes could not settle on any one facet of the abomination. The abhorrent nature of the being was such that Amos dared not accept its reality. The malformed lip, a twisted flap of ruddy flesh, trembled as the creature regarded Amos.

Gathering himself, Amos focused on his daughter, trying to reach her through the fugue. "Sadie dear, come away. Come to Papa."

The creature's clawed hand stirred and then lifted in a languid, jerking motion. It threaded its grotesque fingers into Sadie's small hand as it continued to stare at Amos. A boil-crowded lip quivered and the damned being whispered one, human word, "No."

Amos found he could do nothing other than force himself to address the loathsome beast. "What are you?" His hand played at the button clasp on his knife sheath. He questioned the Lord, deep in his heart, for the best action.

The creature spoke in a rasping echo that wouldn't quite settle in Amos's ears. "Go from this place—you are not welcome."

Undeterred, Amos took a step forward, an uncovering of temper committing him to course, and drawing the keen edge of his knife. His voice, though trembling, still held solid authority. "You will let her go, demon!"

The puckered face of the creature contorted into something resembling a smile as it wrapped a deformed arm about Sadie's waist. Sadie's sweating face lolled back; her eyes were closed and her mouth parted in ignorance of her situation. "I am no demon, sir," the creature said slowly, as if having difficulty forming each word. "And you are no saint. We two—are fathers both. And this is *my* daughter."

The rage mounting within Amos broke forth and he lunged explosively, slamming his considerable body into the terror and toppling end over end into the rusty creek. Sadie was flung to the side and her thin nightgown tore with a loud *rip*. The garment was transformed into a long shred of cloth still snagged in the scrabbling creature's claws. Amos closed a large hand onto the leathery neck of the monster and began to squeeze, sending its milky, yellowish eyes rolling round in dark sockets. "You lie. You...agent of Hell," he managed between hard breaths. "Why do you speak such?" To his left he could hear that Sadie had come around and she was whimpering at the sight of the violence.

"I...it is true," the creature gasped, struggling in the shallow, red water. Amos increased the pressure. "You must...believe me. My crime...was to wish for a better life...for my daughter."

"No!" Amos shouted, wrestling his fingers tighter around the neck as he tried to make sense of what he was hearing. "You lie. I will wring every drop of truth from you!"

"No, sir. I traded them...our children are born normal, before they become...like this." The creature patted a limp claw against its own withered, blemished chest as its voice oozed out in a labored growl. "Your daughter…*is dead*. So, I took…mine back. Do with me as you will, but know this: she is not born of you—"

The knife plunged into the creature's abdomen seemingly of its own will, seeking to cleave these lies from God's earth. Amos's hand was merely the power behind the questing nature of the blade. The familiar hotness of the blood on his skin was welcome, for it doused the blazing forge inside him. The creature's deceitful tongue died off, imprisoned between its deformed jaws.

Amos stood, his chest heaving with effort and relief as he looked down on the gutted shell of the horror; its dark essence mingled with the sludge in the stinking creek.

He turned to find Sadie.

The little girl was cowering near the pitted wall of the creature's hut. "Darling," Amos said softly. He wiped at his hand, trying to clean the tar-like blood from it. "Sadie dear, come to Papa."

The little girl looked up through her mess of tangled hair, regarding Amos with yellow-tinged eyes. Her bare body, what was previously hidden by the nightgown, was covered in a wheal of ripe boils taking hold of her skin and beginning to contort and discolor it. Amos pulled the struggling little girl close and she slapped weakly at his wrist. Seeing the bold enmity and horror on her face rived his heart. Amos tried to hold her against him, to will comfort into the husk of his daughter, but the spark of what was once Sadie was now gone. He could see that she recognized him no longer, for she was not truly of this world. This notion settled into him now as a new, solid conviction.

Amos's lip trembled and the tears flowed hot from his eyes. His hand only briefly faltered in its course, and then he tightened his grip to set the tip of the knife just left of her breastbone.

"There can be no God for me, while a thing such as you still exists."

The Best Of Intentions

"Today I will do everything right."

This is the morning mantra I say to the mirror now. Actually those six words have become a refrain bookending every decision since David's death last week. I stare into my own sleepy and tear-reddened eyes for one more moment before giving into the tyranny of contacts. I run a bit of pomade through my still damp hair, and feel at my sandpapery face. A memory comes – that of David's chapped chin after our first time kissing, and the sound of his laughter as he stroked my cheek. Plenty more tears are still in supply, but I swirl up some cream and focus on the razor. Just enough time for a shave before I have to brave the highway. The shave is quick, and with only minimal accidental bloodletting. The aftershave sting feels good, and wakes me up more than my coffee. Like a bolt I remember that I will have to face David's mother and father at the funeral, where they'll bring the full burden of blame along with them. The old me would have skipped such a potentially confrontational occasion, but not now. No longer. I give myself one more look in the mirror, straightening hairs and wiping away a missed dollop of shaving cream from my earlobe. "Today I will do everything right."

Then I'm in the Audi listening to Soft Cell's "Tainted Love," and weaving between idiots. I'm late. A bolus of anxiety and irritation has settled into my gut. David always said he'd wanted to be cremated, but here are the parents, burying his dear body in a hole in the family plot. David wasn't even particularly religious anymore, and yet I'm sure they'll be having as high a church service as they can muster. I resist the urge to lay on the horn at a young mother with three brats in the back of her minivan, and take a deep breath. "Today I will do everything right." I adjust the AC, and try to ignore the sweat already accumulating inside my suit.

The traffic is mercifully starting to thin out. As I reach to turn up the music my eyes happen upon Starkweather – the figurine of a white horse wearing a monocle and black tuxedo that dangles from my key ring. The horse is smiling and raising an eyebrow in a decidedly devilish fashion. Starkweather is by far the kitschiest thing I own. David had surprised me with the stupid trinket from the Greymantle hotel gift shop in the Blue Ridge Mountains two years ago, setting it on my pillow while I'd been in the bathroom. When I came out he'd neighed, "Good evening, Sir Michael," in the silliest horse voice he could come up with. Starkweather had been named for the dour concierge of the hotel, and it fit perfectly. David had always had the quickest and wittiest sense of humor. The memory brought forth a smile. God, how I miss that crazy man. Of all things, I just happened to find Starkweather in my kitchen catchall drawer yesterday. That's where I must have stuck him when David and I had parted ways; but now he's back on my keys, and I don't think I want to take him off again. Starkweather grins his feisty horse grin, happy to be back in play. I pull into the church parking lot, very late.

Over the course of ten minutes the funeral spirals into a slow disaster. I try to be as quiet as possible as I slip into a back pew with my program. The simple oak casket is up front, with a tasteful arrangement of carnations, mums, snapdragons and Monte Casino atop it. I'm noticed by one of the grandmothers (I forget which palsied old lady is which), and the atmosphere almost immediately shifts from somber to hostile. More eyes are looking back than forward as the minister tries gamely to continue. He begins to truly falter as the whispers start. A quarrelsome, sharp little voice is hissing. That's David's mother, and I can see black flames in her piglet eyes. The minister stops outright when David's Marine father stands up, smooths his dark suit and strides down the aisle. I'm seized wordlessly by strong hands and hauled up. My dress shoes clack against the tiles. Floundering about, I try to break the martial hold on my lapels. My back is used to force the wooden door open and I'm thrust into the hot sunshine I'd just come from. The hands let go. I'm falling down the steps but I manage to wrap an arm around the rail so I just sort of skitter down two or three, scuffing the back of my leg on the stone lip of one. My suit sleeve rips in the violence and I teeter, trying to gain my balance as David's father slams the church door shut. My calf stings, and my heart wants to gallop through my ribs. I start up the steps, meaning to charge back inside, but I stop myself as the mantra surfaces. "Today I will do everything right."

Jacket off. Tie off. In the Audi I have another cry. I notice the funeral program wadded up on the passenger seat and I spread it out against my thigh. The spider web of crinkles running over the paper does nothing to diminish David's beautiful smile.

"Wipe your eyes, sir," Starkweather instructs from where he is hanging by the steering wheel. It's David's voice of course, rendered slightly British and equine in my mind. "Just go on home and have a glass of wine and celebrate David's life in your own way." Starkweather jangles about as I twist the key and flee the church grounds.

I do want to celebrate, but I don't want to go home. The Lashbrooke Family Vineyards are only half an hour away. A drive in the country is exactly what I need right now. I'm singing along to

"Reptile" by The Church, loudly, and it's helping me forget about what just happened. I don't go anywhere without my music.

The suburban sprawl disappears, swallowed whole by crawling blankets of kudzu. The hills are bright and cheery in the sun, and the roads are nearly devoid of other cars. The funeral procession would be moving out to the grave by now. At least the weather's cooperating. No doubt there are still lots of solemn head nods and back-clapping going around at the ouster of the unsavory element known as Michael Creel. I don't care anymore. I did the right thing, coming *and* going. The same can't yet be said for my problems with The Treaster Fund. This is the Gordian knot I've yet to sever with the blade of my simple mantra. It had taken some time maneuvering myself into becoming the office manager for the charitable organization so I could twiddle my wand at the numbers to turn them in my favor. Dr. and Mrs. Robert Treaster began the business to provide food aid to the people of Tanzania, and they spend almost all their time over there, leaving the cat (me) to watch over the mice (their money). The ridiculous part of it is that I don't even need the money. It's just fun to steal from them. The problem now is that putting money back, or covering my tracks, will expose me immediately. But David's death has woken me up permanently, and there's no going back. I need to do something.

"Should I Stay or Should I Go" by The Clash comes on and I laugh. It's just too perfect. I can relate with ol' Mick Jones. Just what the hell kind of catch-22 did he get himself into anyway? Couldn't be worse than this. I glance at Starkweather, wondering if he might have something to say on the matter. "You've made a pretty bed to lie in, Sir," comes the horsey David voice.

"Thanks," I mutter as I slow down to take the sharp curve around a heavily forested hill. They say it takes three weeks for a new behavior to become a habit. Right now doing the right thing at all times requires constant vigilance. I wonder if it will ever be second nature? The road straightens back out and I see an overpass up ahead. A graffito reads: MARY ME CARLA. I wonder if the spelling-challenged Romeo got hitched or not. The sun is glaring through my windshield and I bring the sunshield down just as I'm passing into the band of shade cast by the road bridge. There, beyond the concrete abutment of the overpass, a car has driven off the road and cut muddy furrows in the grass. It's a beat-up classic in a baby shit brown color that could only have been loved by the '70's. The back tires are flat and the passenger side door is open, but there's no one around. I give a face shrug and buzz on by. "Sucks for them."

"Sir?" a horsey voice asks.

"Fine," I sigh, and my foot moves from the gas to the brake. I angle the Audi onto the soft shoulder and stop. "Today I will do everything right." Rearview. Reverse. Now I'm out the Audi and walking toward the old Nova. What am I supposed to do anyway? What's "right" here? Call a tow truck? The car is on a tilt and I walk down to the passenger side door. I should at least look and see if there's any contact info inside, but I find the glove box bare. No registration, no insurance card, not even a single abandoned Snickers wrapper. The inside of the car smells off. It's tangy like the chicken coop we kept out back when I was a kid. The leather upholstery is worn through in many places and the dashboard is baked apart, splitting into long cracks. The keys are missing from the ignition, and are nowhere to be seen. I'm working my way back out the car, planning on shutting the door and saving what's left of the interior from rain at least, when I notice a bundle on the rear floorboard. A faded turquoise rag is bound up, gathered into a wad the size of a loaf of bread. I grab the thing and set it on the hood of the car. I only unwrap a few layers of the musty cloth before I see a couple of droplets of red. My mind hops about. Oh, God, please don't let it be an aborted fetus or something like that. I can already tell it's not though. There's something hard, and somewhat sharp inside. I unwrap the rest, and what I find is somehow even worse. A chisel, a serrated kitchen knife, three long ten-penny nails, and a hammer, all covered with smears of what is very likely blood. Besides the tools there are broken chips of what appear to be teeth.

I hear a thump from the trunk.

I jump, and the tools clatter on the hood. The teeth chips fall into the grass. The day is still. I look at the empty road. My brain is kaleidoscoping. Maybe someone else will happen along. Can *they* take over for me? Can *they* do the "right" thing? Can *they* make the decisions? I hear the *thump* again. Call the cops? Clearly. But should I open the trunk first. Maybe they need air? Then again, who says it's a person? Maybe it's a wild animal. Some redneck stowed their pet raccoon in the trunk for a laugh. But Starkweather neighs from my pocket. "You know what to do, Sir."

Max Dowdle

"Today I will do everything right." I state my mantra with sudden conviction, as if all answers to the mystery of human existence were wrapped up in those six words. I walk to the back of the car. The thumping has become more insistent. The trunk's locking mechanism appears to be broken, and it's done up in bailing wire. Any question as to whether a person is within disappears when I see the tips of three fingers sliding along the bottom edge, trying to gain purchase and force the trunk open from the inside. I quickly unwind the bailing wire, careful not to cut my fingers in the process, and the trunk springs open with a whoosh of hot air. I am instantly horrified by what I see.

A sweating man in a soiled, beige linen suit is crammed into the interior. His hands are bound with zip ties in front, and they reach out pleadingly. His face, below a sweep of greasy dark hair, is badly bruised, and a bloody gag has been tightened about his mouth. He looks to be in his mid-thirties, but it's hard to tell for sure. His heavy-lidded blue eyes are bright though, the whites shining out of the blood and grime. They appear very clean in contrast to everything else. And they are full of great suffering.

He grabs my frozen hand and I jerk back, thinking that he's trying to pull me in there with him. He softens his grip and I realize he's trying to get out. I grab his forearms and ease him over the lip of the trunk. His clear eyes squint shut with the effort as he steps out, feet clad in old, road-bitten boots. Staggering to stand, the wind is a soft gust, and I can hear birds singing in the trees. I feel like an actor on stage as I lead the limping man to the hood and use the kitchen knife to cut the zip ties. He's shying away from the tools so I flip the cloth over to cover them up. The man rubs his wrists and then gingerly removes the gag from his mouth, disgorging a wadded-up, blood-soaked cloth. I retrieve my phone from the Audi; it's time to call someone to take care of this. Goodwill can only do so much. The man puts a hand over my phone and shakes his head. Fear causes his eyes to widen to great, panicked circles. He's trying to talk but his wrecked mouth can't form around the words. I don't want to look at the extent of the damage. He winces and gathers up the gag cloth to press against his bloody lips.

I realize I've yet to say anything. "I'm calling you an ambulance."

He shakes his head again. I'm staring at his thumb, which is bent back at an uncomfortable angle, almost certainly broken. For someone with so many wounds he's remarkably mobile. The man is making a gesture in the air with his right hand. It clicks home.

"Write?"

He nods.

An attaché case is in my backseat. I grab a stubby pencil and legal pad. The man scribbles with his grimy hand. The pencil sounds like it wants to tear through the paper. He finishes and holds up the message. *No police. No hospital. Dangerous.*

"Dangerous? Why?" My fingers are hovering over the buttons. I don't care what he says; he's clearly in need of help.

Perhaps seeing that he's yet to convince me of his sanity he shakes his head and fishes around in his suit's inner pocket. His hand returns with a small picture. It's a school picture of a smiling little girl, all gap-teeth and with scrunchied brown hair. She looks about eight. I can't ever tell the age of kids though. He's writing quickly. *Dangerous for HER. Cops or hospital and SHE DIES.*

I find I can believe this. He's very clearly been tortured. My nerves are all jangly as I try to decide what's best to do. This is too surreal. This shit just doesn't actually happen. Wasn't I just headed to the winery? I think about what I know of David's death. If there had been someone there for him, maybe things wouldn't have happened the way they did. I hear Starkweather in my ear. "What now, sir?"

"Alright, look." I put a hand lightly on the man's shoulder. "I want to do the right thing here. Is there anywhere I *can* take you?"

The man bends over the paper. Scratch, scratch. *Motel, two miles that way.* He points, and then writes more. *Safe there. Need rest.*

I'm frozen, looking the man over. He wants me to drive him somewhere. The man's clearly badly injured and he wants to hole up in a motel. What kind of person doesn't want to go to a hospital? A criminal, that's what kind. But, underneath the grime and his wounds there's this innocence, this kindness in his clear eyes. They're piercing and intense and completely locked onto me. *Genuine*, that's the word. Then there's the little girl. A daughter? What could it hurt to take him to a motel? It's the very least I can do. Most importantly, it seems like the *right* thing to do. Would he try to carjack me? I don't think so. I just saved his ass from a broiling trunk after all. Seeing my indecision he writes, *I can walk.*

"Absolutely not. Come on." There's a Navajo blanket in my trunk and I spread it on the passenger seat to try and save the fabric from this man's blood. I help him into the Audi and I'm about to get into the driver's seat when I see the rag with the tools on the Nova's hood. It seems weird to leave them there so I gather them up. I cast about in the weeds for the teeth bits, but I don't see them. Back in the driver's seat and I search my companion over, looking for signs of crazy. I know crazy, for I've seen plenty when assisting the Treasters on local food bank outreach for the homeless. This guy isn't crazy. Despite his pain he's completely, almost supernaturally lucid. "Ready?" I ask.

He nods and I pull onto the road.

"Good choice, Sir," Starkweather's horsey voice intones. The little figurine is bouncing back and forth with the drums of Ah-Ha's "Take On Me," which I immediately turn off, trying to center my thoughts.

The man has his eyes closed and the wind from the rolled-down window is swatting his hair around. I sneak glances at his abused face. Mediterranean features. A noble nose underneath the swelling. Good chin. There's a sort of familiar quality to his face that I can't quite figure out. "What's your name?"

The man cracks an eye and scratches out four letters. *BARD.*

"Okay." First name? Last name? That will have to do. I'm still not sure how to act with him. He's strangely relaxed for someone so injured. Shock? "Okay, Bard. I'm Michael." The questions I have for this man could fill that notebook up, but I let him rest. It only takes a moment before I have the Audi in the parking lot of the Miero Motel. It's no Greymantle. It's one of those by-the-road-all-in-a-row-twenty-five-dollar-a-night-roaches-in-your-pillowcase-trucker-porn-under-the-mattress type of dumps. I've seen this place a thousand times on my way out to Lashbrooke, but I never thought I'd have a reason to stop here. Bard is fumbling about in his pockets. His hand comes out empty. He writes a terse, *No $.*

"It's fine," I say as I take my keys (I'm not stupid) and head toward the office. "On me." How far does doing the "right thing" extend? Can I really just dump this guy in a room, dust my hands, and call it a day? I watch Bard through the smudgy office window during my transaction with the aged mole behind the counter, but he doesn't budge. I'm back with a key. Bard's limping his way out of the Audi, and we head towards room 116. Miero Motel is no prettier on the inside. The lights flicker and the odor of cigarette smoke is aggressive.

Bard hobbles to the sink where he drinks from the tap for a long while. I'm just standing in the doorway, unsure what to do with myself, so I start to jabber. "Hmm, look, checkout is at eleven tomorrow, but I can just run back and book another two days if you need, or whatever." Bard collapses on the bed and begins to snore. So…shit.

I sit in the Audi. I twist the ignition and crank up Bowie's "Jean Genie." The mole behind the counter in the office is staring at me. Think. Are my duties as the "good guy" done? Rescue a man from a trunk and then go relax with some wine? All in a day's work! I rub at my stinging contacts and shake my head at the dirtied Navajo blanket. The rag with the implements of torture sits in the backseat like a hot coal. I want to get rid of them, yet there they remain. Why hang on to them? Are they evidence? Starkweather is glaring at me through his monocle. "Sir, this is an extraordinary situation. I think there might be a little more one could do. Just a suggestion, of course." Shit.

"Yeah, yeah," I say. One more thing. But then I'm *really* done. I squeal on out to the twisty country road. Lashbrooke is more than a winery. A whole little town grew up around the industrious vineyard, including a movie theater, hotels (nice ones, not like the Miero), auto-body shops and a grocery store with a pharmacy inside. Half an hour later I'm through the automatic doors with a shopping cart. I fill it up. Cotton, gauze, two different first-aid kits, antibacterial cream, disinfecting alcohol, hydrogen peroxide, a selection of the strongest painkillers I can find, soap, shampoo, a pack of plain white t-shirts, I hesitate for a second and then throw in a pack of Hanes, hoping he's a boxer-brief kind of guy, sports drinks with electrolytes, and bottled milkshakes in chocolate and vanilla. Also, a tootsie pop for myself. The total is $157.35, but it doesn't matter. I have more money than I know what to do with. Is that the price tag for a clear conscious? Let's hope so.

I'm back in the Audi with the tail end of "Personal Jesus" by Depeche Mode. I drive. Miero is right where I left it. Bard isn't where I left him though. The shower is singing and sending a cloud of steam out through the open bathroom door. I'm hauling bags onto the bed when the water cuts off and a moment later Bard exits the bathroom, naked and still drying his hair. His well-chiseled back is facing me, and it's a mess of scars. New cuts apparently overlay the old ones. I'm trying to talk around the cherry tootsie pop. "Mmph - sorry. I'm sorry. Didn't mean to intrude." Weird he didn't lock the door.

If he was startled by my return he didn't show it. He simply dropped the towel and wrapped it about his waist before turning. Cleaned of blood and grime I can now see that he's quite handsome, although still very mangled. Bard spots a pad of paper and pen on the bedside table and writes. *You didn't have to come back.* He eyes the supplies. *Thank you. I can pay you back.*

"Don't worry about it," I say. I take a seat in a flimsy chair, trying to decide what to do with myself. Bard starts pawing through the bags. "There's some naproxen in there." He's already found it and is downing the blue pills, chasing them with great gulps of chocolate shake. His hands skitter over the first-aid kits and attempt to rip the outer wrappers. I can see him wince every time he tries to use his screwed-up thumb. "Here, let me." I unwrap the kit. It's easier than watching him struggle. Before I know it I'm dabbing alcohol to the cuts on his face. I'm a nurse now. The inventory of his wounds is frightening: shallow lacerations all along his cheeks, neck and forearms; swollen nose, and companion black eye; clotted gash on scalp; deep bruising along ribs and thighs; the broken thumb; a badly bleeding knee; and four of his front teeth are chipped off at the gum line, making him look like a hockey player when he opens his mouth; and then there's the issue with the jaw itself, painful enough to keep him from being able to speak. Bard still possesses his unusual level of calm as I tend to him. What's more, he directs me by writing down the proper way to clean and dress his wounds. This certainly isn't his first time playing patient. We're finishing up when I say, "So, you gonna tell me what happened?"

He hangs his newly bandaged head for a moment and then looks toward the dresser where he placed the picture of the little girl before removing his ruined suit. Pen on paper. *Thank you for your help. I can't tell you. This is my problem.*

I scoff and go to wash my hands. "Bullshit. You owe me that at least."

Starkweather is eyeing me from the table. "Sir, if I may? The essence of altruism is not to seek reward. The good deed of doing the right thing should be reward enough."

The damn horse isn't wrong. Bard is about to write something when I say, "Forget it. Never mind. Tell me if you want. Or don't. Makes no difference." I grab a sports drink and down it. Yuck. I forgot how much I hate orange.

Bard is thinking. He resembles some kind of unfinished mummy now with the gauze wrapped around his scalp wound. Pen on paper. He stares at the message for a long while before sharing. *Why did you help me?*

I tap my knuckles on the table next to Starkweather's head. I could grab the keys and leave right now, but something wants me to see this through. The elusive "right thing to do?" I'm looking at Bard and it finally occurs to me why he seems so familiar. He looks almost exactly like my first real crush. Coach Caruso was my track coach in seventh grade, and he sported the finest set of legs I've ever seen in my life. Despite the scars and bruises Bard's are a close second. Sitting there on the edge of the bed, hair cleaned, wounds tended to, fantastic Gregory Peck eyebrows above eyes so clear and gentle, he's a God damned European matinee idol. This would be the part of the movie where the adventuring hero has suffered at the hands of the villain and is nursed back to health by the willing local. Why was I helping this man? How could I not? I steal a glance at Starkweather, and I'm honest with Bard. "I lost someone near to me recently. I made a promise to their memory, and turns out you're part of that now."

Bard nods as if this makes perfect sense to him, and then writes. *So we both have promises to keep.* It's my turn to nod as if that makes sense. Bard writes more. *What happened?*

Hmm, he wants me to share. Okay. I spew. "My lover...ex-lover died and we were on bad terms, I never let them know how much they meant to me and now I regret it. Now I'm trying to set things right in my life, I don't want to make that mistake again."

I'm sorry for your loss. How did he die?

I take a deep breath, briefly wondering how Bard caught on that my ex-lover was male. "*He* was instrumental in the construction of a new nightclub in downtown Durham. He was on the grounds after-hours doing God-knows-what and something went wrong. Either he was followed there or someone tried to break in. He was robbed and shot and left for dead, though they said, if you care to know this much, it took him a long time to bleed out." I wipe at a tear that's trying to break free. "It might have even been someone he knew that did it. David's been poking around in some bad shit the past couple of years. His parents blame me. Think I was a bad influence." I drop my head and murmur, "Today was his funeral." I don't want to talk about this anymore.

33

Bard seems to sense this. He reaches forward and puts a hand on mine, letting me know that nothing else needs to be said. His clear eyes are beautiful, and my heart reaches out to this man that has endured so much. What must it have been like to be tortured in such a way? Left for dead. Just like David. His hand lingers on mine for a moment longer, and then lets go.

I must look like I'm about to vacate the room because he quickly starts slashing the pen across the paper. *Will you stay longer?*

Is he making a pass? No. He's clearly just mixed up and fond of me for taking care of him. I'm not sure what to say or do at this point so I stand up and look at the picture on the dresser. My blood is hot under my skin. "Who is she? Your daughter?"

Bard shakes his head and writes. *Madeline. No. But I must protect her.*

More evasion. It doesn't appear that I'll ever get a straight answer out of this guy, but I decide that's okay.

I have to get back home. TOMORROW. He scratches this word over twice, making it bold and jagged. Important.

"Where's home?"

Greensboro.

That's about two hours away. I'm mumbling. "Today I will do everything right." The act of driving Bard to his destination, and ultimately his destiny (whatever that might be), could be the right way to close the chapter on this "grand act of kindness" I've embarked upon. But I have reservations. There's danger here. It's in the periphery at the moment, but I could very well be thrusting myself into the crosshairs as well. I need time to think. "You should get some sleep and we'll figure things out tomorrow."

"Consider the alternative, Sir." Somehow I knew Starkweather would be in support of the trip. I'm convinced this stupid bemonocled horse is Bard's biggest advocate. "Will you just leave this poor man here to his own devices?"

Patience in Bard's eyes. The pen is tapping the paper. He's not sure what to write. Finally. *You're very kind.*

I don't know about that. I'm probably the only Good Samaritan who accomplishes his works kicking and screaming the whole way. "It's fine. Really." I'm staring at the single bed. I need my own room. "Look, you get all the relaxation you can. I'm going to get another room. We can talk again in the morning."

Bard tries to smile, but his mouth is obviously a source of pain. I want him to go to a dentist first thing in the morning, but it doesn't appear anything will deter him from his duty.

I don't go to the office. I go to the Audi and crank the music. "Just Like Heaven" by The Cure washes over me and tumbles my thoughts all over the place. Bard. Madeline. The hot trunk. The bleeding wounds. The bundle of implements. The trusting Treasters. The unlucky nightclub. The calamitous funeral. David. David. David. Once again I consider cutting out while I'm ahead. Weighing the options. Go home, grab some wine, watch television and sleep, always wondering what happened next? Or get a room next to Bard's, wake up, drive to Greensboro, and then what? Protect Madeline. Protect her from what? Whatever did the savagery to Bard, clearly.

A haughty voice. "Do I really need me to tell you what to do at this point, Sir?" Starkweather's not on a high horse, he *is* the high horse.

I let the song play out and then I exit. A minute later I've had a second interaction with the counter mole and I have my own key. Room 118. I give a knock and Bard opens his door. "If you need me in the night I'm right next door."

Bard's wearing one of the white t-shirts I bought for him. He waggles the makeshift splint on his broken thumb in a sort of comical thumbs-up. He also stares at me with those blue eyes. They rove a moment, skating over me, taking me in. I can't read the expression. Should I stay or should I go?

"Well, goodnight!" I say, and shut the door. Back to the Audi and I'm gathering up anything of value. Nothing stays in this hellhole parking lot overnight. Before locking the door I consider grabbing the bundle of tools from the backseat but veto the idea. *They* can stay. In my room, which makes me instantly long for home. It's only slightly better than Bard's. There's a hideous orange accent wall that reminds me of the rec center hallways from when I was a kid. I set my phone to play music while I get ready to bed down with some television and then sleep. "Burning Down the House" by the Talking Heads bumps along and it occurs to me that I haven't had anything for dinner except a tootsie pop. I decide I don't care. I could stand to shed a few pounds. And as far as work goes in the morning: I make my own hours when the Treasters are abroad.

I'm amazed at how tired I am. I turn out the lights and crank up the clanker of an air conditioner. The television's soft blue glow swims about the room and I forget what I'm watching. I'm drifting. I think about Bard in the room next door. Who is he, really? A bodyguard? Is it a ransom situation? Is he a soldier from the future, here to protect the child iteration of humanity's only hope? I give a little chuckle. Maybe he's a mental patient. Maybe he's a kook that got into some bad drugs and ran into some unsavory types that had their way with him and dumped him in a trunk. No. The eyes. His story is all in his eyes. I have no doubt that Bard is telling me the truth, if only part of it. My thoughts turn from his eyes to his body. The memory of attending to his damaged physique. The hard muscles under the olive skin…a knock on my door.

Peep through the peephole and I'm seeing Bard's bandaged face. I open the door without turning on the light. Bard is staring at me. A fat moon is perched above his shoulder like a glowing familiar. He enters wordlessly. We don't kiss, for that would pain him too much. We are gentle, taking our time to work around his wounds and find pleasure. Neither of us manages to sleep much.

Hours later dawn beats at the cheap curtain. Starkweather is awash in a slice of sunlight. "Did you enjoy yourself, Sir?" I roll away from his arched eyebrow.

Bard is awake and sitting on the edge of the bed away from me, his scarred back like an old road of pain. He's holding a piece of paper. He passes the message over when I sit up. *Will you take me?*

I crumble the note. "Of course I will."

We don't speak about the night.

Stare into the mirror. "Today I will do everything right." Change the bandages. Drink some milkshakes. Turn the keys in to the office. Zip the Audi out of the parking lot. Duran Duran's "Hungry Like the Wolf" seems apropos. Breakfast beckons so we land at the Waffle House outside Lashbrooke. Lard-laden pancakes and imitation strawberry syrup. Jesus, I'm going to regret this later. Due to his teeth and jaw it's all Bard can do to manage another milkshake. I go for a second cup of coffee after tearing apart my breakfast. Bard's bandages garner lots of looks from staff and patron alike. The Audi is roaring down the road again. I'm wondering what's going through Bard's mind, but he's mute. A pall of inevitability has descended upon our venture. For better or worse, I am a part of this now, whatever *this* is. I punch the stereo and bring up "One Way or Another" by Blondie. The road is open to us and I let the playlist fill it up.

I turn it down when Elvis Costello comes on. I can't stand that weasel voice. "What will you do when you get home?" I ask Bard.

He writes. *Protect Madeline. That's my only job.*

That's all he offers up and I'm once again left to wonder at the nature of his relationship to her. Greensboro is approaching. My empty gas indicator is lit, as well as the bladder full indicator so I stop at a service station. Bard offers to pump. I go in, powder my nose, grab two bottles of water and head back out.

The Audi is gone.

I left the keys in the ignition. A cold prickling starts at my calves and runs up over my shoulders. How could I have been so stupid? I imagine Bard and Starkweather zooming off over the horizon; the stupid natty horse haranguing its new master.

Honk!

I look to my left. Bard has moved the Audi from the pump to an empty parking space. Stability locks my heart and stomach down again. I give a little half smile as Bard heaves himself over into the passenger seat again. He's put his soiled linen jacket back on over the clean white t-shirt. He looks odd in the obviously once expensive suit. His old, badly-beaten boots only add to the strangely disheveled appearance. I'm thinking homeless drug lord on vacation in Cancun.

Greensboro city limits. Beat-up strip malls and rusted trailer parks returning to the earth. Bard is running a finger over the surface of the photograph. A spot of strawberry milkshake has stained the bandage holding down the thumb splint. Bard is directing me by pointing through this old southern city. It's taking a while. We need to backtrack when I make wrong turns. It's not the most efficient way of getting around. Starkweather is oddly silent. Guess I'm doing the "right thing." Winding down roads, through neighborhoods. Stop light. Turn. Stop sign. Turn. Through this intersection. Left. Right. No, left. Bard's edgy. There's a current running through him as he fidgets in the passenger seat. He's taken the picture out and put it back at least a half a dozen times. Now he's gesturing to slow down and pointing at the curb. I stop. We're in a well-appointed neighborhood called Broadview on the northern edge of the city. It's idyllic if you're drawn to this sort of quasi-suburban living space. There's a manmade lake off to the left dotted by gazebos and trees. The sky is bright and blue through the spaces between the leaves. The houses are mostly digressive brick affairs done up in just enough variation to make the place seem like it can claim character.

I go to open the door but Bard clamps a hand to my wrist. He hurriedly begins to write. *No. **You can't come. Don't want you to get hurt.***

For once I don't want to argue. This is it. I do feel as if I have accomplished something. I did the elusive "right thing." I nod. "Look. I'll wait here for a bit. I can't pretend I know what's going on, but if you need me…I'll be here." Can I pretend that we have more than this?

Bard twitches his lips into a pained smile. Those genuine, sane, beautiful eyes bore into me. He clutches my shoulder tightly in camaraderie and then leaves. Just like that, Bard is exiting my life. Born from a deathtrap trunk he's now wandering off to some unknown fate in a tucked-away suburb. I watch him cross the road, and when he starts up the lawn I turn away.

"Was that it then?" I wonder. Starkweather just dangles there, saying nothing. I'm waiting for the sense of euphoria that should come with finishing a job well done. But there are too many unanswered questions. I glance in the rearview, watching Bard's slowly limping form. My eyes happen upon the evil little bundle of tools. I reach back and grab the faded cloth, wondering what to do with these damned things. Something is off. I unbind the bundle. It feels different. Lighter. Unwrap. Blood stains. The bundle is unfurled in my lap. Chisel. Serrated kitchen knife. Three long nails. Hammer. Wait, where's the hammer? It's not here. Not on the backseat. Not on the floorboard. I look in the rearview where I can still clearly see Bard. He's at the front door. He knocks. His arm shakes a bit and the hammer drops from his sleeve into his waiting fingers.

A smiling little girl answers the door, all gap-teeth and scrunchied brown hair.

Madeline.

"Sir? Quickly now." Starkweather clears his throat. "What are you going to do?"

Beyond The Verge

The auburn tabby's sniveling breath was the suffering song of a blistered afternoon. The cat's step weaved and its back bobbed, sending the slack fur to shudder like a shredded battle flag in lazy wind. Clearly the feline was thirsty, hungry, sick, or maybe all three.

Another sad scrap of life struggling through its final allotment of harsh days.

Ezra gained on the cat as it made to settle into a ditch near a narrow feed store. In the high heat of the day no other living thing was about. Ezra mopped the brow beneath his hat, reached into his poke and drew out a fold of wax paper that held the last smears of goat cheese. His mother had been fond of cats. There'd been twelve of them when he was a child in Galveston. One named for each month of the year. This tawny fellow could have been kin to November. The cat watched Ezra draw closer with curious eyes, gave a sad *mrow*, and stretched, all loose bones in a cat-shaped sack.

"There, lil' one. Don't fear. I've got-got somethin–" Ezra's hands slowed to a stop midway though the action of unfolding the treat. November's cousin wasn't tabby at all. What Ezra had taken for orange fur was a series of raised welts, livid with golden-yellow pustules, populating the cat's flanks and slackened belly. Ezra stepped back, for a puff of desert breeze had pushed a nostrilful of the cat's stench toward him.

Death.

The cat emitted the odor of something that had been long dead on its feet. He knew the smell. The creature's mood changed from pitifulness to confusion. It's head trembled and twitched, not unlike the little rose-bellied lizards that skittered over the sands all across the state. A miserable yowl burst forth as it twisted onto its ungainly feet and bunched up its shoulders in the most unnatural fashion Ezra had ever seen. Ezra pressed his fingers together over the sweating wax paper, realizing he still held it. He backed up and flicked the cheese toward the cat, less as a peace offering and more so he could free up his hand. The cat's head weaved from side to side, as the ferocious little eyes bore into Ezra. The slowly weeping sores along the cat's body shone like snail leavings in the blistering sun. Ezra's hand stole down to the butt of his gun, which he liberated from its holster.

The cat was still within pouncing distance. Its body wound tight into a rigid, trembling pile of weeping flesh. Ezra's trigger finger, forever quick to make decisions, reacted to a shift in the cat's balance, and squeezed tight. The old Colt Dragoon spat a wad of lead down into the target's small head with a thunderous bark that echoed off the clapboard buildings. The big bullet felled the little cat, and pushed its light body back several inches. Like as not there were eyes at the windows that had seen the stranger put the cat out of its misery, but no one ventured forth into the heat to claim the sad creature as their own. Ezra slid the warm steel home and wiped at his brow once again as he strode over to the carcass.

Cat, steer, or man. Taking any life always felt the same: a new measure of emptiness in the world that could never be regained.

Ezra poked at it the dead cat with the toe of his boot and the dishrag flesh tore as readily as antique lace. Stifling a retch, he hunkered down to get a closer look at the peculiar, sore-laden body, and the orangish ichor that seeped from the damaged head. A tiny yellow gnat, no bigger than a mustard seed, lingered about the hole. Ezra could take no more of the smell and he made as if to stand. Then, a flood of the little gnats exited the cat's wound and circled Ezra's head, seeking out his eyes, nostrils, and mouth. He snatched off his hat and beat it about himself to fend off the invasive pests. Eyes clamped shut. A blast of air exiting each nostril. Mouth locked tight. The gnats stuck to the sweat on his brow, burrowed into his hair and clustered about his ears, searching for egress. Ezra opened his eyes long enough to register orientation and then bolted toward the Marshal office at the end of the street, dousing himself with the contents of his waterskin along the way.

"Dammit all!" Ezra snarled as he fumbled his way into the office and slammed the door behind him. He stood there, hands on his knees, snorting and spitting for some time, unmindful of the two men that had frozen midway through their perusal of a sheaf of papers.

"Are you –" the older, balder of the men started, but Ezra's hacking cut him off. He waited until the fit had passed and the newcomer seemed steady on his feet before drawling out, "You the census taker?"

Ezra snuffled and ran his hands through his hair to ferret out the last of the crawling bugs. Reasonably certain he was free of the gnats he approached the men. "You've got the wrong fella. I'm Deputy Marshal Ezra Bittern. *Kaff!*" A tickle in his throat led to another coughing fit. The men, for their part, waited patiently. "*Krrrrhm* –late of Galveston. Called out to Hart's Stream by Marshal Amos Reginald."

The younger of the two men, a freckled youth with a notable underbite, struck a toothsome grin and said. "No, you our census taker. Ol' Mr. Reginald up and died last week. This who in charge now," he

41

indicated the older man, "Marshal Beau Garrett. An Marshal's are stuck with the census task. Han't you heard?"

"No, I," Ezra began to clear his throat.

"Was that you discharged your firearm in the street, suh?" the older man asked, pointing to the iron on Ezra's hip.

"Yes, I – *hhhrack!*" The tickle continued, and the sensation of crawling bugs still lingered in his hair. He swatted at his temple.

The younger man whacked Ezra on his shoulder. "One a them widow's pussycats. Nasty shits keep turning up."

Marshal Garrett shook his head. "See to our visitor, Leland. Get him settled afore he coughs hisself to bits. We can revisit these duties shortly."

Leland gave Ezra another clout right between the shoulder blades followed by a shot of Garrett's whiskey from the sideboard. The coughing subsided, and Marshal Garrett began to list off the census duties. Ezra's head still swam from the heat outside and the little bugs he'd been assailed by, but he managed to compose himself and listen to his new boss.

Marshal Garrett flipped to the next page and adjusted his spectacles. "Continuein' on. *Deaf and dumb, Blind, Insane, or Idiotic. Great care will be taken in performin'* this work of enumeration, so as at once to secure completeness and avoid givin' offense. Total blindness and undoubted insanity only are intended in this inquiry. Deafness merely, without the loss of speech, is not to be reported. The fact of idiocy will be bettuh determined by the common consent of the neighborhood…"

Ezra glanced at Leland, perched on the bench next to him before the great desk Marshal Garrett occupied. A fly buzzed drunkenly around Leland's sweat-matted hair. Ezra's head drooped. He was tired and over-hungry. A single soft-boiled egg, gritty coffee and a scrap of toast for breakfast, followed by the goat cheese later in the day, were simply not enough. The whiskey offered by the Marshal and his deputy had only quelled the hunger pangs momentarily. There didn't seem any hope of a meal anytime soon, not with the Marshal slowly growling out every line of the census directives.

"…avoid unmeanin' terms, or such as are too general to convey a definite idea of the occupation. Call no man a 'factory hand' or a 'mill operative.' State the *kind* of mill or factory. The better form of expression would be, 'works in cotton mill,' 'works in paper mill,'

– hnh, ain't no mills around here no how. At any rate…do not call a man a 'shoemaker,' or 'bootmaker,' unless he makes the entire boot or shoe in a small shop. If he works in, or *for*, a boot and shoe factory, say so." Marshal Garrett let the paper droop and peered over it. "You lookin' a bit pale there, Ezra."

"I'm fine, sir," Ezra said with a huff. "Go on."

"Continuein' then. Do not apply the word 'jeweler' to those who make watches, watch chains, or jewelry in large manufacturin' establishments. Distinguish between…"

And on it went. Ezra settled onto the bench as the long list of instructions marched by. After the Marshal finished his litany he retired to a backroom and had Leland show Ezra about the office. Holding cell for transport of prisoners, small safe, armory, it was all standard and much like the office he'd known in Galveston, though on a miniature scale.

"Travel long?" Leland asked as they stepped out of the office into the Hart's Stream evening. The day had cooled considerably and there was now more bustle on the street.

"Ride took most of the day. Overfull as trains can be," Ezra said. Looking down he saw a crushed yellow gnat caught in his lapel, which he flicked away with lingering distaste. "Feeling road-soiled, and very hungry."

"That's fine. You gonna stay with me at mine 'till we get you set up proper. I got a pallet all laid out." Leland, gangly and full of a kind of nervy energy, led Ezra through the center of town. A dry wind kicked the dust up into small devils whirling in the sunset. Galveston had been surrounded by water, and when Ezra felt hygienically overdue he was accustomed to letting the saltwater wash over him in the twilight hours. A dip in clear water would set him feeling aright. "Where's the stream?"

"The what?" Leland asked.

"Hart's Stream. Where is it?"

Leland gave a little chuckle. "Misnamed. There ain't no stream but the arroyo west of the verge. Muddy crick a few hours after it rain and then the land drink the water right back up dry."

"I see." Ezra chewed his lip, more frustrated than mad. Was this the right place to start over? Hart's Stream was going to test his proclivity for cleanliness.

Max Dowdle

Leland gave another little laugh and clapped a friendly hand to Ezra's shoulder. "Don't look so disappointed. We all know you're a big shot. Heard how you caught that Will…Willard what has his name?"

"Willis. Whip Willis."

"That's it! Whip Willis. Cousin to the mayor in yer parts, weren't he?"

Ezra nodded.

"You caught him dead to rights 'n outdrew him. I heard he was quick'n too." Leland near bounced with excitement. Seeing a dark shadow pass over Ezra's face he said, "Look, Mr. Bittern. Close to the border as we are…plenty to keep you busy out here. *Plenty*. I promise."

"I'll do whatever is required of me," Ezra mused, faraway in the gulf's warm embrace.

They passed the spot where the cat had perished. Ezra cast an eye at the splotch of stained dirt where the vital fluids had leaked out. The carcass was gone, perhaps carried off by some carrion bird. Ezra felt ill once again thinking of the little feline's ravaged, pestilent body. "You said something before 'bout a widow?"

"*Oh*, you want excitement. Nagel. That's the family name. Dutch. Been around these parts a long time. Got them a patch south a here, whole buncha cats. Well, husband caught sick. Died. Children caught sick. Died. Some of the cats died too, I guess. Nagel woman keeps to herself now, but…I hear she dances nekkid in the moonlight, away out there in the desert." He raised an eyebrow. Seeing that this did not excite Ezra he continued, "Well, them cats that are left wander all about. Awful, diseased things they is. Look as like they been turned inside out, huh?"

"Hm." Ezra squinted out at the desert. His new obligations hovered over him, an unforeseen facet of his posting. "Marshal Garrett wants me to be about the census taking on the morrow then?" He looked up and down the dusty little town, counting up maybe two dozen buildings. "Don't 'spect it's going to take me very long," Ezra said, swallowing to subdue the tickle that had formed again in his throat.

At dawn Ezra awoke feeling rejuvenated. A hearty meal and long bathe, furnished by Leland, had done him right. As he shaved he mused at the close press of riders on the train: ill individuals coughing into their calloused hands, or availing themselves of the provided spittoons. The slight scratch in his throat was still there, and he worried now that he might have caught something contagious. He slapped at an imagined sensation of gnats crawling on his neck, and cleaned up. An old-fashioned mangle sat in one corner, and Ezra set about pressing his shirt.

Rest had done nothing to temper Leland's jumpiness as he led Ezra, clean and presentable, to the Marshal's office to receive the census materials. Marshal Garrett had little time for formalities as he sifted through his predecessor's unfinished work. As Ezra stepped outside, attaché in one hand, Leland called out, "Just come find me if you get lost or have any questions!" Ezra gave a nod and turned left. Might as well start next door.

By eleven AM he'd already covered the north and south end of the main avenue and started down a side street. The first paper, ruled into a series of tiny boxes and rectangles, had gradually filled up. Dwelling houses were numbered sequentially, and poor houses and hotels counted as one dwelling, no matter how many people might live under the roof. Names and ages were recorded, and Ezra was happy to witness that his questions were received with very little suspicion. His cough was worsening, no doubt exacerbated by all the questioning and talking, but a pause for water would usually quell the hacking.

Ezra readjusted his hat and knocked on the next door. A stooped woman answered and stepped to one side. Ezra ducked inside the dim home. "Morning, ma'am. I – hhh-Keck!" He pressed a handkerchief to his lips. "Excuse me. I wonder if I might ask you some questions for the census?"

The ancient woman, face and neck seamed with lines of age, only stared at him.

"Ma'am?"

The woman raised a crooked hand to her ear and pointed. She shook her head. Then she pointed to her mouth, and shook her head again.

"She's cain't hear well," a small voice said from deeper inside.

Ezra squinted, and saw a young girl curled up on a mottled mattress near a small window. She was tiny and thin as a stalk of wheat, but her voice was sweet, and nearly musical. Ezra judged her age somewhere between seven and nine. "My gram can't speak no more neither." The little girl stood up and took the old woman's hand. She led her to a chair and helped her sit.

"And what's your name?"

"Amelia."

Ezra spoke softly, trying not to upset his throat again. "Where's your daddy, Amelia?" Ezra asked, taking a chair next to the old woman. He looked about the sad little home, wondering how these two were able to survive in a place like this.

"Don't know. Grampa went down to Dallas last week."

"And your momma?"

"Died," Amelia said, tucking her chin into her chest. Ezra's heart lurched. This girl no longer had any parents, and here he was, a man who no longer had a family. He drew forth his papers and asked a hasty series of questions. There wasn't much to enumerate in the shack, and he wanted to get it over with quickly. The little girl proved knowledgeable enough for his purposes, but the old woman stayed mostly still for the duration, staring at a patch of dirt floor.

When he was done Ezra looked about the poor interior and chewed at his lip. The girl was bright, and he felt badly for her being in this place. He put a hand to her shoulder, and cringed inwardly, noting how thin she was. "Are you and yours doin' okay here? Got enough to eat?"

"Yes, sir," she said without raising her head.

"Just to be sure." Ezra fished in his pocket and pulled out three new shield nickels. The old woman's eyes widened, but she began to shake her head as Ezra laid them on the table. "Nonsense." He raised his voice for the grandmother's benefit. "Have your husband stop by the Marshal office when he come home. He can pay me back then." With that he stood and tousled Amelia's hair, eliciting a smile from the little girl.

As Ezra gathered his leather case back up he said, "I'll call on you again tomorrow. Promise." The sun was bright and powerful back outside. He glanced up and down the dusty streets of Hart's Stream, deciding which way to go next. A swirl of sand kicked up and Ezra began to cough. His stomach burbled and he realized now just how hungry he'd become under his workload. He was midway back to Leland's for a break when the cough turned into another fit and he doubled over, feeling a stab of heartburn. The arid nature of the town did not agree with sinus and throat accustomed to a wetter climate. The apothecary he'd visited earlier in the morning for census questioning was one building over. Within a few moments Ezra had procured a bottle reading, *Patented Southern Gold Bitters.* He crunched two of the chalky tablets between his teeth and washed it down with a swallow of water. Nausea bucked his stomach and he decided to forego any food. The census job was begun, and he aimed to finish it so he could get on with real work.

Several hours later, soaked in sweat and feeling a pervasive twist in his gut, Ezra found Leland at the Marshal's office. With an air of resignation he slapped a stack of paper on the front desk and said, "That's that. All's done." He coughed and chomped another bitter.

Leland riffled through the papers, sticking out his lower lip all the while. "Looks 'bout right, Mr. Bittern. Hey, got yerself a bellyache there?"

Ezra shook his head. "Fine. It's nothing."

"Well. I'll leave these by for Marshal Garrett, and you can get started on the rest tomorruh."

"The rest?" Ezra said. "That's the lot of 'em. I saw to every person in Hart's Stream today."

"So you did, but yer just gettin' started. Lotta people live out in the verge. All types. Each 'n every one need to be catalogued."

"Here. Marshal Garrett brought Argus over while you was shavin'." Leland handed the reins to Ezra. The appaloosa dipped its head and snuffled at Leland's palm. "You gonna be fit to ride today? Didn't seem like you slept all that well last night."

Ezra rubbed at his eyes and nodded. "Just...upset stomach."

Leland nodded. "We're working on a room for you at the Queen Mary. Should have a bed of your own tonight. Well, look here, Argus is a good horse. Just a bit skittish. Hold on to 'im tight and he'll do you fine."

Ezra swung up into the worn saddle. On his chest he wore the shield of office. On his right hip was the iron to enforce it, and on his left, the bowie knife given to him by his father. He checked the bags on either side.

"Marshal put your map of the verge and other sundry paperwork in there. Should be everything you need. I put a lunch in the other pouch. Water. Them bitters to settle your belly."

Ezra pulled his hat low to combat the morning sun's brightness. "You're a good man, Leland." He eyed the horizon. "Gonna start with that widow. Which way should I go?"

Leland pointed off to the right, to a dusty trail that led into the scrub. "You wanna head south there if you're going out to Widow Nagel's. You'll run into ol' loony Hyrum Tallmadge first. Tell 'im 'howdy' from me, less you get your head blown off."

Ezra touched his brim and gave Argus a nudge. The horse was gentle, and soon enough the huddle of buildings known as Hart's Stream was receding at a steady rate. The up and down motion, however mild, was enough to set Ezra's stomach on edge again though. Truth be known, it wasn't just his belly that had kept him up, but hauntings of the mind. Though he'd lain on the pile of blankets Leland had provided for the entirety of the night, it had been a fitful and fever-vision addled doze. The moon's wan light had painted the rough walls of Leland's small house in midnight blues; and try as he might to sleep it was Clara's pale face that coalesced out of the stucco textures.

Clara Kilcannon, sweet, demure, short of stature and daughter of the butcher. Ezra, son of the barber next door, had grown up wading the Galveston gulf with her, and had thrown a bouquet of pink wildflowers into the surf on the day of her burial. Clara Kilcannon Bittern, sweating, flushed, with panic in her wet eyes. Her face turned up to Ezra as she asked through trembling lips, "Is everything okay?" A slice of seeping red at Clara's abdomen as the blue baby was pulled forth, cord wrapped about her delicate neck. Clara ripped roughly in two, with gouts of yellow gnats pouring forth from the violence.

Ezra shook his head. His stomach twisted in another knot and he held tighter to the reins, peering at the scorched horizon over Argus's black mane. A large barn came into view, smudged and blurred by the heat waves. Ezra withdrew the map and spread it out on the back of the horse's bobbing neck. A circle marked the town of Hart's Stream, with a thin, meandering line weaving off north and south, presumably the dry creek bed. Hatch marks accompanied by family names peppered the rest of the paper. There was an 'X' due south of Hart's Stream labeled Tallmadge, and the one a considerable distance beyond that had the name Nagel scratched next to it.

The barn leaned heavily westward, as if it had travelled the desert waste, grown tired in the heat, and collapsed at the top of a hill in a heap. A small corral held a clutch of skinny cattle, mindlessly chewing at a splintered trough. A thin man, brown as Ezra's saddle, and twice as sun-cracked, materialized in the open doorway wearing a union suit stained yellow at the pits and crotch. "Hyrum Tallmadge?" Ezra asked. The man gave a curt nod, his round head, still populated by a few flyaway strands, bobbling on the wiry neck. Ezra dismounted and pulled forth the census materials. "I'm Marshal Bittern. New to the office in Hart's Stream." Seeing the dubious glint in Tallmadge's eye he added, "Leland gives his regards. Think you could find your way to answering some friendly-like questions for me?" Tallmadge nodded again. "You speak?"

"Damn right, *I speck*," Tallmadge said, spitting a string of brown into the dust beyond his threshold.

Ezra raised a conciliatory palm. "Okay then." He looked over the first paper with its sectioned out little boxes and sighed. "Accordin' to the map, your land runs right up to the Nagel plot, all the way, what – fifteen miles south of here?"

Tallmadge sniffed as his face contorted into a wad of wrinkles. "Don't a single Nagel come round nary 'gain!" He kicked dust up with his bare feet, furious. "E'r since last year I missed three a my herd. Found one, ripped open 'n emptied out just over that hill."

Ezra frowned. "Wait. You're saying the Nagel family took your livestock?"

"Yessir. And kilt one a 'um. Bones all broke. 'Testins all missin'."

Why Leland hadn't mentioned any of this baffled Ezra. "Did you report that?"

The old man got a sly look and reached inside. "Reported with this." He withdrew a fifty-caliber buffalo rifle near as big as he was from behind the jamb. "They ain't come back. But jes the night afore last one a them cats come over here and bit muh Polly."

"Your what?"

"Muh. Polly. You deef?" He pointed a crooked finger into the barn where an ox lay on its side, laboring with shallow breaths. Flies buzzed about the great beast's swollen abdomen as it vainly flopped its tail to and fro. "She got a sickness. Collapsed on me."

"That cat. You kill it?"

Tallmadge gave a smirk. "Shot 'er out there as she was struttin' away, pleased as may be. T'weren't nothin' left."

Ezra groaned as his breakfast threatened to rise. He gritted his teeth and hurriedly put the census papers away.

"You okay, mister?"

"Excuse me, sir. I – I'll be back." He swung up into the saddle. There was something wrong at the Nagels'. Surveys and samples be damned, he had to know right now. With a kick to the ribs he set Argus southward, leaving Tallmadge behind.

Here was the line where the scrub gave way to real desert. The verge spread wide in every direction, a shimmering lip of sun-baked orange against a blistering white sky. Ezra coughed long and loudly. He pulled Argus to a stop and leaned to one side, retching. The remains of eggs, fatback, toast, and coffee landed in a sickening mélange beside the horse's forehoof.

Ezra took a deep pull from the water skin and paused to get a breath. Clara's voice whispered in his ears, *Is everything okay?* The sun was on the downside of the day. The Marshal straightened his shoulders and set Argus to trotting again. A dwindling pocketful of bitters, the warm water, and the slight breeze that cooled his sweat-soaked clothes were the only allies Ezra had for quelling the mounting nausea. As afternoon passed to evening a billow of dark clouds took position on the horizon before him.

Though the verge was a sea of sand and rock, Ezra was confident of his direction, and that he should be upon the Nagel plot within the hour. His energy waned, but his stomach balked at the idea of the meal Leland had packed. Ezra clucked his tongue at Argus to pick up the gait.

The tower of clouds loomed large, mountainous and black. Ezra could see a heartbeat of lightning within, though it was still many seconds before the thunder reached him. His current course took him headlong into the stampede of clouds where man, horse and land would be soaked alike. Panic had not yet fully set in when Ezra espied the low sod house crouched amidst a cluster of boulders.

"Good boy, Argus. Just a little farther now." Ezra tilted his head back to take in the vast thunderhead before jabbing a heel in Argus's side to spur the horse on for the last thousand yards. "Hie!"

Thunder grumbled portentously and Argus shuddered. Ezra bent low over the horse's tense neck and whispered assurances, as much for his own comfort as the beast's. Sprinkles of rain dotted and darkened the thirsty dust in rapid number. Ezra took the horse headlong into the storm's hot breath, a great wind that blew low over the verge like the roar of a freshly awoken colossus. The sun had been occluded entirely by the army of black clouds, and all the land showed in muted color, drained away by the storm's power.

The sod house, a type of ramshackle hovel prevalent in remote parts such as these, abutted the largest of the boulders. The gnarled, wind-blown remnants of a dead tree protruded from a bunch of rocks near the front of the house like a deformed bone bleached by the sun. Ezra descended his mount in haste, tangling his boot in the stirrup. With a comforting pat he pulled Argus closer to the tree and proceeded to hitch the reins when a blaze lit up the sky near to their left. The echoing crack, like the riving of creation itself, reverberated through Ezra's very being, causing his teeth to clack together in fear. Argus reared back, wrenching the leather from Ezra's hand. The next flash silhouetted the big appaloosa and then Argus bolted around the side of the largest boulder. Ezra gave pursuit, but by the time he'd rounded the outcropping of rock Argus was disappearing into the encroaching storm's gloom, saddlebags and all. The rains lashed Ezra's clothes through, quickly soaking every inch of him. He jerked his hat low and sprinted toward the Nagel residence, hallooing all the way.

The crudely hewn door gave way easily and Ezra found himself pitching forward onto the dirt floor of the dark interior. It was immediately plain that there was no one home. Even before Ezra's eyes began to adjust to the dimness the smell informed on the state of the residents. Smells had always been a quick avenue to vibrant or traumatic memories for Ezra, and the odor inside the Nagel house, though faint, was no different. It was the same smell wafting free from the rotting feline in Hart's Stream, and the same smell aboard Whip Willis's hideout, the rusty steamer christened *Drusilla's Reward*.

Ezra coughed and got back to his feet, casting his gaze about the sod house. Lantern and flint rested on a low bench near the door and he set about coaxing a flame. The walls came alive with flickering shadows. He expected to see a body, given the smell, but there was nothing. The humble furnishings seemed right at home in the little hovel as Ezra settled down, listening to the storm. Another bench, a handmade bed, a small woodstove and a warped cabinet populated the far end of the narrow room. The storm roared and Ezra's guts grumbled in kind; but the sickening stench lingering about quelled any desire to eat.

The door remained open and flickers of lightening cracked by, lighting up the deep shadows that the weak lantern could not illuminate. Ezra looked toward the bed and with the next flash he caught a glimpse of something pale beneath it. He bent down on creaking knees to inspect what lay there. It was a hand, long-nailed and shriveled by the desert air. Ezra grabbed the wrist and pulled, revealing a grotesque horror the like of which he had not seen since stepping onboard *Drusilla's Reward* those many months ago.

The shape of the body had once been human, but violence and distress had rendered the corpse something that now resembled a gutted fish. The desiccated skin and torn clothing clung to the splintered ribcage, leaving a gaping, empty hole that yawned open in the blackness. Most of the entrails were missing or dried up, but Ezra could hear maggots still foraging the moist interior. The size and dress indicated that this had once been an adult woman, and Ezra could only assume it was the tortured remains of Mrs. Nagel. There was something else as well. A golden-yellow, web-like tissue caked the edges of the abdominal cavity.

Ezra yanked the stained sheet from atop the bed and spread it over the body. He tucked the edges underneath and then grabbed the cold, bony ankles, dragging the grotesquery to the door. He hesitated, looking out at the growing pool of water in the dooryard. The puddles chattered with the unending pelt of heavy drops. Ezra deposited the ragged husk of Mrs. Nagel into the corner nearest the door. A Christian burial would have to wait.

For a long while Ezra sat, looking from the covered body to the slate-colored sea forming outside. Faintly, beneath the plash of rain, he thought he could hear a high, singsong melody, like a young girl reciting nursery rhymes. Though hearing things was nothing new. He was familiar with the tricks the plains could play on a lonesome and beleaguered mind. The imagined sound brought to mind Amelia, and his promise to visit the young girl. It seemed that would have to wait, and the thought filled Ezra with regret. Finally the pain in his gut became too much and he caught himself reaching to where he would have stowed the saddlebag, if only Argus had not run off with it. He needed food. No matter how sick he felt he'd have to find something and force it down. Miss Nagel's pantry was bare except for a burlap fold of cloth with three tack biscuits serving as residence for a colony of weevils. Ezra picked the weevils free by the light of the lantern and slowly chewed the tooth dullers. The biscuits didn't stay put for long. A spasm rippled up Ezra's torso and kicked the masticated mush free in a mucus-laced vomitus with a stench that added to the already ripe confines of the sod house.

Pain stitched itself in Ezra's side. He knew from when he was a child and suffered from migraines brought on by a flash of light off the gulf waters that the only sure cure for pain was sleep. Ezra reluctantly hauled himself to the dead woman's mildewed mattress while the thunder shook overhead. Flashes traced the outline of Miss Nagel's feet by the door. Ezra shut his eyes and gritted his teeth.

"I surrender." Willis sat cross-legged, smiling a set of broken teeth that crawled with yellow gnats. His hands, palms out and slicked with blood, glowed dully in the setting sun slanting through the windows of *Drusilla's Reward*. A small child, flayed and missing his boy parts, was slung across one knee, the shredded skin thrown into the corner like the discarded shell of a crayfish. "Go on an' haul me in, lawman," Willis whispered.

Ezra's finger made a decision his mind could not, pulling the trigger and letting the bullet loose from its chamber to find a new resting place in Whip Willis's right eye socket.

Ezra rubbed at his burning temples. It wasn't a dream so much as an admixture of assorted memories boiled in the heat of fever. The thunder and rain had subsided overhead, but the rumbles continued in his gut. Ezra leaned over and retched long and painfully upon the dirt floor. Presently he opened his stinging eyes and saw that light pierced the ill-patched cracks in the walls to illuminate the dim form of the widow's corpse where it had sat watch all night. Sore, and still very tired, he swung his legs over the edge of the bed and looked down to see an unwelcome sight. His belly, normally flat from years of physical activity, was distended by bloat and tight like a sack of grain.

He resembled Clara after four or five months of pregnancy; and the twisting pain inside, a mixture of nausea and hunger, was excruciating. As Ezra braced himself and stood he broke wind, releasing enough of the damnable pressure that he felt able to walk. A noxious smell mingled with the fetid interior of the house and he gagged. Wishing to avoid another vomiting fit, Ezra careened from the hovel into the bright heat of morning on the verge.

The vivid sky assaulted his eyes and he staggered in the dooryard, feet tangling beneath. The pressures inside Ezra's torso mounted and he paused on hands and knees to allow the gas passage, but a more urgent need began to present itself. He hurriedly undid the picture agate belt buckle and tore his denims down, unmindful of modesty or location. What followed was both messy and painful. Ezra kicked mud over his leavings, but not before spying smears of blood within them. Dysentery, he was sure. He needed to return to Hart's Stream before the illness got any worse. Aware of how quickly dehydration could claim a victim in the desert he stooped to the rain barrel and drank deeply of the fresh water. This calmed his belly by a few degrees, which allowed him to think clearly. Though the sun was climbing toward noon it was still early enough to tell the cardinal directions. The map in Argus's bags had shown the namesake creek bed traced just west of the Nagel plot. He could follow that north back to town, if he could find it. Ezra drank another deep helping, finally pulling free and gasping before setting off westward into the deeper verge.

Progress was slow, for every shuffled half mile or so Ezra had to squat and expel another runny pile of blood and mucus-laced ordure. A mocking part of him mused that he could always find his way back to finish up census duties by following the befouled trail he now made. As he regained his feet he grabbed a wind-bitten length of wood to bear his weight. He was growing weaker, and his distended, rumbling belly worried at his fevered mind. How far until the creek? Another mile? *Two?* The land all around was mostly flat, but Ezra was now slowly making his way up a small rise, hoping to see the basin of the creek on the other side. As he crested the rise he saw something else that made his bowels lurch.

Twenty-feet in front of him, partially buried in mud, lay the disemboweled carcass of Argus. The horse's body parts and viscera were spread out in a shaky line, as if something had unraveled the

Appaloosa like an old quilt. Horseflesh baked in the sun, and the small bit of wind meandering over the verge tugged at the remains of Ezra's census materials, also cast about in haphazard fashion. Ezra gathered up one shredded saddlebag and found the remains of his water skin, similarly sliced open and empty. Most likely coyotes or wolves had gotten to Argus during his fearful gallop the night before. The horse didn't appear eaten in any way, just killed and scattered about. This needled at Ezra, cutting through the pain and urgency he felt.

The sun began its descent, and Ezra's intestinal distress worsened. He forced his feet to move westward, shaky as they felt beneath him. Fat clouds massed along the horizon once again, but they were still very distant, content to let the sun continue its scorching reign. The wind kicked up, carrying a soft babble to Ezra's ear. He squinted, and there, amidst the heat-wavering sand, he saw the rift in the verge. What's more, the torrent of the night before had flowed into the arroyo, filling it with fast-moving, murky water that flowed southward. Ezra's step increased and he cast the stick aside as he hurried toward the water. Though he was still many miles from town, the creek's presence did much to leaven his moral. He plunged his head beneath and drank. The urge to vomit reemerged and he stopped. As he collected himself the wind upstream carried a peculiar sound, much like the song he'd heard in the sod house the night before. A low, singsong lullaby, like a youthful voice, wavered just beyond reckoning. Hallucinations, it had to be. But he began to imagine Amelia was calling to him. *You can be my daddy*, the voice could be saying. Sometimes it nearly resembled crying, or laughing, such was the uncertain nature of it. Ezra scrambled in the mud and began to lope northward, pendulous belly swaying with each step.

The song continued, and a sharp burning twisted in his groin, sending electric jolts into his bowel and spine. This time he was too late trying to get his pants down, but he was beyond caring. He waded into the sluicing water to clean himself. The current tugged at his loose gun belt, dragging at the big iron like an anchor. His hand, agent of the fevered mind, reached down and liberated the gun, letting it disappear into the cloudy stream. Beneath the surface he toed his boots off, and let them go, feeling the squish of mud between his toes. Ezra watched himself do these things with a sort of detached curiosity. They were just *things*, and he didn't need them anymore. The pain he felt was purifying, teaching him what was really important in life. He wanted nothing more than to strip off the rest of his clothes and feel the water slide over his tortured, weakened body as he would have done in the Galveston surf at twilight. The lullaby grew louder, but no more intelligible. At least, the words were nothing that Ezra could have written down, but he felt he still knew their meaning deeply. He laughed, a razor-sharp sound echoing over the soft trickle of the creek.

The bank on either side grew taller, and the bed of the stream took to twisting back and forth between a series of hills. From up ahead came the active sound of a cataract. Ezra, still wading through thigh-high water, flung his hat aside and tore out of his shirt. He opened his mouth wide and plunged it into the runoff, tasting the silt and earth swirling there. The song, high and close, spurred him on now. *Drink, Daddy, drink.* A giddy snuffle started to emerge from Ezra. He felt ecstasy and belonging like never before. The pain in his distended belly had turned to warmth, and the steady expulsion of blood that ran from his backend to fill his soggy denims was forgotten. The song filled his ears, as bright and all encompassing as the cloud-free sky above. He knew now it wasn't Amelia, but something far more enthralling. "I surrender. I surrender," Ezra mumbled happily, and wept.

Another bend in the stream and he saw it. The creek cracked the plain sharply here, and a jumble of boulders filled the arroyo creating a natural waterfall for the runoff. There, beneath the torrential downspout, was the source of the song. A being of unnatural and incomprehensible physique twisted in the water. Ezra wiped the tears from his eyes, trying to ascertain the reality of the thing he saw before him, distorted further by the cascading sheet of water. The leathern and rust-colored habitus folded and shifted and turned with every movement. The many-taloned limbs that bent and flailed at improper angles on bulging joints were contrary to any beast's structure that Ezra had ever known. The flesh of the creature, or very substance in fact, appeared to be able to stretch and reform, powered by some terrible, foreign will. The song, clear and sweet, came loud and fervently from a fang-ringed orifice centered in the beast's body.

Ezra crawled out of the creek, grinning in obeisance. His belly was now as round and taut as Clara's had been at full-term. The unspeakable organism, commanding and magnificent, left the shower of water behind and bowed in front of Ezra. A tendril of flesh slithered along the ground to lap at the underside of Ezra's belly. The Marshal's denims, sodden and soiled, clung to his thighs, and though his gun had been lost, the bowie knife was still safe in its sheath. Ezra drew it forth and held it before his eyes. "I surrender to you," he said as he slid the tip of the blade into his torso just below the ribcage and steadily sliced along the ribs, using them as a guide. His entrails spilled forth with surprising ease, and suddenly the pressure was gone.

With a soft moan Ezra fell to one side as a golden-yellow, webbed sack twitched free of his abdomen and flopped to the ground. He watched as another smaller, gristled and many-jointed creature tore free of the golden-yellow membrane. It's mucus covered length glistened warmly as it basked in the afternoon warmth. A soft song, in a higher pitch, harmonized with the first. Cool peace was stealing over Ezra. He felt his life draining away into the muddy creek bed. His tear-rimmed eyes dimmed as he beheld the two creatures come together for the twisting flesh of their bodies to twine about each other in a lovers' embrace, and there was a new measure of fullness in the world.

Max Dowdle

Koko

"Do you have any dog-friendly rooms?" Sarah leaned close to the grimy grate in the window. There was the spicy-pungent smell of Vietnamese cooking wafting out from within. The dreary deluge of rain misted under the narrow awning, sprinkling her forearms. A flash lit up the streets, followed by a formidable grumble of thunder. This

58

was one of those bottom-heavy storms that squalled in and shadowed the early afternoon in twilight gloom.

The girl behind the counter, perhaps fourteen or fifteen, flipped through the worn book and then tapped at the keys on an ancient PC. Two young boys sporting black bowl cuts chased each other with squirt guns through the living quarters beyond the tiny office. "Uh, no. Wait, yes! What kind of dog, please?"

"What kind of what?" Sarah had been distracted by a woman tottering in six-inch heels under the bus stop shelter flanking the humming avenue alongside the drenched parking lot of the Econo Lodge Motel. "Oh, Koko? Koko's just a German shepherd mix."

"Oh, big puppy okay, yes, there is one room. Second floor, okay?" the girl asked in her clipped accent. This was the kind of girl that Steve had always referred to as a China doll, not caring whether she had actually been Chinese or not. "It is only two twins. I am sorry."

"Yeah, fine, whatever," Sarah said with a shrug. She didn't care about the format of the room; as long as the sheets were relatively clean, she'd have no problem sinking into them for a nap. Then it was off to find an apartment when the storm finally cleared, preferably something with little to no deposit. Her brother, Will, who'd lived in the city until three years ago, had said, *City's on the move, easy to start over in a place like that. You could look into nursing homes. Have you thought of that?* Of course she'd thought of that, but she knew that there was little chance the stewards looking after the coffin dodgers would take her after what had happened. But Charlotte was the place Will had gotten back on his feet after he'd been laid off. So maybe it would pan out for her as well.

"Forty dollars for one night. You pay now. Pay cash?"

Sarah dug around in her purse and found the cracked leather wallet Steve had given her for their third anniversary. Why was she still hanging on to *that* after all this time? *At least those happy bullshit days are over.* She reminded herself that as soon as she had some extra cash she'd replace it. With some hesitation, she pulled two of the five twenties out of the wallet's fold and slipped them into the tray under the window. *Bye-bye, boys,* she thought as the duo of Jacksons disappeared into the money drawer. The stewing odor of the proprietors' lunch, mingling with the stench of the open dumpster a few feet away, eliminated any appetite she might have still had after downing three bags of pretzels on the flight from Detroit. She wished she could have just gotten a direct flight from Boston; she hated layovers, especially at Detroit Metro. Sarah glanced back at her rental car, a cherry-red Aveo that looked and drove like a toy—a far cry from the reassuring bulk of a GMC ambulance. Koko's ears twitched, a lupine silhouette in the rear window.

"Just sign here, okay? Checkout is eleven," the girl said over the slap-patter of rain, and slid a slip of paper and pen under the window.

Sarah made her mark and smiled back at the sweet girl. She was just trying to make her way, just like everyone else.

The clerk set a key into the tray. "Room twenty-eight. You let me know you need anything."

Sarah picked up the key and ducked back into the cool rain. It was a real, honest-to-goodness key, not a magnetic card. This was definitely a throwback, reminding her of the place she and Steve had stopped on the way up to their honeymoon in Niagara Falls; a thousand years ago before he'd even enlisted in the Army. Sarah clicked the bulky fob, unlocking the Aveo's doors. As soon as the passenger door was open, Koko's snout was pressing against her wet hand, eager to explore the new territory. "Hold on now, girl. That's my big bad wolfie," Sarah cooed as she clicked the length of red leash onto Koko's collar and led her under a large tree to the side of the motel. Koko was a good girl but Sarah didn't trust the busy street, still flashing white and red as vehicles sped toward downtown, or, as they called it, "Uptown" here. She could see the gray, muzzy silhouettes of the new skyscrapers through the storm, standing dark sentry over the city. Koko threw all of her sixty pounds into the perusal of the mortar at the base of the hotel, seemingly unconcerned with the water gushing down on them. "Come on, baby, don't make me stand out here in the damn rain." Sarah strained against the leash, willing Koko to find a suitable spot for her business.

A gaunt man in a gray t-shirt was leaning against one of the doors on the first floor, lazily hammering a fist against it, bawling, "Dottie, let me in, baby. It's not fair." Sarah shook her head in resignation at her lodgings. She knew things could only get better from here. Finally Koko squatted and baptized an already drowning weed. "That's my girl," Sarah said with a chuckle.

Bag slung over one shoulder and the collapsible dog crate braced under the other arm, Sarah and Koko headed up the rain-slick stairs to the second floor and came to twenty-eight, the last on the right. She managed to force the key into the grimy lock and turn the loose knob without dropping her burden, but once she clicked the light on the crate clattered to her feet. "Econo Lodge my ass. Econo shithole is more like it." Koko dove into the room and gave a great shake, spraying the walls with drops of rain. Sarah picked up the crate and walked carefully, watching where she stepped on the mottled old carpet. The place brought a memory of a call her partner Darius and she had responded to in East Boston, a three-year-old boy, blue in the face after trying to swallow a used condom he'd found on the floor of a supposedly clean hotel room. And that was exactly why Sarah and Steve had never had Kids. Kids were stupid. She remembered how Darius had cleared the airway and then waxed all night about the payday that boy's family would get. "First thing I'd do is buy a helicopter, man," he'd said. "Motherfuck this traffic!" Good times those…

Sarah sighed and set her damp things on the twin bed Koko had claimed. "That's the one you want, huh? Yeah, don't worry, I'm not gonna make you sleep in the crate. Long as you behave yourself." The pervading aroma of industrial lemon cleaner seemed to accentuate the cloying tang of mold and stale cigarettes. The peeling, nicotine-tinted walls were interrupted only by rectangles of insipid prints and spreading water stains. Sarah scanned for the amenities boasted by the marquee outside. Color TV? Check—though it had a knob, making the relic roughly the same age as herself. She pinched the edge of the bedspread on the far twin and peeled it back. Clean sheets? Check—as long as she ignored the curly black hair sitting on the pillowcase. She blew hard, sending the offending hair onto the camouflaged surface of the floor where it could disappear forever. Koko stood and trotted in a little circle, instinct directing her to flatten the tall grass that wasn't there into a suitable nest. "Nasty place, eh, Ko? Seen worse, I guess." Koko perked her ears and turned her head, intent on her mistress's words. Sarah swore the dog understood her sometimes. "That's right, we're just two ladies out of a job. I know your career didn't work out either, sorry. Least we have each other, huh?" At the sing-song tone of Sarah's voice, Koko's tail slapped excitedly against the bedspread,

Max Dowdle

sending a fluff of dog hair into the air. A boom of thunder sounded, but Koko remained unruffled.

"Hmmm, okay, how about I give you food, get a shower, and we ride this thing out? Would you like that?" Koko bolted upright at the mention of the "f-word," which was the term Steve used for it. The dog watched intently as Sarah dug into her bag for the plastic container filled with kibble and freed the top, setting it in the corner so Koko could happily lap it all up. "You're gonna choke one day. I always say that." Jeez, just like that poor kid, Sarah winced.

Ever since Darius and she had found the skinny pup on a call, suffering from malnutrition, the worms in her gut stealing any food she could forage in that dump apartment she'd been trapped in, Koko had inhaled every meal set before her like it was the last she'd ever see. *That pup just keep on keeping on, huh?* Darius had said, which summed her up perfectly. She'd been "Koko" ever since.

"Momma's taking a shower now. You behave." Sarah stripped her flannel shirt off and threw it on the bed. As she reached behind to unclasp her bra, she caught sight of the front door in the mirror by the bathroom. Remembering the door didn't have an automatic lock, she made her way to it and twisted the deadbolt. It spun easily in her hand, round and round, never engaging. She closed her eyes. "Seriously?"

Sarah walked over to the phone and dialed the office. When it had rung more than ten times without answer she hung up in frustration. Twitching the curtain aside and looking down, Sarah noticed that the office window was now darkened. The only person in the parking lot was the tart in the high heels and zebra skirt who was now leaning into a car window by the bus stop. "Trashy ass place," Sarah muttered as she engaged the chain lock on the door. But she was going to be all right. That was the point of being here after all. She could take care of herself. "You're on guard duty, Ko. Anyone comes in, you bite their nose off."

Koko wagged her tail, seeming all too happy to comply. Sarah unbuttoned her jeans. She avoided her reflection in the mirror, denying the slow accumulation of fat around her midsection. Middle age and an on-the-go diet were having their way with her large frame, conspiring to turn her into her high school nickname, "Sarahsquatch." Though she'd been christened that more for her height and dominant nature on the volleyball court. She grabbed her toiletry bag and reached for the switch by the door.

The bulb in the bathroom buzzed, illuminating the toilet and bathtub. "Would you look at that?" A series of cigarette burns were arranged in the shape of a smiley face on the toilet seat. Black, unknown material clung to the spaces between the cracked floor tiles. *Welcome to hell*, she thought. Despite the defaced seat and suspicious floor, the bathtub seemed surprisingly clean, without a ring or errant hair marring its smooth surface. Sarah set her travel bag on the back of the toilet then skinned her jeans off. Groaning, she bent forward to turn the knob for the shower. The pipe clanged and the showerhead sputtered, but she was rewarded with only a thin trickle of scalding water. With a shake of her head, she twisted the knob again and a torrent of water spilled out of the bath nozzle. Bath it was then. Sarah hated trying to fold her long legs comfortably into a bath, but she needed to rid herself of the grime from the five-hour layover in Detroit. A good soak with a bar of soap would be just about right. She checked the porcelain once more for detritus and slipped into the hot water. The tub filled and she twisted the handle with her toes, plunging the close room into sudden silence. Sarah slid down into the water, causing her legs to rise like fleshy mountains from the depths. The curse of the tall person—at least half of Sarah was always out of the water. The hot water was already doing wonders to her sore muscles and the steam was momentarily clearing her perpetually clogged sinuses. Set adrift in drowsiness, Sarah awoke to the singing of her phone from its place in her jeans' pocket. She sat up and reached for the phone, careful not to let any water from her face drip on it. She checked the message from Darius. *Boston ain't the same without you. I want you to know that no one here agrees with the ruling. Least no one who counts. Political mutherfuckers! How you holding up, S?*

What strange twists her life had taken that her best friend was a black man pushing sixty who had a new baby younger than his youngest grandchild. The one thing she could count on with Darius was that he always kept things real with her, but even his unflappable optimism hadn't been enough to save her job for her. A momentary lapse of judgment was all it took to upend the applecart, it seemed. Sarah typed out her response. *Gonna miss you too crazy bastard. Don't be a stranger Big D. In the wag now?*

Just had code purple, nasty sidewalk soufflé. Translation: jumper, dead on arrival. They didn't call it a meat wagon for nothing. Sarah sunk back into the water and ruminated on her idiotic misstep. A cold day in March a year and a half ago, fresh powder on top of slush on the Mass Pike and a six-car salad topped by a snowplow. Chaos when she and Darius had responded. Two bodies already assuming seasonal temperature and a third man that was hysterical, bound and determined to bleed out from a severed foot, were the worst of it. Sarah and Darius were superfluous on the scene, assisting rather than gathering. Chaos when Sarah had knelt and pulled the mass of unidentifiable flesh from underneath a t-boned station wagon. Three toes still clung to the twist of red muscle and bone. There had been no way that something so destroyed could be reattached; if it could have been, she would have immediately reported it. Steve had balked at her lunch cooler's contents when she'd come home, but by then they'd moved far past the point of considerate discussion and into the territory of shouting reproach. That chaos had spread fully, swallowing up everything when Sarah had acted on her decision to teach Koko without Steve's blessing.

As it was, there were so few affordable places to get good training for a prospective cadaver dog. Why would Sarah pay four hundred dollars when she could easily teach Koko to find dead bodies herself? A good cadaver dog could pull in a few hundred extra a month, a welcome supplement after the loss of Steve's income. She still wondered if her misstep had been taking the foot, or had if it been mentioning her plans to that loudmouth Camilla? She should have known better than to have done that. Bitch had always had it out for her. Whatever, it was all moot now anyway. She could have dealt with the fine and six month probation but then the single-footed Mr. Joshua Farrig had heaped a suit on top of it. Something Boston EMS wouldn't get behind her on at all. She guessed that had been the end for Steve as well.

A guttural growl and then a sharp bark sounded in the other room. "Kokie, mama will be done in a minute." Koko's series of barks turned into a long howl and Sarah sat up. "Shush, Koko! You'll get us kicked out," Sarah hissed through the closed door. "Crazy pup, what the hell is she barking—" Sarah was cut short when she heard a load bang. Suddenly the water felt cold. She cocked an ear. There was another bang and a small boom and she heard Koko jump down from the bed and begin to snarl. "Koko?" Sarah asked in the momentary silence. A metallic *clink* and then a much louder crash caused Koko to resume her barking. Sarah stood and slipped in the full tub, dropping her phone into the splashing water. She cursed and then righted herself and reached for a towel. "Who's there?" she yelled.

"God dammit!" came a gruff shout from the room. Koko's barking had turned feral, intertwined with the surprised bellowing of the unfamiliar voice. A tear of fabric was followed by a sour yip from Koko, the unmistakable cry of pain, and then the man screamed, "Fucken mutt! Get out of my room!"

"Don't touch her!" Sarah's skin crawled as she gathered the towel around her shoulders. She flung the bathroom door open. The room was in disarray, the chain lock swinging broken from the side of the thrown open door. Koko was nowhere to be seen but the man, wild and out of place, wheeled on her. Sarah's attention fixated on the smallest, inconsequential details as he advanced. The tufts of white hair in disarray over each ear. The wrinkled skin of his neck. The gray t-shirt featuring the cartoon broccoli mascot of a farmer's market. There was a glint of metal and she saw the cleaver in his hand, the sick red of blood painting his fingers and smeared across the grinning cruciferous on his shirt. "Koko?" Sarah called, her voice weakening as the man's lip curled and he began to close the distance between them. She stepped back and slammed the bathroom door shut. The lock in the bathroom worked without a snag, clicking closed just as the handle began to jiggle under her grip.

"Come out of there, bitch!" the man roared. The sturdy door trembled under a blow as Sarah stared, wide-eyed.

"What have you done with Koko?" she screamed. "What have you done?"

"Get the fuck out of my room," the man replied, continuing to beat at the door, seemingly oblivious to her question.

Sarah took her hand from the door, the fingers closing into a tight fist as anger began to steel over her fear. She'd run into her share of crazies throughout her career and there'd been plenty of times that there hadn't been a single cop on the scene to protect her or Darius from pharmaceutically gifted space cadets or wife-beating husbands. "This isn't your room, asshole! So help me, if you've hurt my dog, you'll be wishing she'd torn off your balls compared to what I'll do to you."

The banging on the door stopped and there was a moment of silence. Sarah knelt down and hastily stepped into her jeans. She gave the drowned phone a rueful look and then turned back to the door.

The light clicked off, leaving her in darkness.

Sarah's face grew hard and her nails bit into her palms. Why did they always put the light switch *outside* the bathroom? There was a crash against the door and she stepped back, her calves bumping the edge of the bathtub. That sharp thump wasn't the sound of knuckles on wood. He was hacking at the door with the cleaver. "Stop it! What are you doing? I have my phone, I'm calling the cops!"

"Good! I'll tell them what you did! What you've *been doing!*" the man continued to chop away at the door. Sarah imagined the cleaver biting deeper with every blow of the heavy blade, wood chips flying into the wild eyes of the stranger.

"Sir, you need to calm down." She had no idea what he was talking about. All she could imagine was Koko lying between the ratty twin beds, bleeding out from some terrible wound. "I'm sure this is just a misunderstanding." She was trying to keep her voice even, trying to speak in the reasonable tone she'd always put on when dealing with a schizoid homeless trying to scam a free ride. "I'm not sure what you think I did. There's been a mistake about the rooms perhaps—"

"NO! You did it, didn't you? You put a secret organ into Dottie, you put it in her, and I—I cut it out. I freed her," the man panted between exerted gasps and hacks with the cleaver.

Sarah ignored the tears on her cheeks, and the weight of her bare breasts against her belly. The man was crazy and she was trapped, completely helpless in the dark. She needed something, anything to gain an advantage if she wanted to get out of this. With shaking hands she probed the darkness, exploring the cold contours of the toilet. Even if she could get the seat free it was the thin, plastic variety, useless as a weapon. Her heart sunk when she reached under her toiletry bag and discovered that the top to the tank was similarly flimsy. The thud of the great knife continued its assault on the defenseless door. A thin crack of light pierced the blackness, sending a shaft of flickering fluorescence across the little room. "Go away!" she yelled as fear and frustration began to get the better of her. He'd come through the door and she'd end with a raw split running down her bare belly, spilling forth her guts so this lunatic could play fingerpaints with them. "Go away, go away, go!"

"Not—until—you—pay," the man huffed between chops. "Just like your doggy did."

With trembling fingers Sarah found the zipper to her little toiletry bag and wrenched it open, tumbling the contents onto the floor with a hollow rattle. In the faint light she groped along the gritty tiles, knocking aside a cylinder of deodorant and her toothbrush before her fingers closed on the tiny cuticle scissors. Her thumb raked against the sharp edge and she grinned. The crack in the middle of the door had spread to a splintered hole the size of a pack of cards. Sarah flattened herself against the wall and waited.

Hack!

Hack!

Hack!

The small room was filled with the sound of violence as the cleaver bit away at the hole, widening it to the size of a softball. *Just a little more, fucker.* Blood beat hot up **Sarah's** neck and into her ears.

Hack!

Hack!

Hack!

The cleaver disappeared and the shaft of light darkened. The outline of a hand stole into the darkness of the bathroom. "You're going to regret this," the man fumed. Sarah lunged forward, twisted his sweat slick forearm against the door and brought the little scissors down, over and over to perforate tiny, deep holes into his writhing muscles. The man struggled, bawling with pain but Sarah held fast, relentlessly plunging the vicious clippers into his skin from wrist to elbow. His arm thrashed and his fingers bumped the doorknob. Sarah could hear him fumbling, seeking out the lock. The scissors slipped from between her fingers but she caught them and they snapped open. With a violent yank she brought them lengthwise down his arm, laying the skin open and wrenching a terrible scream from the man's lungs. The door bucked under his insistent weight as the lock was freed. The bathroom was filled with light and the man's other arm came through, wielding the cleaver. A searing burst ignited in Sarah's bare shoulder. She shrieked at the pain, but it was impossible to tell how badly he'd hurt her in the frantic scuffle. She bit down on her lip, ignoring the pulsing sting in her shoulder and focusing on not losing control of the door, or her attacker's flayed arm. With both feet braced against the base of the tub she succeeded in pushing the door shut again. "Let go of me!" he yelled.

Max Dowdle

The slick, shredded arm finally slipped out of Sarah's grasp and disappeared through the hole in the bathroom door as the man gathered himself and put his full weight against the door. Sarah pushed back with equal ferocity. Another surge from the man and the door began to open in on Sarah. He began to work his head and upper body into the room. He flailed blindly with the cleaver and Sarah made one more attempt to press her solid mass against the door. The stranger's head was pinned momentarily between door and jamb. Sarah, ignoring the throb in her arm, lashed out at the man's face with the scissors and felt them connect with a *pop*. A great yowl and the man's grip loosened on the cleaver. It fell to the bathroom floor with a sharp echo. He staggered backward and Sarah's foot bumped the door shut as she dropped to her knees and felt over the sticky tiles to put her hands on the blood-caked cleaver. She looked out of the hole in the door and spied the man, face half-painted red, and the scissor handles like a tiny, metal "B" jutting from his mangled left eye. He felt at his face, a bleat of horror escaping his lips at what he found.

"Don't try to come in here again. I'll do worse next time!" Sarah yelled through the hole, uncaring of the man or the damage he'd suffered.

She watched as the crazed stranger seemed to be trying to find a way to pull the scissors without doing any more damage until finally giving up. With his uninjured left arm he reached behind and pulled forth another, smaller knife stuck into his waistband. Following a string of hoarse, unintelligible syllables, he charged and then threw himself at the door again. Sarah's hand shot out and closed on the doorknob but her fingers slipped on the lock. The man succeeded in getting the door open enough to get a hand through. Sarah didn't hesitate. The cleaver connected with the thick wood of the jamb, severing three of the man's fingers in one clean stroke. A spray of hot blood showered Sarah's face and the man staggered back. His shoulder must have hit the light switch for Sarah was instantly bathed in the fifty-watt glow of the bulb above. The carnage, pools and streaks of red rendered the small room a lurid tapestry.

The man was a gibbering pile of puling expletives on the other side of the door. Sarah waited, readying herself for another assault but it didn't come. Instead she heard footsteps and shouts from farther away. It felt like there was bustle back at the doorway of room twenty-eight. Was he leaving? She put an eye to the hole in the door and saw

68

the man slowly getting to his knees, his attention drawn to something across the room.

"Stay right there, sir. Hands, let's see your hands." This new voice was curt and full of force. Even through the haze and exhilaration of fear Sarah could recognize the authoritative tenor of a police officer.

The man stood, unheeding of the command. He stumbled forward, away from the bathroom.

"Sir! Put the knife down!"

From this angle Sarah could no longer see what was transpiring in her hotel room. Another order and then a gunshot. Sarah dropped the cleaver and covered her ears. Two more bangs and then a dull thud as the man slumped backward and fell onto the tiles in front of the mirror.

"Somebody in there?"

Distantly, a dog barked over the light patter of rain.

"Koko?" Sarah whispered, her heart swelling at the sound.

Cops, paramedics, firemen. The circus of catastrophe busy under a freshly cleared sky. Excited onlookers craning over the rail of the second floor walkway, lit orange by the evening sunset. The hussy in the zebra skirt watching the scene and smoking by the Pepsi machine. The Vietnamese girl, wide-eyed, and holding a bawling two-year old as she tried to give her story to an attending officer. The crackle of service radios. Lights flashing blue. Lights flashing red. The press standing in leftover puddles behind the yellow line. A cobalt body bag being carted down the still wet stairs.

Oh, they're blue here, Sarah thought dimly. She sat in the back of the ambulance, allowing the EMT to tend to her shoulder.

The detective whose name Sarah had already forgotten, heavy and broad in his brown suit, plodded over. The red leash was wound tight in his thick right hand. "Someone wants to see you. This one's better than Lassie, comin' down to get the girl in the office!"

Sarah woke out of her daze. "Koko! There you are, my baby, there you are." She wrapped her arms around Koko's warm neck and nuzzled into it, inhaling the familiar smell of her fur. Koko's back end was wrapped in gauze, looped around her tail and left thigh.

Max Dowdle

"Don't think she's gonna have too much trouble. Seems our Mr. Delatorre only got a little of her derriere with his knife," said the detective. He gave Koko a good rub behind the ears.

"She just keeps on keeping on," Sarah said absently, searching Koko's happy eyes deeply. "That she does. What about the woman he talked about?" Sarah wondered. "Did you find her room? Did he do *something* to her?"

"Man wasn't even staying here. Got no prior record, and no indication of a wife. That door you say you saw him pounding on. Empty room." He shrugged. "Can't say for sure yet if he visited anyone *else* before you tonight or not though." The detective gave Koko one last stroke. "We'll be out of here soon, then we can get you down and take your formal statement." The man rubbed at his weary, heavy eyelids. "Weird shit. We still haven't found the, ah—fingers. Not that the bastard needs 'em all that much now. You didn't happen to see where they went did you?"

"Toilet, maybe. Might have flushed them in the confusion," Sarah mumbled.

The detective stood up and gave a great belly-laugh, wiping at his brow with a handkerchief. "Oh ho, I hope you did!" He turned at the beckon of some colleague and began to shuffle away, "We'll catch up later, Ms. Randolph. I want you to talk with the counselor now."

Sarah nodded.

Koko gave a little yelp and sat happily. She snuffled and her nose moved to a bulge at Sarah's hip. Sarah smiled and nodded. "That's right, girl. I think we're gonna find us a job yet." She slipped her hand into her jeans pocket to close over the small bundle of toilet paper wrapped around three fingers.

70

The Account Of Gavin McNabb

"We cannot conceive of
any end or limit to the
world, but always as
necessity it occurs to us

Max Dowdle

that there is something beyond."

— Francis Bacon, 1620

Monday, May 26ʰ, 1828
Schicksale Atoll, Day 1

This very morn I observed that loathsome banker, Mr. Downs, squatting where the water runs up over low, broken black rocks, and tapping at a large sea snail with his claw-handled walking stick, delighting in harrying the small animal over a surf-slick rock. The snail reached the edge of the rock and paused, perhaps deciding to enter the water as a means of escape, when the diabolical man brought the silver claw down sharply, crushing shell and contents therein. He undoubtedly did this solely for my provocation, for he stood, peeled the viscous, crushed creature from the rock and with a wink assailed me whilst I took my coffee beneath a swaying palm. "Break your fast, McNabb?" he said jovially, flicking the destroyed snail into my lap and leaving. The bestial man was actually chortling to himself as he strode toward the remnants of the abandoned village of Erlabrunn. Oh, how I do abhor that Horace Downs!

Conus Marmoreus. The marbled cone snail. Venomous, and a predator of other cone snails. Though the glistening entrails still pulsed with life, this snail would hunt no more; its existence cut short by an Act of Man. Upon the completion of my meal I endeavored to find an unmolested specimen to draw, if only to preserve one for posterity and set right the actions of the Downses of the world. I ambled westward over the jumbled rocks. It appears that the atoll is chiefly composed of two materials, bright white fragments of the coral reef, and various-sizes of massed, black, colorless basalt. Past a small hill of this black rock my searchings were quickly rewarded, for not far from our anchorage was a veritable paradise of cone snails and other rare mollusks. A coral outcropping, bleached to plaster whiteness, provided a haven under which dozens of snails sheltered in a shallow pool. I selected the shell with the finest patterning and recreated it here in graphite. It is not altogether dissimilar to the shell depicted in the etching by the famed artist Rembrandt van Rijn. I look forward to the other wonders the atoll has to offer, for here we have truly found a rich and abundant oasis, a tiny bustling planet of vigor in the center of this vast ocean.

Life, it seems, misses no opportunity to flourish. *Figure one.*

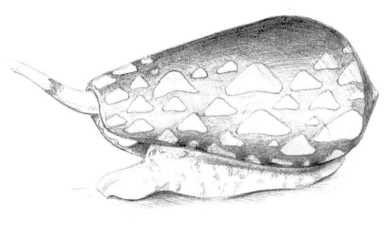

Figure 1. Conus Marmoreus

Monday, May 26th, 1828
Schicksale Atoll, Day 1 (later)

After my excursion westward along the shore, I returned to *The Polyphylax* to replenish my water flask. There I was called upon by Mister MacCurdy, the boatswain. He was insistent that I join him on an excursion to Erlabrunn. I had no more than a fleeting interest in the lost village, or the mystery of its inhabitants (my charge being to catalogue the Natural wonders of the atoll), but I did not want to appear rude or ungrateful for the invitation. Mister MacCurdy, being a fellow Irelander (though from Tipperary, not Cork), is one of the few members of the crew that I feel wholly comfortable around. While we walked I was able to take in an overview of the island proper. Though vegetation was sparsely gathered in most areas, there was a dense cropping of palms to the north, past the dark lagoon that inhabited the center of the atoll. Our perambulations afforded plenty of time for MacCurdy to amuse me with tales of seafaring lore. When I remarked upon the rope tattooed about his wrist he assured me that I could get one as well, if I were keen to learn the ropes of the deck. I declined the offer with a laugh. His tales ranged far but he had some especial interesting stories where concerned Schicksale. What follows here is a synopsis of our conversation as best as I can condense it, in which as we navigated the rocky shore, Mister MacCurdy delivered an historical timeline of Schicksale Atoll, from discovery to eventual dissolution of the first settlement. I would not include this here, except that the tale-end differed significantly from the agreed upon chronicle that I read before embarking on this adventure.

The record of discovery by the German explorer, Captain Johann Schicksale aboard his famous vessel *Die Forscher*, and the establishment of the settlement of Erlabrunn, does not deviate from common knowledge. There were no natives on the small island when Captain Schicksale landed, but a trio of savages he had retained as guides referred to the coral ring as "Erdrunavaya," or the "Gift of God." Erlabrunn, as the settlement was christened, was intended to become a waypoint for ships traveling this corridor, but the settlers who had stayed were vanished before a single calendar year was concluded. The next ship of note to land, *The Caelum*, Captained by a Frenchman, one Monsieur Antonin Du Bocage, reported the desertion of the atoll, with nary a body to be found. It was assumed that the denizens had been kidnapped by hostiles who had raided them for their stores. MacCurdy had more to say on this point however.

The first significant difference that I note is that there is a strong undercurrent of superstition amongst the crew as to the fate of the Erlabrunn villagers. According to MacCurdy, the majority seem convinced that a wave of madness took the villagers, and they extinguished themselves from this mortal plane. Here there were two prevailing theories. Either they slew each other to the man, until the last living settler died of starvation, or the whole of the group swam into the ocean with stones strapped to their midsections to sink to deep blue graves. MacCurdy was of the latter mindset. "If you were to walk upon the bottom of this ocean, you would find it littered with the fish-picked bones of those good Christian men and women." MacCurdy had said this with a most sorrowful shake of his head. He had much, much more to say on the matter, but I shall not write the extended, dreadful details here. It was not unknown for an outsider such as myself to be put upon by the crew, Lord knows I had suffered my share of good-natured jocularity on our extended voyage, but I do trust MacCurdy unreservedly. And I trust that *he* believes what he told me, no matter how likely it may or may not be.

Erlabrunn, which at the count noted by Schicksale, numbered forty-three when he debarked, had been left with stores enough for a year. Upon *The Caelum's* arrival nine months later, Captain Du Bocage noted the coral foundations of twelve huts, fashioned from locally sourced materials, but nothing else. All materials, remnants and souls had gone missing, save for aforementioned foundations, and a small chapel at one end of the village clearing. This very afternoon when MacCurdy and myself crested the slight rise at one end of the atoll and beheld the village remains, I saw that it was just as described by Captain Du Bocage. Twelve rings of coral, arrayed in two rows of six, with the one-story, roughly erected black chapel standing sentry at the far end, as if waiting the return of its damned flock. We paused here a moment as I recorded the view from the coral dune. *Figure two.*

Figure 2. Erlabrunn

Whatever adventurous crew had come to view the ruins had already left for other parts of the island. I saw no sign of Captain Lyon, First Mate Wm. Flatt, or Horace Downs, though there were plenty of tracks about where crewmembers had clearly inspected the foundations and outcroppings of rock around Erlabrunn. Striding through the center of the village I was struck by the abject solitude of this place. The low structure of the chapel was the only real evidence of civilization; and even that, crudely formed as it was, only hinted at the works capable of Mankind. The rude, four-sided hovel bore the remnants of a thatched roof that had largely been removed by the pressures of wind and rain. The only indication that this structure had indeed once been a chapel was a whitewashed cross starkly painted on the keystone above the doorless opening.

I must admit that I did peer inside the chapel but I *did not* go inside. Though I do not normally consider myself superstitious, I did experience a pervasive notion at first that it would be a breach of decorum to step foot over the threshold. My observation of the interior, albeit fleeting, was nonetheless indelibly committed to memory, and only served to grow the pit of disquiet germinating in my soul. The slant of sun through the ruined roof on the narrow rows of stone benches, crouched contritely as they were before the tumbledown alter, was an eerie culmination to our jaunt through Erlabrunn. Upon seeing the chapel's haunting aspect I begged MacCurdy to return me to *The Polyphylax*, for I felt that today's expedition was definitively concluded.

I wished to see no more.

*Monday, May 26*th*, 1828*
Schicksale Atoll, Day 1 (evening)

I supped tonight with the officers on the beach. It was a welcome change from the cramped mess aboard *The Polyphylax*. Captain Lyon had the writing table in his quarters unbolted and brought to the beach, where I, first mate William Flatt, second mate Peter Forsyth, and Horace Downs joined him for a meal of salted pork, biscuit, tinned preserves and wine. We dined until far after sunset, when the abundant spill of stars, and the silver face of the full moon became our only light. Throughout the meal I suffered in a perpetual state of disquiet, a fact remarked upon more than once by Mister Downs. His attempted probings and jibes were met with indifference as I held my composure at the Captain's table. The Captain for his part, a man demanding of respect and admiration, ignored this display, quite content to hold forth with Mister Flatt and Mister Forsyth about their observations gleaned that day on their circumnavigation of the atoll. Of course the topic of the chapel was broached. I listened intently, though I endeavored to appear more interested in the soft susurrus of the surf lapping the nearby shore.

There were indeed some interesting gems in the ensuing exchange, and I will note some of what was said here. Captain Lyon was speaking of his belief that Erlabrunn had been beset by a storm or perhaps sickness that had quickly ended the settlement when Mister Flatt said, "Sir, begging to differ, but as was recorded in the logs of *The Caelum*, there really is no evidence of what may have happened, one way or t'other."

"Ah," replied the Captain, "but there you are wrong. You saw the evidence yourself this very day!"

Flatt, Forsyth and Downs waited in patience for the answer, while I began about packing my post-supper pipe.

"The chapel, my good men. Don't you see?" In the wan moonlight I observed the expression of sure confidence I'd come to expect on the Captain's broad face. "The chapel still stands as a testament not only to the mercy of God, but to the piety of the men and women of Erlabrunn." He measured out another round of wine and continued. "Ask yourself this: *if* savages had attacked the settlement, surely they would have toppled the chapel. *If* some "madness" had taken hold of the settlers, surely they themselves, in a fit of heathenism, would have razed that symbol of all that is good and just in the world."

"But a sickness," said Mister Flatt with some doubt still in his voice, "would there not be graves? Bones?"

"Precisely why I tend toward the belief that a monsoon must have wiped the settlers away," Captain Lyon said sadly. "We sailors well know what havoc the sea can manage."

"But the chapel stands still?" Mister Forsyth exclaimed. "Would it not have become lost in a surge from the ocean?"

The Captain's faith was unshakable. "Nay, Mister Forsyth, God saw fit to protect the chapel as a message to those who came upon it. So that we may know that the people of Erlabrunn believed in Him completely, even through the horror of such a frightening tempest."

I knew the Captain to be a pious man, and I could see how his explanation made perfect and utter sense to himself, but for my part I remained unconvinced. I said nothing about this though. It was not my place to counter his narrative, but I could not stop myself from adding,

"It is always important to remember just where we stand in the great expanse of Nature."

The Captain and his crewmates raised their cups to this. "Indeed," said the Captain.

I pressed on, afraid I might be putting too fine a point on it. "Equally important to remember just how impossible it is to reign in Nature. It can never truly belong to us."

Again the Captain and his crewmates raised their cups. Horace Downs, though, looked ready to spit. He eyed me contemptuously and said, "Naiveté. Pure naiveté. Mankind has every right to go where he pleases."

Mister Downs was edging toward a particular tender area for me. I eyed him right back. "Land like this can never really belong to Man. Look about us." I gestured to the crashing waves all around. "We are at the mercy of the Sublime."

There were some mumblings of approval from the three seafarers.

Mister Downs was perhaps deeply inebriated at this point, but he continued, wheeling on the Captain, Flatt and Forsyth. "This island," he slurred slowly, just before swallowing a mouthful of wine, "it is very vulnerable to storm surges such as this…in your estimation?"

"Oh, indeed," said the Captain.

Mister Downs seemed to ruminate on this for some time before asking, "And what might one do to protect an island like this from the caprices of the weather?"

The Captain, Flatt and Forsyth stared at each other in shocked silence for a mere moment and then broke into great peals of laughter. I admit I was delighted by the twist of humiliation that distorted Mister Downs's features, for he had utterly walked into this. Mister Flatt gained his senses and said, "Protection? You jest, sir. There's nothing one can do against the unmitigated power of a monsoon."

I did not offer "prayer" as a form of protection, not wanting to dampen the point that the seasoned seamen were making. It was not long after this embarrassment that Mister Downs began to pandiculate with great exaggeration before exchanging pleasantries and excusing himself for his berth. I continued to smoke my pipe in peace, reveling in the small victory over that repugnant creature.

Tuesday, May 27th, 1828
Schicksale Atoll, Day 2

Further Description of Schicksale Atoll

I left *The Polyphylax* alone early after morning breakfast call to facilitate a proper reconnaissance of the atoll in entirety. It is time I fully describe the most salient natural features of Schicksale. The climate is of course tropical, with the temperature never wavering far from twenty-five degrees Celsius. Though we are squarely within the rainy season, the weather thus far has been pleasant and we seem to be avoiding the worst of what Nature has to offer. The ocean waters are warm, and inviting, though the tides can be rather forceful if one ventures too far from land.

By my estimation the sum total of the island is described by an oblong ellipse, more than ten kilometers in circumference. Here is my impression of a bird's-eye-view, with notes.
Figure three.

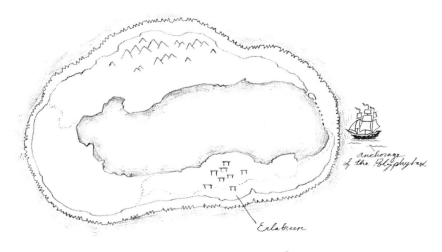

Figure 3: Schicksale atoll

The northernmost side is dominated by a jagged, volcanic outcropping that towers to what appears to be thirty or so meters. The view from the top is extraordinary. Even the ponderous bulk of *The Polyphylax* looked to be nothing but a toy from the top of the scarp. The rest of the atoll is relatively low in elevation. The surrounding reef is exposed during low tide on three sides, but is largely absent from the eastern end of the atoll; this is where *The Polyphylax* is anchored. The aforementioned basalt and coral are the only geological accretions of any note.

Overview of Flora and Fauna:

Schicksale Atoll's beach is in the main suffrutescent, broken by patches of grass and shrubbery, with the occasional thickets of coconut palms standing in scattered groupings. Most of the spiny grass nearest the ocean is constantly pruned and eaten by terrestrial crabs, likely *Johngarthia planata*, a slow process, which I witnessed myself. The grass beneath the palms, on the slightly higher elevations, is mostly untouched still by the bright orange crabs. Most of the other flora is either the white-flowered *Heliotropium curassavicum,* or the succulent *Portulaca oleracea*. What is unclear is whether these are native, or were somehow introduced to Schicksale.

Separately from the crabs, the only other land animals I have detected are two species of reptiles, being the dusty, tan *Gehyra insulensis,* and a very swift skink that appeared to be *Emoia cyanura,* or related. The fowl I have seen have uniformly exhibited the peculiar tendency to take flight at the slightest provocation, as if they are accustomed to remain constantly on the move, though there are no natural predators for them here. Most of my identifications have been from fleeting airborne specimens, but so far bird species seen include terns, boobies, noddies, frigates, coots, martins, and warblers. I believe I may have also seen a single duck as well. I will elaborate on the list of birds when I am able to gather more information.

The Central Lagoon

By far the most interesting geological feature is the expansive lagoon at the heart of the atoll. When standing on one shore, the other side of the ring is more than halfway to the horizon. At high tide, waves intermittently spill over the north-western rim into the lagoon, replenishing the stagnant, freshwater reservoir. The water is much cloudier than the surrounding ocean, so that visibility becomes obscured within the depth of a few inches. The underwater shelf of the inner shore falls at a very steep declination, leaving a swimmer unable to touch the bottom in a mere matter of moments. The ultimate depth of the lagoon is unknown.

The body appears to be wholly devoid of fish, or any other marine life. In fact, one would expect the water to be highly eutrophic, and veritably bursting with seaweed due to the likely abundant concentration of vitamin and mineral content, but not a single shred of seaweed was observed within the murky inner lagoon. Though the water is quite foul of odor, it is believed to be potable, at least by the crew of *The Polyphylax*.

Tuesday, May 27^{*th*}*, 1828*
Schicksale Atoll, Day 2 (later)

Finally I have fully come to understand the crux of that rogue Horace Downs's animosity towards me! Now that I have collected myself fully after a heated encounter, I believe I can find the words to explain properly. Near noon I was apprehended by the villain on the far side of the atoll. Whilst in the midst of exploring the volcanic escarpment, I heard the distinct tapping of his silver-clawed walking stick on the rocks below. He called up to me, his studied banker's voice straining with the effort. The man cannot be more than fifty years old but the sourness of a venal and grasping life has clearly aged him prematurely beyond his years. I reluctantly left my examinations of the bird droppings upon the highest bleached rocks there and treaded my way cautiously to *terra firma*.

There I was met with instant hostility as Mister Downs hurled accusations that I had been rummaging in his belongings upon *The Polyphylax*. I denied this, for of course it was not true. I am not sure whether my words were any salve, but Mister Downs quickly shifted the conversations to questioning me as to whether I had witnessed the Captain's peculiar behavior that morning. I said I had not, and asked him to elaborate. He was clearly distressed, and could not focus on any one particular topic for too long. In point of fact, he continued with accusations of my character before telling me that the Captain had rounded up the crew, as well as Mister Downs himself, and dressed them down for perceived mutinous tendencies. This was an allegation that seemed wholly out of character for the Captain, and indeed for the crew. I was not sorry that I had missed the display. What's more, the Captain had apparently been clutching a small wooden elephant in his hands, a crude thing the likes of which no one had yet seen on the voyage at any time. When approached by Mister Flatt during the tirade, the Captain accused Flatt of trying to steal the doll. It was then that the Captain warned them off of any further behavior of this type and then retired to his quarters for the rest of the morning, taking the elephant and leaving Mister Flatt in charge of the daily duties.

Upon Mister Downs's finishing delivery of this information, he once again employed an accusatory finger toward me, going so far as snatching at my leather satchel, and demanding to search it for a missing gold pocket watch that "meant much to him." The irony of his accusations, and their strange mirroring of what he had described about the Captain and the elephant were lost on Mister Downs. At this point I could not even tell if he was giving me a straight story at all, and in a fit I upended my own belongings on the sand, spilling my inkpot, and losing a small sheaf of paper in the process to the wind. I could see by the scoundrel's eye that this satisfied his curiosity, and in fact the discomfit that it caused me amused some malevolent streak deep within his character. Oh, how I hate to see that scar-like leer upon his white-whiskered face!

It was then, when I was on my knees gathering my scattered implements and cursing him under my breath, that Horace Downs delivered the death stroke, and I comprehended to what allegiance his shriveled heart was truly magnetized. "There's a handsome sight. Supplicate yourself, McNabb, and make your pitiful notes. For this is the last time that anyone will see this island as a useless ring of sand in the middle of the ocean. Come this time next year, Barker and Company will have transformed this disgraceful, forgotten reef into a waypoint of activity. The Gateway to the East, McNabb." He indicated the vast lagoon. "Fresh water and prime positioning. Nothing can stand in our way. Bet on it!" I began to protest, to argue for the pristine haven of Nature when he *whacked* his walking stick across my back, and kicked a tumbling piece of paper out of my grasp and into the lagoon. Thus satisfied, he made off, derisive laughter taking flight in the steadily blowing wind.

There it was. Evidence of an overriding contempt for Nature, and the full machinery of Her mysterious workings. His kind wishes nothing more than to see every animal and plant entered into a ledger and then subjugated or smote beneath the wheel of Great Progress. The very land itself is more important than anything that may have originated upon it from his corrupted, fully debased locus. Given the plans of his Barker and Company now revealed, it was more important than ever that I preserve what I could of this mysterious ecosystem. Tomorrow I will make a point of quickly gathering what other small samples I can for transport back to the archive store of the Raleigh Club, for now I must administer a compress to the throbbing welt on my spine.

Wednesday, May 28th, 1828
Schicksale Atoll, Day 3 (morning)

Panic is the order of the day.

At dawn, First Mate Flatt delivered the news that the Captain had not been seen for some hours and that we would be breaking into four parties to search the island in an attempt to find some clue as to his fate. I was partnered with MacCurdy the boatswain, Musters the cook, and crewmembers Sullivan Peters, and George York. We were assigned the most south-westerly quadrant of the atoll. This portion of the ring is mostly flat and devoid of feature other than the occasional palm or rock grouping. Despite this we spent the completeness of the morning devoted to uncovering any clue as to the Captain's whereabouts. None of the crew was in the best of spirits, but MacCurdy seemed to be taking the fact of the missing Captain particularly hard. Indeed, moral was clearly draining away quickly in the absence of the popular Captain Lyon.

Because Captain Lyon was well known for wearing a particular square-toed boot, it was tracks of this variety that we paid especial attention to. Since during the Captain's exploration of the atoll he had already trod quite extensively about the island, and so thus, there were plenty of tracks for us to examine, though none seemed to offer any real answer as to where he may have disappeared to during the previous night. During our search I questioned MacCurdy about the Captain's demeanor the previous day, as I had not encountered him upon returning to *The Polyphylax* in the evening. Returning late I had missed dinner, but he had apparently not been present for his meal either. All of this was of course very distressing to MacCurdy and to the other members of the crew. When I inquired about the unusual wooden elephant, no one seemed to know anything about it, and MacCurdy swore he had never seen such an item in the Captain's quarters or anywhere else on the ship, though it was possible it might have been stowed in the Captain's personal chest.

An hour later I finally saw the elephant with my own eyes. When we returned to the ship, the group that had searched the south-eastern section of the ring, the section that contained the lost settlement of Erlabrunn, had already returned and had found the little doll half sunk into the sand on the lagoon side of the beach near the black stone chapel. What's more, the Captain's square-towed tracks lead inland, toward the lagoon where he had evidently sat and then stood and continued down into the lagoon itself. No tracks led away from the water.

This was taken as incontrovertible evidence that the Captain was lost for good and as such Mister Flatt took command of the ship, assuming the mantle of Captain. While we waited for the rest of the crew to arrive he drew me aside and showed me the small elephant. It was a rough thing that had seen many years. The trunk was broken off long ago, for the nub had been worn smooth. There was no paint or other decoration upon the wooden surface. The figure clearly did not originate on the island for it was whittled from applewood. I have reproduced it here.

Figure four.

Figure 4: The Elephant Figurine

I reported my observations to Captain Flatt, surmising that it may have belonged to one of the lost villagers. The Captain confirmed that it indeed was not from the island, and that it *did* belong to Captain Lyon, at least according to his words. This had been conveyed to Flatt shortly before Lyon had disappeared, Lyon claiming that it had been lost when he was a child and indeed *found* in the crude chapel in Erlabrunn. Neither I nor Captain Flatt knew what to make of this claim, and I remarked on the fact that it was more likely that given his behavior, Captain Lyon had been suffering from some debilitating fever and had either found it, assumed it was his, or *had* actually brought it and forgot that detail. At any rate he was no longer here to clear this up and we were left dumfounded as to the true origin of the figure.

Wednesday, May 28th, 1828
Schicksale Atoll, Day 3 (later)

I find I do not have the energy or wherewithal to continue cataloging the features of the atoll today. The enigmatic fate of Captain Lyon has paralyzed the crew, myself included, and no one feels entirely safe any longer. There are whispers that the voyage may be cut short prematurely of the planned three weeks. I cannot say I entirely disagree with this. No decisions have been made yet, and I am confident that I will be able to rally tomorrow for another excursion onto the atoll. Furthermore, in light of the recent events, Captain Flatt has ordered that no man shall debark unescorted from *The Polyphylax*.

Wednesday, May 28th, 1828
Schicksale Atoll, Day 3 (evening)

No one left the ship this afternoon. The atoll is now regarded as cursed by much of the crew and it has been decided that we will set sail the day after tomorrow. The meal this evening was a quiet, solemn affair. Even Mister Prior, who is known to customarily lead a shanty or two after a meal, was conspicuously silent as the crew scattered to their berths or duties after eating.

I had been avoiding Mister Downs like a pestilent beggar since our encounter at the escarpment, but while returning from the privy I overheard him discussing his "lost golden timepiece" once again. This time he had buttonholed George York (without recriminations). I paused to take in what the odious man was saying, and was surprised when I heard his plans to visit the stone chapel on the morrow, convinced that the watch would be somewhere within the rude structure. I couldn't imagine how it might have been lost there of all places, but I slipped off quickly after that, wishing to hear his grating voice no more. Little do I care what that man does with his time anyway as long as he is away from me.

Thursday, May 29th, 1828
En voyage to England

We have left even earlier than planned, and I am relieved.

Let me chronicle here what has happened so that there may be no mistake Schicksale Atoll truly is a cursed place, and no man should set foot upon its execrable beaches. The events unfolded thusly:

I awoke at early call, ready to make a final reconnaissance of the island, and gather what specimens I could before what was to be our departure on the morrow, the thirtieth. According to Captain Flatt's orders I was not able to leave the ship without companionship, and since he had no duties at the moment I employed Conrad MacCurdy for the role. MacCurdy is a sailor through and through, but he has privately divulged to me that he does indeed suffer from a spot of nausea when ship-bound for too long. Being that we were slated to spend the next several weeks on the open ocean he was all too happy to take a final stroll on solid ground.

We debarked early, alone, for no other crew wished to spend any more time upon the island. Whilst leaving I did witness Horace Downs speaking with deckhand Martin Billet about a final trip to the ruins of Erlabrunn, but Billet did not seem amenable to venturing forth. Mister Downs of course did not want to accompany *me* anywhere.

MacCurdy and I had a fruitful morning. I must say my affection for the man has grown inestimably over the course of our adventuring. MacCurdy is a rare soul who balances an equal measure of humility and nobility upon his broad shoulders. I should be so fortunate as to call him "friend" after the conclusion of this expedition. MacCurdy proved himself to have a good eye for shell specimens that, once checked for vacancies, were washed and deposited in my satchel for eventual careful packing and return to England. We decided to make a full, final trip around the atoll, moving clockwise, and only giving a cursory search of the escarpment, as I had thoroughly scrutinized that area the day before.

The day was reaching a very hot noon, with the sun high and burning bright in the center of the sky when we came upon the remains of Erlabrunn. Thinking to luncheon there we sought out a sprawl of shade beneath a clump of palms near the chapel, as neither MacCurdy nor I wished to take our meal within the confines of that curious structure. As we drew closer it became apparent that someone was within the chapel though. A scuffle ensued, punctuated by muffled shouts, and then Horace Downs shot forth, navigating the rocks and sands in an alarmed, clumsy run back toward *The Polyphylax*. He did not look over his shoulder, and did not see MacCurdy or I from our place in the shade. I was about to call after him when we heard more noise come from the chapel. A moment later newly promoted first mate Peter Forsyth stumbled out of the chapel, clutching something small and brightly shining in his hands. MacCurdy and I *did* call out to Forsyth, who either did not hear us, or chose to ignore our entreaties. Forsyth shambled in a sort of dazed fashion down the central path of Erlabrunn and turned right, inland. MacCurdy and I followed at some distance, calling out all the while. After stumbling over the inland dunes Forsyth came to the edge of the lagoon and went to his knees. I still could not see what he had clenched so tightly in his hand. Forsyth brought his lips low and drank deeply from the lagoon for what seemed a long, very long while. MacCurdy and I were nearly behind him when he abruptly stood and dove fast and straight out into the lagoon, disappearing beneath the murky surface.

MacCurdy and I waited for him to surface, unsure what the man could be thinking. The seconds passed slowly, feeling like an eternity. Finally MacCurdy lunged forth himself, diving beneath the placid water and similarly vanishing. I was dumbstruck, completely irresolute at what my next move should be when MacCurdy finally surfaced with a thrashing Peter Forsyth gathered under one iron-thewed arm. MacCurdy navigated his way back to the shore, dragging Forsyth behind amidst great splashes and oaths. Once they were beached I aided MacCurdy in subduing Forsyth who made as if to throw himself back into the lagoon. Ultimately it took both of us, and the leather thong from my satchel gathered about Forsyth's wrists, to force Forsyth back to *The Polyphylax*. During the struggles back to the ship I finally could see what it was that Forsyth held with such a fierce death grip in his hand. A tiny silver thimble.

Captain Flatt observed our return to the ship and had two deckhands join in lifting Forsyth aloft, and after some explanation from MacCurdy and I, carrying him to the brig where he was isolated under lock and key. Martin Billet attempted to wrest the thimble from Forsyth, and was bitten in the process so badly that it was agreed that the man should be allowed to keep his trinket. I inquired after Horace Downs, and was told that he had returned to his berth in an agitated state. After the episode with Forsyth I could see the crew was utterly shaken. Captain Flatt clearly came to the same conclusion for he ordered at that moment that we pull up anchor and begin our voyage home.

Thursday, May 29th, 1828
En voyage to England (evening)

Captain Flatt called an hour ago and conscripted me into visiting Forsyth to help ascertain the tenor of his mental state. I am shaken by the encounter and I will endeavor to record my thoughts here, though I am no expert. When I arrived in the brig the ship surgeon Robert Peck was administering a compress of witch hazel to the fevered brow of Forsyth, who was tethered to a cot in the small dark cell. The thimble was still gripped defiantly in one hand, the silver edge peeking out between fingers and catching hints of lantern light. Peck, for his part, was tired and rather hungry. The laconic doctor was more than happy to hand the compress over to me without comment and take his leave. Before he left though I enquired about the thimble. He said that Forsyth only mentioned it once when the doctor tried to slip it from his hand, gripping tighter and saying that his mother gave it to him. With that Peck left. Having some very distant and cursory medical training in my youth I set about easing the discomfort of Forsyth as best I could.

It was my intention to question him about what he had experienced in the chapel that had driven him to such rash action, but I soon learned that no amount of coaxing could get through the veil of madness that had took hold. I had very soon heard the extent of Forsyth's ramblings, for they were encompassed by a repeated series of sentences, uttered through clenched teeth that went thusly:

"Lovely Heaven below.
Mother, I am coming.
I have done all that I can do.
When will you show yourself?"

This was almost poetic, and seemed nearly familiar, but I could not place a source. For some time I listened to Forsyth mumble these words over and over, sure that I myself might be driven mad by the unceasing incantation. After some time I attempted to engage Forsyth once more, asking him what role Horace Downs had played in the incident at the chapel. Forsyth abruptly terminated the recitation and inclined his neck to get a better look at me. Seeing him lick his parched lips I was sure he was ready to actually deliver some new detail when he rudely spat directly into my face. His wheezing breath devolved into maniacal tittering, and I chose to take my leave.

Now more than ever I was convinced Horace Downs had played some dastardly part in the day's sequence of events. I sought out the monster, finding him still entrenched in his berth, blanket pulled fully over his bald, sun-reddened head. I pulled him quite roughly from the bunk and shook his wiry frame to bits, demanding answers; for I am sad to say it now, a bestial rage had fully taken control of my faculties. I stared into the eyes of a sobbing mess. Mister Downs was crying, and making no effort at all to fight back. I let go and the man fell to a heap at my knees. His hands scrabbled at my boots, and I took a step back. "Away. We have to get away," he was saying. I asked him what had transpired between he and Forsyth in the chapel and he gave me no answer, only repeating his pleadings. It was then I removed myself from the pitiful scene and retreated to the slop room where I knew I would have some privacy to collect myself. The whole of the ship feels mad to me, suffused with some abominable hex woven by *that place*. Schicksale atoll, *Erdrunavaya*, as it was known, should be stricken from any and every map.

Whatever shall I do now?

Thursday, May 29th, 1828
En voyage to England (night)

I have been startled awake by screams from amidships. I must have fallen asleep here in the slop room. The screams grow closer, but

89

Max Dowdle

I cannot tell whose voice…it is many voices…screams of pain, not anger. I dare not move from this place. I have barred the door with store barrels and crate wood stowed here. No one knows I am here but the rats, and even they are frightened by the noises outside the door.

I will wait it out here, and see what the dawn holds.

Friday, May 30th, 1828

Insanity has taken hold of *The Polyphylax*, and all is lost. It is here, in the Captain's quarters that I am sure my existence will come to an end, and I can only hope that someone will find this journal and know what tragedy befell us. Beside me is Horace Downs, breathing his final lungful, and as far as I can tell we are the last two living souls aboard the ship, excepting whatever damnable thing Forsyth has become. I may have just enough time to tell the tale, for we have barred the door and Forsyth is otherwise engaged.

Upon waking once again in the slop room after the terrors of the eternal night I found that the ship was quiet. There were no portholes in the slop room, but hunger overrode my fear and I decided to venture forth to seek answers. I removed the barricade I had created and opened the door to find a sepulchral quiet. The soft slap of water on the hull outside, and creak of ship timbers were the only noises. I sought out the stairs, seeing the splashes of inviting sunlight slanting through the deck slats. Above deck my eyes were assaulted by the bright sun of midday. I stumbled, slipping on something as my eyes adjusted. When I looked about I found unimaginable horror. Streaks of blood painted the deck from one end to the other. Ragged holes were torn in the lower sail and it flapped vainly in the breeze, trying to billow full. A severed hand rested against the base of the mizzenmast in a pool of red. A rope was tattooed round the wrist. MacCurdy. I retched, spilling what little contents I had in my stomach upon my boots.

A voice called to me from the quarterdeck, and there I beheld a fearsome haunt at the helm. Peter Forsyth, shrouded in a blood-drenched length of canvas cut from the sails, leered at me over the wheel. His muscles jumped with a feverish energy, and his tendons stood tautly beneath his sallow skin. His eyes blazed with an intense madness I did not think possible in a human face. The whole of his being seemed animated by some dreadful power as he left off the

90

wheel and approached. Even amid this madness I saw the silver thimble on his finger, shining starkly in the sunlight. Disoriented, I could not think of what to ask him. How was it he came to be free? Where was the crew? "Lovely heaven below," he said, continuing his chant from before. This time he changed it though, adding, "We go, McNabb. Erdrunavaya calls." With this he cast aside the sailcloth, revealing a blood-soaked cutlass. I dove down the stairs of the companionway before he reached me, hearing the bite of the blade in the wood of the hatch behind me.

I fled through the aft hold where I found the berth deck transformed into an abattoir, so much so that the creosoted ceilings dripped moist with the spilled lifeblood of the crew that had rose up against the carnage Forsyth wrought. I slipped again, trying to gain purchase in the gore strewn about the floor as *The Polyphylax* creaked over the bucking waves outside. I could hear the fury of Forsyth behind me as I made my way to the forward hold, trying to ignore the snatches of horror I saw from the wan light of the skylights. Faces, these familiar crew, dead. Many had died quickly from slashed throats, or cleaved breastbones, others looked to have suffered more protracted, painful fates.

A small voice called to me in the dark and I strained to hear what direction it came from. I moved toward the voice, when my satchel was suddenly caught short by something along the way. I panicked, pulling, imagining the grasping hand of Forsyth had seized me. I reached back and found the loose nail I was caught on and freed myself. In the hatch leading to the orlop deck I found the shivering form of Horace Downs. "This way," he implored in a barely audible whisper. I had no choice but to follow the man down, deeper, below the water line and into the black, cable-filled space of the orlop. We waited there for some time, discussing our options as we listened to the stampings and searchings going on above us. Our options really only seemed two: To sneak above and take the lifeboat, or to rush Forsyth and subdue, or more preferably, kill the man. As we had no weapons, and both of us were well past our prime we decided on the former idea, and that is assuredly where we truly made our last mistake.

We crept over the oiled cables toward the stern, as we heard Forsyth headed in the direction of the bow. When we found the stern hatch we wriggled through quickly, and intended to head toward the ladder to the spar deck when we were waylaid by Forsyth. The fiend had doubled-back and interrupted our escape. He brandished the cutlass, jabbing at us playfully, backing us towards the Captain's quarters. Downs, for his part, made a last heroic stand and lunged at Forsyth, only to be answered with a swift cut to the belly that stopped him in his tracks. Downs grasped at his suddenly bloodied midsection in complete surprise. Forsyth smiled and leaned against the wall in a casual way that belied the venomous power coursing through is veins. I grasped Downs's coat and pulled him through the door to the Captain's quarters, slamming the heavy door behind me and barring it.

Downs collapsed on the bed, staring at his reddened hands and the place where his shirt was parted to reveal a deep gash in his skin. His intestines strained at the cut, brimming over his belt. He looked upon me with an expression of profound loss. We both knew what this meant. I gathered the captains bedding over the wound and implored Downs to hold pressure there as I endeavored to bar the door further.

A small tapping had started at the door, and I imagined Forsyth on the other side, striking a beat like that of a tiny metal heart with the small silver thimble. He called our names, and then began his litany. The gibbering at the door, like the fevered mumblings of an opium addict who had too long existed without a draw on the pipe, gave me the feeling of a trapped rat. This lasted for some time, as I tried to ease Downs into some more comfort. At some point the tapping and raving stopped and Forsyth went away. It was then that I searched the Captain's belongings, but we were woefully under-supplied in this room. No food or weapons had been left in here. Seeing that Downs had equalized I set about writing these words here in this journal.

So here I sit, writing this in a splash of dimming sunlight from a porthole too small to escape through. We are headed back to the atoll, prisoners captained by a madman. I have the sketches of a theory, settled upon by my observations, as to why this is happening, but it is still fairly incomplete. Nevertheless I shall try to muddle through my fatigue. The chapel acts as a sort of hallucinogenic agent that induces a madness in anyone that stays too long within its walls. I might go so far to say that it is likely there is an animalcule at play that impacts the nervous system on some microscopic level. I have no hard scientific basis for this, and it is cut from the whole cloth of speculation. As far as the mysterious objects, I cannot account for the elephant or the thimble and their associated meanings. Both Lyon and

Forsyth seemed to have believed these items to belong to them, though no crew member had ever seen them before, leaving one to assume they came into each respective man's possession on the island itself. But how? I have not figured out how Horace Downs's search for his watch figures into the narrative, and he his beyond the asking now. Whatever it was that drove these men to these absurdities it is wholly beyond my ken, and I feel stretched too thinly mentally to decipher this further. Perhaps some other explorer in the future will be able to solve the mystery, but if it were up to me, I would warn off anyone from spending a moment on that awful piece of blighted land.

Downs's hands, tensed to ridged claws, can barely hold the pale coils of his bowels in place any longer. I fear he may already be dead, and that there is nothing I can do for him now. When I finish writing I will seal this journal in oilskin and secret it in the Captain's waterproof trunk so that it will be known what tragedy befell the crew of *The Polyphylax.*

I know now that I am doomed no matter what I do.

Even if I were able to somehow overpower Forsyth and take command of the ship, I would still be hopelessly lost at sea.

The sweet salt-tinged wind washes over my face, as we sail back toward that cursed island. I can just now see one bright edge of the coral reef creeping into distant view.

I hear the tap-tapping once again at the door.

Peter Forsyth has said his piece and left. Those final ravings echo in my ears still.

"You were right all along, McNabb. The Gift of God does not belong to us. We belong to the Gift of God. We belong to *Erdrunavaya.*" I cannot help but shudder as I write the final words Flatt called out as he ascended the ladder back to the wheel above.

"*And Erdrunavaya must be fed.*"

Before me is an ivory-handled letter opener found among Captain Lyon's belongings. The point is sharp…and tempting. I dare not let Forsyth take me to the island alive.

I do not wish to learn what lurks below the waters of the lagoon.

Gavin McNabb, 1828

Max Dowdle

The Picker In The Shade

Once again I willed the boy to look up at me. He wasn't one of the dormitory pickers. He lived nearby on a corn farm, but made the six-mile walk every morning before sunup to the strawberry fields to earn extra money for his family. Those were the only things I knew about him. That, and the fact that he was beautiful. Though his body was tall, broad-shouldered and powerful, he stooped lightly in the rows and gathered each berry with the gentlest of care. His skin and hair were fair, and he preferred to pick in the shade, so he always made sure to get here early and claim the rows nearest the tree line. That's where he was now, and I wished that just once he would glance up and meet my waiting eyes.

When he'd first been hired on a week ago, I could not take my eyes off of him. Near midday he would strip his loose linen shirt from the knit muscles of his chest, splash himself with water during his only break and then head into the vast fields again. He was quicker than most, delivering his baskets to the owner's wife and trading them in for empties. The other dormitory pickers noted my interest in the boy, and they chided me, shamed me into undertaking my ogling in a more furtive fashion. Not one of them even knew his name, for he was a shy boy, who returned home every evening without a word to the other pickers.

Picking can be punishing work, tough on the back and knees. I was near ready to quit, and perhaps take up as a washerwoman down by the creek, when the boy first arrived. His presence became a salve to my blistered fingers and throbbing muscles. Every day his body shone twilight blue beneath the shade of the great oaks that ran the length of the fields, and I studied him, from the plowed furrow in his brow as he concentrated on his work, to the way his well-formed calves minutely tensed each time he snapped the stem of a strawberry. When he inevitably pulled an overripe berry, and burst the skin, he would lick his fingers with the soft length of his tongue, and I would die a little with desire. I had known men before, but the country innocence of this boy left me feeling blissful flutters in my chest every time I saw him. At night I would lie awake in the humid dormitory, slapping at mosquitos and letting my hands wander about my own hills and valleys as I dreamed of the boy.

I made it a daily goal to claim rows near the boy, and to stay abreast of his pace. Today I was making good time despite the full heat of the day, clearing nearly as many baskets as he, but I'd been unable to catch a row near him at daybreak. He was three pickers over, working the furthest edge near the trees, with his back to me. Once again I despaired I'd ever get to know him. I looked down at my hands, reflexively testing the tenderness of a berry's skin before slicing the stem with my long thumbnail. When I glanced back up, the boy's eyes were locked on mine.

With the slightest of nods he set the basket down and raised a hand. A wave. Or near as I could tell, some kind of beckoning gesture. My heart quickened. I looked around. Was he signaling me? Every other picker's back was bent into the fields. I looked toward the boy standing in the shadows beneath the tree, still waving his beautiful hand at me. He stepped back into the deeper shadows, still staring at me, lips spreading into an inviting smile. My cheeks flushed in anticipation. Could he really be asking me beneath the trees? If so, we wouldn't be the first pickers to briefly escape duties for the fulfillment of lusty desires. I'd heard talk.

I searched far down the field for the owner's wife, saw her dozing beneath a faded parasol, and dropped my basket. I began to hop over the rows, feet born light by the promise of gratification, and eyes locked on the boy who was receding slowly into the cool interior of the forest. It's easy to get used to the sun, and the way it commands the day while we toil in the fields below, but all of that suffocating heat drained away as I stepped from the furrows of strawberries into the wild underbrush beneath the oaks. I tore my hat from my head and let my hair fall where it may. I was feeling uninhibited like the forest around me, and I wanted the boy to find me as irresistible as I found him. The shade was deepening here, and our fellow workers would not be able to see whatever it was we got up to. The boy stood in a cleft of darkness between two trees, smiling, and still waving that slow wave. I paused a few paces away to unbutton my shirt. The boy's hand continued to wave, but the wrist went limp.

I halted, three buttons down, questioning the moment. All at once, something seemed wrong with the boy. His arms and head moved in a subtle, puppet-like fashion, and all of a sudden his body tumbled to the weedy ground in separate, blood-leaking pieces. The once beautiful head lolled on the forest floor, pale eyes drawn toward the heavens, and a rivulet of deep red seeped from the torn neckline. A thickening, tangible blackness behind where the boy had stood reared up, repulsive and all encompassing. I turned to flee, and the bright field tended by the oblivious pickers burned into my vision as a hand of darkness descended over my weeping eyes.

And then it took me.

Max Dowdle

Matchmaker

This is the only place I can truly get lost anymore. The sun's hot fingers are massaging my back with every pedal stroke, wringing the stress from my muscles, as I zip far away from where I left my car in tiny downtown Pittsboro an hour ago. Good, clean sweat paints my cheeks and brow beneath my helmet. I speed down another hill, and revel in the blissful exertion of body and bike shooting through the summer wind as one. There's nothing like taking an aimless ride in the country for clearing one's head. Every mile peels another layer away. *Whizz!* No more spinning my wheels temping and answering phones at Falco Water Treatment. *Zoom!* No more churlish barking from the neighbor's miniature pinscher. *Swish!* No more mailbox stuffed with overdue credit card notices. *Whoosh!* And, of course, a break from Jamie. *Foom!* Three more glorious hours of this and I might be able to face that cluttered world once again. I reach the bottom of this hill and on a lark I take a left toward the hundreds of acres of cornfield that lay west of town, expecting I'll be home just in time for a shower and dinner. I don't know it yet, but I've just done something I will come to regret for the rest of my life.

Going for a ride? Be back by six. We've got Estrella's dinner party tonight, Tara! My boyfriend Jamie's last words to me as I broke for the door are the only nuggets still rattling around in the ol' brainpan. I know I should just break up with him and let sassy Estrella sink her teeth in. He's just the kind of meal she likes anyway. Jamie's a sweet kid, but do I really see myself chained to a financial anchor like that? A last minute switch to a visual art degree with a focus in "conceptual installation"? Come on! I really don't know what the hell I was thinking getting together with this dud. Dad would never have approved. Well, it doesn't matter right now. Nothing does. Pushing the thoughts from my mind, I focus on riding farther away from town, from cars, from businesses and from houses. The roads narrow as the countryside opens up, willing to embrace me with wide, corn-laden arms, and I take great pleasure in turning randomly at intersections.

A powder-blue Ford pickup buzzes by. Cracked windshield. Rusted wheel wells. Shirtless gentleman leering over a beer. I'm in the country, all right. Up ahead I spy another cyclist. He slows to take a long pull from his water bottle. I speed up, intending to pass him quickly, when I notice something that makes me chuckle. We're wearing the exact same orange Firegear Durham racing jerseys. I tick along beside him. I can see now that he's long and lean, tan and very comfortable on his bike. Solid thighs. The curls springing out from beneath his helmet shine like copper wire. His earnest blue eyes say he might be interesting, and *interested*. "Twins," I say, thoughts of Jamie far away. Nonexistent.

"What?" He looks down and smiles, showing a great set of teeth. "Oh, you too huh? Do well?"

I shrug. "Not my best." The truth is I have nearly no time for training while trying to keep both Jamie and myself afloat. The Firegear race in May had actually been my worst time in three years.

There's that award-winning smile again. "Maybe better next time."

A dusty intersection approaches. Part of me wants to continue our conversation, but that's not why I'm out here. I want solitude. He's angling left. I turn right. "Next time," I echo as I pedal away from the looker. Bye, bye, Solid Thighs.

There's little in the way of house or barn out here. Field after field of tall corn flanks me on either side as I settle into the pleasurable rhythms of the road. Here the roads often turn to gravel, and sometimes even dirt. I'm not worried about getting too lost though. Dad always said I had a knack for directions; that's why he'd let me play navigator on sales trips during the summer. I miss that time with him. Though I don't miss roadside motels.

A silver van boils toward me, churning up a plume of dust behind it. GMC Safari. Maybe 1990. Another thing road trips with Dad were good for: learning cars. As this one goes past I see it's got the curtains in the back windows; a "rapevan," my friends and I would have called it in high school. I hold my breath and squint my eyes as I go into the great cloud of swirling dust. There's an engine rev behind me and then I hear a honk. Must be another car trying to get by. I wave whoever is behind me by, but the honk sounds again. I look back and see that the van has turned around, and it's creeping up on me. The vehicle pulls alongside, and I stop pedaling as the passenger window rolls down.

A woman is there. Early twenties, skinny and freckled in a pink halter-top. She's got braids in her dark, sweat-matted hair, and a giant set of sunglasses that cover the top half of her face. She just kind of stares at me, chewing a big wad of gum. The driver, who's harder to see from the shade inside the van but looks to be a guy closer to thirty, leans over the girl and with a soft southern twang says, "Hey, do you know Eric Shepherd?"

This break is a perfect excuse to drain some of my water bottle. That buys me some time to think. *Did* I know someone named Eric Shepherd? Common enough name. I shake my head. "No."

101

He rolls this around a bit and then says, "You never heard of him at all?" The girl just keeps staring at me from behind the black lenses.

I shrug. "Nope." Feet back on the pedals and I'm already pulling away from the van. A hundred or so yards ahead I look behind and see that they're working at a five-point turn to drive off down the dirt road in the opposite direction. Good riddance, weirdoes.

I take the next road I come to, which finds me back on asphalt. The bike likes this better, and so do I. I cycle through the gears, forever marveling at the engineering of such a contraption. Carbon fiber frame, internal cable routing, bladed spokes, all coming in at under five pounds. Oh, how I missed riding this bike! Three thousand dollars on the barrelhead. One of Dad's favorite sayings pops up. *If you can't get it on the barrelhead, don't get it at all.* Well, that was in better days when my wallet had been made up of more green paper than plastic card. I've tried to stick to your lessons, Dad. Sorry.

Jamie's potato-round face bobs into my mind and I blink it away, replacing it with a rakish smile from Solid Thighs. I sigh, and turn east at the next unmarked intersection. The road I choose terminates with a chain and a "No Trespassing" sign so I double back and go north.

A vehicle is approaching. The sun glints off the wide windshield. It looks like another van. *Another* GMC Safari? No. It's the *same* van. Were they that lost? This is close to two miles from where I first saw them. I catch a quick look at the driver this time as they pass. He's got this big grin like a kid looking in on monkeys copulating at the zoo. I give a little wave and move on, picking up my speed. The van vanishes down the road I came from.

I'm guessing the "Elusive Eric Shepherd Meth House" still hasn't been found. They must have nothing better to do on a Sunday than meander around the countryside. I laugh then, realizing that's exactly what I'm doing. Still, did I really look like a friend of a friend, or what? Dad's voice, croaky with cigarette smoke, pipes up. *Never forget: some folks have nothing but cooked vegetables in the ol' brainpan, Tarasaurus.* I'm not exactly worried, but I do pat the pocket with the folding knife Dad gave me as a sweet sixteen present. It's there, with his pet name for me inscribed on the six-inch blade.

Nothing to do but pedal on. I'm zipping down the roads, taking turns casual-like. North, west, south, west, north, east. The sun is still turning up the heat. Not a cloud around to block it. I'm aware that part of my mind has turned to the "Jamie problem," and has been dissecting it for the better part of the afternoon. He'd been so kind when we met, bringing me lunch when I'd temped at that gallery on Mangum. And that first month of sex…never have I met someone so attentive. The gears stick for a moment before clicking into place. Hmmm. It's not enough. I think it's time to call the whole thing off with Jamie before I fall any deeper into that hole. I don't want to get into a situation where I have to tell him "no" while he's down on a knee doing a ring thing. I can see that's where he wants this to go. He'll bounce back, especially if Estrella warms his belly with the artistry of her Peruvian cuisine.

What then?

I turn south, and not twenty feet ahead of me is that damned van again, parked on the side, and hugged up close to some tall stalks of corn. As I begin to peddle by, the driver side window rolls down and the man waves me over. I stop. I can see him well for the first time. He's probably in his late twenties, though it looks like a wild adolescence took a mean toll on his baby face, leaving it overly scarred and prematurely lined. He has at least two-weeks invested in his patchy beard, and a rolled up blue bandana to hold his dark brown locks at bay, à la Bruce Springsteen. The girl continues chewing her gum. *Smack, smackity, smack.* I keep expecting the guy to say something, but he just stares at me with that off-putting smile. At least thirty looooong seconds have gone by. I'm starting to feel nervous because the guy and girl are just looking me over. I'm trying to think up some witty quip I can lay on them before hitting the road again, when the girl nudges him and he says, "Hey, do you know Eric Shepherd?"

What? The same damn question! Okay, what gives? Why are they fucking around with me? He's not smiling anymore, and he's staring me down. The girl is nudging, nudging. She blows a bubble. *Pop!* Are they high? I'm rolling my bike back slowly, and I say, "Nope. Still don't."

The girl pistons her sharp elbow into him again.

"Well, what's *your* name then?" He pulls a cigarette free with his teeth, and cracks this strangely charismatic grin.

"Tara Gill," is out of my mouth before a sense of self-preservation can override my automatic response with something

Max Dowdle

made-up. Is that a steamed bunch of cauliflower sitting in my brainpan? Why the hell did I just tell them *that*?

A smile tickles the girl's lips. "Ta-ra Gee-ull," says the guy, spreading my name out with his country boy drawl. "That's a nice one."

I'm already directing my bike forward, fumbling at the pedals with my feet. "Sorry I don't know your friend. See ya!" I yell back. I'm picking up speed now, getting the hell away from these creeps. I hear the van engine gun behind me and my furiously pumping legs seize up. This is the moment they'll come for me. I know it. I brace for the impending impact, imagining clumps of my hair twisting in the front grill as I'm pulled under the wheels, but when I hazard a look back the van is pulling a U-turn, spraying gravel from under the front tire, and then receding. I remember that I need to breath.

I pause and look to my left and right, realizing just how isolated I am way out here in the country. There's not a house or another vehicle in sight. Hell, there's not even a power line overhead. Woods and cornfield are all I can see. The van's gone, and I have no interest in running into them again. It makes zero sense that I've already seen them as many times as I have, and in such disparate places. Here comes Dad's voice again: *Never attribute to evil something that can be explained by stupidity.* Normally words to live by, Dad, but I'm through with the locals for the day. It's time to go home.

As maze-like as these roads are I'm confident I can get back to Pittsboro's little historic downtown fairly easily. I know that Highway 64 runs north of me, so I turn down the next right, a gravel road cleaving between two vast cornfields. At this rate it will probably only take me about a half an hour to get back to my car and start hooking the bike to the rack. The quicker I can get there the better. It's going to be a long time before I venture out into this town's environs again, given the loonies that populate these parts.

I pedal harder; already ready to be back to report this whacked-out story to Estrella's dinner guests tonight. I can just imagine her roommate Danielle squealing and shaking her head in disbelief when I lay on the details. The vulnerable sensation creeping across the skin of my neck is lessened now that I'm away, and heading home, imagining the faces of friends I'll see tonight. Maybe one of them will have heard of this Eric Shepherd fellow. Or not. Who the hell knows? I pedal, pump, and hurry, knowing I'm close to 64. The gravel road begins to veer left, and split into a dirt road on the right. I hear them before I see them.

The silver flash of the van takes most of the road's width up ahead. Dammit! I scramble in my pocket for the folding knife. This is foolish. I remember that if they want they can just run me down with the van. I won't let that happen though. Lester Gill didn't raise his only child to be snuffed out in some godforsaken cornfield. As they get closer I ready myself to ditch the bike and disappear into the cornrows; but the van slows. The driver's window rolls down once again. He leans out the window. I don't even think of stopping. I speed up, flying past the van and choosing the way they hadn't come, cycling as fast as I can down the dirt road on the right. A quick glance back and I see that the van is just sitting there, growling and puttering exhaust.

I pound at the pedals, following the dirt road's curve, until I can't see the van at all. Then I stop. I feel like a rat being forced through a maze. This might be my only chance to change the game. I dismount, legs twanging from the exertion, and drag my bike into the corn. If they truly mean to follow me and do me harm it would be easy enough for them to turn around and be on me in a second. My only chance to get away is to see which way they're going to go. I crouch and slide through the rows, dodging ears as I go. The dry corn leaves whisper against my sweaty skin, and the knife handle is rubbery and hot in my hand; "Tarasaurus," says the glinting blade. I find a spot where I'm well concealed and I can still see the van, idling there in the middle of the road. I'm watching the vehicle from the rear of the driver's side, and I don't see him at all in his window. I hear the passenger door open, and see the curtains in the window twitch. There are the girl's feet, skinny sticks in sandals beneath the van, and then she slides open the rear passenger door. A shape falls slack and heavy onto the gravel in the van's shadow. The girl's feet skitter back into the vehicle and I see the driver's silhouette pop into his window. The van revs and jerks into gear, tearing off down the road, leaving the dumped shape in the dust. The vehicle has disappeared again.

I skulk forward to see what was left behind. With a cough I enter the dirt cloud, already starting to disperse as the summer wind whips it away. My knife is heavy in my hand. I can see orange and red. Huddled and broken in the gravel lies the shape of a man. Long and lean. Tan skin and solid thighs. His jersey has been shredded, and darkly stained. I kneel to roll him over, and the bulk of his body flops limply. A ragged gash has nearly separated his head from his body. Most of his blood has leaked through this wound to paint the gravel beneath him. I can now see that the jersey has been almost completely ripped free from his chest. There, carved deeply into his flesh, are sharp letters.

They read, *Tara Gill.*

The Cicadas Have All Died

Joaquin's magic eyes turned cold at the teal string bikini I'd just revealed by removing my overshirt. He frowned at me like a cat trying to bury shit in a tile floor. Here we go again. "Andrea, come back here a minute."

Drew took a tug at his beer, clad in a kitschy bottle-sized wetsuit, and winked as I grumbled and stood. The boat bucked and I pitched toward Drew, catching myself on his pink, scrawny shoulder. He steadied my waist with his free hand and then stuck his tongue out to blow a raspberry. "Watch it, *Ann Diarrhea*." I smacked his shoulder. "*Aiee*, that stings!"

"Good." I stumbled toward Joaquin in the captain's chair beneath the canopy, and nearly fell again as the boat began to pick up speed, jouncing across the crisscrossed wakes leftover by a squadron of jet-skis scarring the surface of Lake Crewse. The kids, legs dangling off the prow, mingled their giggles with bursts of spray kicked up by the wind. We hit another bump and I toppled onto the soft bench next to Joaquin. He'd done that on purpose. I could tell by the thin-lipped smirk. "*What?*" I hissed.

Joaquin raised an eyebrow. "Really? You need to ask? Or is it just me that sees what goes on?"

I already knew what he was going to say. I rolled my eyes upward, and closed them. Took a deep breath and tried to roll my eyes even farther, back, back, back, out my ears, and out of the boat where they could float away and not have to see the ridiculous jealousy residing in the lines of my husband's face. I opened them. I saw it. And I gave the requisite response he was waiting for. This was the dance. "Sees what?" I checked to make sure Drew wasn't listening to us. He faced forward and nursed his beer. Over the wind and sound of the motor it would have been impossible to hear us anyway, unless Joaquin decided to mine one of his patented *Ruiz shouting veins*.

"*Drew*. The way he looks at you, at your," he gestured toward my breasts in a swirling motion. "Eyes all over this."

"Jesus, he's my *brother*." This wasn't the first time Joaquin had made this sort of claim; I'd just hoped that things might be different this year.

He forged on, undeterred, "And what was that? The way he grabbed at you?"

"I *tripped*. It was your fault anyway – no, forget it. I'm not doing this today, Joaquin. Not in front of Drew, not in front of the kids. A quick look toward the front of the boat told me that everyone else was still focused on having fun. Boats swarmed the lake, alighting on the scattered cypress-furred sandy islands like fruit flies on a spilled bowl of molding oranges. Joaquin, tension knotting the center of his oak-like countenance, stared forward, focused on piloting the craft. I stroked at the solid knee beneath the frayed hem of his cutoffs; a soft, white explorer snaking over the dark surfaces of a foreign desert. "Look, behave yourself, mister, and maybe we can find a little nookie nook later." The oak split, minutely, into a smile. "Huh?" Gooseflesh pricked under my touch. Three years into our relationship, and ten months into our marriage and the best thing that could be said was "we still had good sex." Even more sadly, sexual excitement was the only thing that could calm the suspicious demon that lived just under Joaquin's skin.

"I guess Drew *is* good for something," Joaquin whispered, favoring me with his magic eyes once again.

"Oh?" I snuck a finger up the inside of his shorts and he shifted his hips in the seat, the smile still tickling his lips. "And what would that be?"

"Babysitter."

I reached behind and grabbed the rough, flower-patterned beach towel on the bench back, twirling it over my shoulders. My tan could wait. This was a fight I'd rather let die off. "Better?"

"For my *ojos* only," Joaquin said, only half-joking as he gripped the wheel tightly and split through a fresh phalanx of choppy whitecaps. "Hnnh, forecast said no rain," he looked relieved to find a way to change the subject, "lake looks like a storm lake though."

The sky above was cloudless, but an insistent wind whipped at the water, torturing it into frothy peaks. Islands flanked us, crowded to capacity with pontoons and rednecks ready to celebrate Independence Day. Lake Crewse was supposed to be a ghost town compared to the more popular, and much clearer, Mazer Lake, but from the looks of the stuffed islands I didn't see how we'd ever find a good place to land. It actually appeared as if last year's festive gathering on Mazer Lake, replete with barking dogs of every breed and a radio arms race of who could play their personal favorite country station loudest, was going to be reenacted here. We'd be elbow to beer gut with the local fauna in no time. I watched Joaquin's face as he searched the horizon, looking for an area of less activity. "How much farther do you want to look?"

"I saw a place about ten minutes ago. No so crowded, but maybe we can do better up here. S'big lake, *bonita*." He shrugged.

Drew's skinny back tensed with every jolt of the boat. He reached a wiry arm out and traded his empty beer for a fresh one from

109

the cooler. I could read my twin's mind from the set of his shoulders. He was intentionally ignoring us out of politeness. Beyond him my son Caleb, long and lanky for a thirteen-year-old, and his little nerd of a friend Zachery, bounced like ragdolls hanging on to the bow rail as if their lives depended on it. Fiona, who'd just had her eighth birthday, sat in profile, staring out at the lake with the normal, bemused expression of a young lady twice her age. Sofi, the tomboy-ish local girl who lived near the house we'd rented for the weekend, sat beside her, smiling a gap-toothed grin and sipping at a juice box. At least the kids were having fun. Wasn't that priority one anyway?

I stood and hugged the towel about my shoulders. "You really think it's going to storm?" The wind *did* feel cooler after all.

"Afternoon sprinkle at most. Like it does sometimes." Joaquin grumbled and squinted as a slash of light cut under the awning when he turned the boat. "Nowhere free," he spat, jamming his sunglasses onto the bridge of his nose.

"Joaquin!" Fiona shouted from the front. She was pointing one skinny, sunscreen-slathered arm off starboard. "Go that way. Sofi says to go that way!"

Joaquin ticked his gaze to the left and spun the wheel. He gestured for the little girl to take a seat on the bench next to his chair. She pushed past me easily, gait steady on the craft, as sure as if she'd been born on the back of a motorboat. Her freckles stood out, sun-kissed and dark on her pink cheeks, and a smear of sugary red juice painted her chapped lips.

"You know somewhere good?" I asked her.

"Yeah, it's around that big bend. You just go around it to a sort of…of…"

"Inlet? Cove?" I wondered.

"Yeah. I went there with my dad. It's tucked away so summer people don't really know about it." She shrugged her little stick shoulders and slapped her thighs. "We all camped there one time."

"Okay, then." Joaquin throttled the boat up to top speed and cut the heads off the waves, making a beeline for the outcropping of cypress trees that Sofi had pointed to.

We passed a low-slung white boat, and Drew raised a hand in greeting. The other boater raised his in kind. Drew turned to me and smiled. "It's a nautical thing, Andrea. You wouldn't understand."

Not *that* same stupid joke again. What, was he ten the first time he gave me that line? I flashed him the finger, quick to conceal it before Sofi saw.

She was otherwise engaged. "That osprey nest," Sofi pointed out a bristle of sticks on top of one of the trees, "turn in there."

The tension was already running out of Joaquin's shoulders now that we had a plan. Really, we were supposed to be relaxing here, and it was already well past noon. Not much day left, and before we knew it we'd be back on the road to Raleigh on Sunday morning. Joaquin back to his CPA work where the quarterly filers would keep him busy until tax time again, and me back to Tangled Up In Boule, the vegan soup and bread joint I started so long ago with my roommate Melanie right out of college. We were gearing up to franchise out a second location in Charlotte in just a few short months, and Caleb would be starting on register part-time to earn spending money when we returned home. God, how the time does pass. There's no way it's been thirteen years since his father and I brought him home from the hospital. I peek at Joaquin's face and think about where Mark might be right now. Saving the world with his new wife, no doubt. Where were they going this year, Tasmania…or was it Tanzania? Oh, who the hell cared where they went anyway?

Sofi's munchkin voice piped up, "Right there."

It *was* a cove. There, unfolded in front of us, but hidden behind a screen of trees, was a pristine, rust-colored crescent of beach. Only one other motorboat was tucked in, like a bright yellow tick burrowed into the flank of an orange tabby stretching in the sun.   "Yay!" exclaimed Caleb, jumping to his feet as we idled in.

"Sit down!" I yelled to the front.

Drew shot me a look that clearly read as, "Oh, please." It was still weird for him to see me as anything other than the hell-raiser I'd been in high school. To him any attempt at parenting, no matter how justified, was a step toward authoritarianism, and that much closer to the worst of all outcomes, becoming just like one's own parents.

Joaquin guided the boat slowly into the bank where it halted, crunching at the coarse sand. "Tie us off, me maties!" he shouted to Caleb and Zachery. The boys sprang down, with anchor rope trailing behind. They rushed up the bank where they found a tangle of cypress knees to weave the rope into. "Hey," Joaquin yelled, "now don't knot that thing up too much. We still need to leave sometime!" He chuckled. The frustration corrugating his brow was gone, and I took my chance removing the towel from my shoulders. I was still determined to get a tan this trip.

Drew heaved the cooler up onto the edge of the boat, balancing it there while he dropped splashily into the knee-high water. The cooler teetered and I lunged forward, catching it in time to hand it down gently. "Thanks," he grunted.

"Cold?" I wondered.

"Fucking freezing," Drew said and tugged at my shorts, knocking me off-balance.

I slipped, not entirely gracefully, down into the water, bracing myself for a shock, but instead found a warm soup that lapped at my knees. Plumes of lake silt floated in the shallows like brown clouds, broken by the occasional twist of algae. That pervasive lake smell puffed up now that we weren't cruising through the wind anymore, reminding me of septic tanks and crawlspaces. "Jerk," I spat at Drew, casting a look over my shoulder at Joaquin, who was crouched to tinker with the motor, missing the incident entirely. I grabbed one end of the heavy cooler and helped Drew hump it up the crumbling sandbank. Fiona and Sofi were already running through the weedy vegetation, searching out the choicest bleached gnarls of driftwood strewn about like the bones of some mutant creatures. We planted the cooler like a flag to stake our territory and I scanned the island. From the top of the bank I could see that the stretched spit of sand was rather narrow, and more of the vast lake sparkled on through the screen of trees. At the far end was the other boat, still buffeting lightly from the last ripples of our wake. It was such a sparse day on the water I wished we'd gotten the beach all to ourselves. Oh well, neighbors it was. A bright red canvas canopy had been erected on the beach beneath the stretching fronds of a cypress. White text screamed, "HOW 'BOUT THEM DAWGS," accompanied by the cartoonish head of the Georgia Bulldog mascot. Four men were tucked in folding chairs within the shade, sharing a drink and looking out at the water.

"Too bad we didn't get the beach to ourselves," Drew said, as he sat on the cooler and clapped the sand out of his flip-flops.

"We don't get everything we want," I said softly.

"Huh?" Drew wondered, promptly thrusting his reshod feet right back into the sand.

"Nothing. Can I have a beer?"

We ate lunch: sandwiches made from too-warm cold cuts, smushed bread, and sweating American; boiled peanuts that stubbornly clung to their shells so you had to pick at them with your teeth; wilted slices of watermelon, accompanied with seed spitting contest into the lake, which I handily won; and endless bags of chips crumbling to dust from being packed too tightly into the beach bag. Sand got in my teeth, my beer became far too warm, and flat too fast, gnats savaged my underarms, but none of this mattered. This was vacation. This was family time. And despite the lake smell, and the sporty neighbors, who really were unobtrusive, this was a sort of paradise, temporarily at least. Joaquin, handsome in his straw hat and cut-off chinos, rushed the lake and dove beneath. A moment later he popped up, hat limp and drooping around his ears. The kids laughed. Caleb and Zachery peeled off their t-shirts and ran to join him. This day could last forever and I'd be okay with that.

"Where's your girlfriend this weekend. Leah was it?"

"*Lena.*" Drew took in a long breath and leaned back on his elbows. He wrinkled his nose. "Studying."

I poked him in the ribs and he recoiled. "SATs, huh?"

"No, *dick.* Stop. She's a grad student; I told you that. Just young for her program. She was in accelerated classes. Besides," Drew said as he munched around a handful of corn chips, "she hates boats."

"You're an idiot." I took the bag from him. "When're you going to settle down?"

"Don't you call me an idiot, fatty."

I looked down at where the bit of belly flab overhung my shorts and pinched at it, sighing, "That's where two kids will get me." Out past the boat the boys wrestled. I watched as Sofi shot out into the lake like a minnow. Fiona stalked the edge of the water, picking at freshwater snail shells with a toe. Beyond her, motorboats appeared, racing out in the open lake, the tinny whine of their motors interrupting the otherwise placid peace here in the cove. Was it too much to ask for a solitary moment without idiots rushing about with their toys wide open?

There was a crunch behind me, and I nearly spun my head off my shoulders, startled by the large silhouette blotting out the sun. "You guys have a lighter?" It was a middle-aged man, maybe handsome at one point but gone to seed from perhaps too many junk food lunches. His pasty spare tire threatened the button on his

Hawaiian pattern bathing suit. "Oh, ha! Sorry, didn't mean to scare you. It's just my dad, he brought a little grill, you know, for burgers, but he forgot a lighter, matches, you know." I couldn't place his accent, other than it being something far north of the Mason-Dixon. The man pointed to the flaming red canopy, and one of the figures waved a slow, big wave.

Drew dug around in the beach bag and fished out a disposable lighter. "Yeah, no problem, man. Here."

"Oh, hey, you're a lifesaver. Thanks." He took the lighter and gave it a little flick. The flame sprung up and snuffed right out just as quickly. "My name's Ben, by the way."

He offered his pudgy hand to Drew and then me. We nodded, told him our names and waited for him to trot off, but instead he just sort of stood there with a gumpy grin, shuffling his pale feet in the sand. Drew gave me a fleeting, "twin look" that said, "Can't this doofus find his way back?"

There was something off-putting about Ben's smile, or really rather his eyes above his smile, like round, dark craters peering out of a fat moon face. What did they remind me of? I was homing in on the memory of my first dentist's intense eyes over his sanitary mask when Ben asked, "You guys from around here? Lake Crewse?"

"No, man. Just here for the fourth." Drew stared out at the water, giving Ben a polite, but firm, cold-shoulder.

"Yeah. Fireworks, you know?" Ben clicked the lighter smartly. "Kid's love 'em!"

Fireworks.

"SHIT!" I sat up quickly, sand flying from my elbows. Drew and Ben looked at me like I'd just yanked open their respective bathing suits and spat phlegm down in them. "Fireworks!" My mind raced over the lake surface, up the dock and through the back door of our rented cabin to the counter where a big, garish box marked *THUNDER ASSAULT* perched. $120 dollars of fireworks were sitting pretty in a climate-controlled kitchen where they'd be doing absolutely bupkis tonight. I looked at the kids, and then to Drew. "I forgot them. Dammit. I forgot them."

"Are you sure?" Drew said, swatting a no-see-um from his neck. "Maybe they're still in the –"

"No. No, they're not in the boat. God, the kids are going to be so disappointed." I was already mentally going through the calculations. Time enough to rush home, grab the damn fireworks and get back out here before sundown? How long did it take to get here anyway? Joaquin would *not* be happy about having to go back. I hung my head. "Stupid!"

"Hey, wait, it's okay," Ben said from behind us. "My brother Matt just about bought the store out. We've got enough to put the Boston Pops display to shame," he chuckled. "You guys just join us."

I smiled. "That's…that's very generous of you, Ben. Are you sure?"

"Yeah. Got a cooler full, completely full of burger meat too." He rocked back on his heels and flicked the lighter again. "Couldn't do anything without this anyway. Looks like we all forgot important things. Must have been destiny you landing on this beach, you know?" He began to saunter away, whistling a little tune. "I'll call you over when the grub's on!" And with that he slipped off toward the low radio music warbling on the other side of the island, lighter click-clicking the whole way.

"Weirdo," Drew snorted.

"I think he's okay." I squinted at the figure coming toward us out of the water. "Was nice of him to offer food. *You* want a burger?"

"Actually, yeah," Drew said, leaning back into the warm sand.

Joaquin stood before us. He looked from me to Drew, and back again as he shook droplets from his arms and plumbed an ear with his pinky. "Who was that dude?"

I stood up and threw my arms around Joaquin's bulky shoulders. I kissed him hard on the lips and pushed him back out toward the water. Balancing my kids' happiness against my husband's jealousy was going to take some finessing. I dragged him out past our nipples, where we were hidden from nearly everyone by the swaying form of the motorboat, and kissed him more, grabbed at his buns and told him all about Ben and his invite to a burgers and fireworks extravaganza. To my surprise, Joaquin was cool with it. Fire and charred meat: the easiest way to win a man's heart apparently.

A gust kicked up, setting the cypresses to shiver, and the wind on my face felt wonderful. The temperature of the lake felt wonderful. Joaquin's muscled frame, tanned skin sliding against mine under the surface of the water…felt wonderful. All of a sudden hands, mine, his, reached down, tugging at bathing suit edges, freeing *us*. Then he was inside. I held him close and nipped at his neck. A distant storm front smeared the horizon like a bloodless bruise. It didn't take long at all. Joaquin tensed against me. There was a far off peal of muffled thunder. Joaquin pulled away, and I felt momentarily empty, as cold lake water filled the void he had left.

Then it was time to dogpaddle back around to the other side of the boat where the boys knocked a beach ball about with Sofi. I told the boys about forgetting the fireworks, but that our neighbors were nice enough to share. They seemed only minutely perturbed before resuming their game. Joaquin pinched at me under the water, where no one could see and favored me with those magical eyes, brimming with contentment. "Stop, enough," I whispered, evading his playful hands. "That storm going to blow off or what?" I wondered, adjusting my bathing suit back to orderliness.

"Storm already came and went," he said with a smirk.

"You're terrible." I gave him my best disapproving schoolmarm look. "Do we need to pack it all up?"

"No. If it was coming, it would have come by now. Oh, wait, I guess it did." He double down on joke, still leering.

"The worst!" I laughed, kicking away toward the shore. My insides still throbbed from our tryst in the lake. If Joaquin had just kept going for another minute or so. *So close!* I was broken out of my reverie by a sharp *whistle-crack!* overhead. I looked up, where a little puff of smoke was slowly disintegrating. Another whistle shot off, signaling that the other group on the beach were getting an early start on the fireworks with a bottle rocket preamble. It was still probably two hours till sunset, but what self-respecting partyer could really wait with fireworks anyway?

"Mom? Can we go?" Caleb called, galloping out of the water with great high steps, and pointing toward Ben's group.

"Yeah, sure," I sighed. "But no lighting any, not yet. Wait till Joaquin or I get over there."

"Okay, okay!" he yelled, tearing off with Zachery and Sofi in tow.

I looked around for Fiona, who was poking about solitarily at the tree line atop the dunes. We'd brought the little local girl along to be play with Fiona, but so far she seemed more content to tag along with the boys.

Drew still sat where I'd left him, and I was completely unsurprised when he read my mind and commented. "Looks like someone's got a crush, huh?"

I toppled a little mound of sand over on to his feet and sat heavily next to him. "I just worry about Fiona. She's…ehm, she's never going to make any friends. It just doesn't come easy to her like it does to Caleb." Caleb was dancing around Ben's group like a frenetic whirligig, gesticulating at the beach, the lake, and the ongoing firework salvos. Entertaining to a fault.

"Come on," Drew said. "She's just like you were at that age."

"Oh, God, don't say that!"

"No, really. Studious, smart, she'll be fine." Drew pushed the sand off his foot and on to mine, toes brushing against my skin in the process. The touch sent a little electric shiver down my leg. I looked for Joaquin, but he was already down the beach, exiting the water and joining the merrymakers. Caleb ran to him, volcanic excitement animating his every movement.

"They like him," Drew said. "He's a good dad to them."

I nodded. "I know." Drew's toe brushed mine again, this time I shied away, playing it off by scratching one foot with another. I didn't let myself think about the games we used to play as kids, or those few, very few, misguided times later. This wasn't the time, or the place. That time and place didn't even exist anymore. I was about to stand, make an excuse, and join the rest of the group when Fiona sat down with a *thump* next to me, bumping my shoulder roughly in her kid clumsiness.

"Look what I found!" She held out a bleached, rib-shaped length of driftwood, upon which was a small, pulsating, butter and caramel-colored form. She was shoving it toward my face, and I recoiled into Drew, feeling his bare chest against my back. "It's really cool. Watch."

"Ah, stop, Fi." I held her thin arm, steadying the show-and-tell back to where I could see it. A carapace, like thin, brown glass clutched the driftwood. Where it was split violently across the back, a pallid creature emerged in an undulating, rhythmic fashion, freeing itself from the inert prison.

"Aw, a cicada," Drew said, reaching a finger out.

"Don't touch!" Fiona drew the stick back. "It's hatching."

"I see that," Drew said as he leaned into my back. I straightened up, away, caught between him and the insect. "Remember Dad telling us how they lived for years, like decades, before coming out and doing that?"

"I know all about them already," Fiona said matter-of-factly. "We learned in school. They only live for a few weeks after they do this. See the wings are little at first, like that, then they stretch out. It will change color too."

"Well, you *do* know," I said, mesmerized by the little show. The cicadas wings were indeed stunted, but they were already unfurling and filling up as some sort of arcane, alien process pumped life into its tiny appendages. It was already appearing less grub-like and more like the classic finished model, though still off-color. The discarded husk squatted on the white wood like a rusted, useless suit of armor. "It's beautiful," I said, lost in this natural moment. The wings fanned, clearly more comfortable in their new form. I was starting to feel bad, like we might somehow upset this delicate process with our voyeurism. "Fiona, take him back where you found him."

"But I wanna keep watching."

"You can. Just set him down and watch." I pointed to the trees. "Right back where you got him from."

"I *will*," she said, stomping off toward the trees with shoulders slumped.

"Hey!" I called. She turned, dark hair framing her little face and I experienced one of those strange, off-putting moments where I could see the woman she would become, and all the good and bad that would entail. "Thank you for showing us, honey."

She nodded, put some pep back into her posture and jogged off with her little discovery.

"You remember what else Dad said about cicadas when he'd send me out with a badminton racket to kill them when they swarmed?" Drew was sitting up cross-legged now, poking twigs into a little circle in the sand. "He was always pissed at the sound, said it was like a bunch of drunks playing with hedge trimmers. Then Mom would say they were singing with 'intoxicated ecstasy' because it was the beginning of spring. Ha!"

"I don't remember that," I said. Caleb was coming toward us, with Sofi hot on his heels. "I don't remember that at all."

"Well, it happened. Intoxicated ecstasy," he repeated, laying sticks horizontally across the top of the first ones, creating a mini-Stonehenge. Or…Stickhenge, really.

"Uncle Drew, Mom, Joaquin says you guys should come over. They're 'bout to cook dinner," Caleb said. He twiddled the red plastic cone from a spent firework between two fingers, and then stuck it between his teeth and chewed the end.

"Caleb, get that out of your mouth." I dusted sand from my rear as I stood and snatched at the little cone.

Caleb was far too quick and dodged me. "Eck! It tastes like gunpowder," he laughed, and shot off down the beach, Sofi giggling behind him the whole while. Drew and I ambled wordlessly down the beach. I could already smell the burgers on the grill and my stomach rumbled. I was so much hungrier than I thought! How long had we watched that little cicada? The light was decidedly dimmer as the world began toward dusk around us. The first stars, or maybe they were planets, popped awake in the pink-hazed sky. New boats still trolled about out on the lake proper, and reports from other firework caches occasionally sounded from other islands. Then we were all together: Ben with his goofy city-boy-in-the-country grin, offering beers and introductions round to Drew and I; Ben's younger and more handsome brother Matt, the University of Georgia grad; their father Cortland, who owned horses and played a harmonica; Cortland's army buddy Red, the local of the group, and a man whose sourpuss old-timer face was more than matched by his sullen temperament. Joaquin gathered me under an arm, and laid claim to his goods in the presence of these other men. Caleb, Zachery and Sofi were still letting off fireworks from the beer bottle plunged into the sand at water's edge. I was happy to see Fiona finally join them, and even happier to see the little threesome accept her without complaint. As if on cue the first cicada began to chirrup in the trees, soon joined by the trilling song of its fellows.

When the burgers were ready Drew ran back to the beach and grabbed our folding chairs. We arrayed them in a semicircle starting with Red on one end, as he wouldn't budge from his claimed spot under the canopy, despite the sun retreating to a diminished toothless orange ball on the bright lake horizon. Though the storm clouds were now bloated and full, they'd pushed far off to the east to be subsumed by the inky twilight.

Max Dowdle

"Thanks again, Ben, everyone." I lifted my burger in salute and took a deep bite. The char and juiciness was just right. I may own a vegan eatery, but I left my rabbit food days behind long, long ago. Whatever else Matt might have learned at the University of Georgia, he certainly could cook a damn good burger. "Really nice of you all."

"Course!" Ben raised his beer. "New friends, you know?"

"I just wish we had a fire." Matt indicated the small charcoal grill they'd brought. "Cooked over real wood is that much better."

Red spat a wad of post-dinner tobacco into the lake and grunted. "You gonna haul all the wood out here yerself then. Them cypress ain't no good for cookin' nohow."

"Oh, Red, that gives it just the right flavor!" Cortland piped up. These were friends who thrived off of adversity and disagreement. It was quickly apparent in every interaction they had.

Red sucked his brown teeth. "Bullshit," he said with no regard for the youngsters around him. He eyed the remains of his dinner on the paper plate in his lap. "Tastes like it came from the ass-end of the cow already. Not sure how cypress gonna make it any betta. Don't matter noways, cypresses here are 'tected. Cain't go about cuttin' em down as you please."

This was a completely useless conversation to be sure. It somehow washed over me the same way as did the cicada drone, and the abhorrent screeches of distant motorboats. These were integral pieces of the lake experience.

"Hey, looky there! More friends," Ben said, pointing over my shoulder.

I turned. Past our dormant boat a motley trio of weathered johnboats cut their motors and drifted into the cove. Just when I'd gotten used to my surroundings there they went and changed again. It looked now like this particular beach would end up crowded ahead of the promised fireworks displays popping up all over the lake. The crafts thudded to a stop in the soft sand and figures leapt ashore, tying off on the cypress tree knees and unloading bundles of camping materials. It was a *big* group. I counted nearly a dozen in total. Though the light was dimming quickly as we approached the magic hour, I could see at least three older men, two women and a gaggle of kids ranging from a girl around Fiona's age to two boys on the precipice of manhood.

120

Drew raised a hand in greeting, but not a one returned the gesture.

"Guess it's not a nautical thing," I chided. He rolled his eyes.

The members of the new group were busy with their individual tasks. They were altogether a quiet group at least. No shouts or merrymaking, no radio, and no barking dogs. There was nothing outwardly peculiar about them, but at the same time I still felt intruded upon, as if this beach had already been claimed so late in the day, and they should have had the decency to push off to another anchorage. As if to blatantly contest what Red had just been saying about the cypress, one of the men walked purposefully to the tree line with a hatchet and began to hack low branches. He dragged them to where the children were clearing a patch of grass and deposited them before returning for more. One of the other boys took up another hatchet and began felling young, straight trees. He piled them in a stack while the rest of the group set about unfurling a foursome of dusty green canvas tents and assembling the skeletons of their frameworks. Everyone had a designated task and approached it with single-minded focus. It was actually rather impressive to watch, despite the fact that they were completely taking over the small beach.

Ben slapped at his armrest. "Welp, I'm going to go welcome them to our humble little beach, and offer some dinner to our new friends." There was certainly still enough food to feed an army. Matt was already stoking the grill in preparation for seconds.

"Let me. I'll do it," Drew said, hopping up before Ben could really get started with his welcome wagon efforts.

"You sure? I'm happy to, you know?" But Ben was already settling back down into his chair where he'd clearly been very comfortable.

"Yeah, yeah. Be right back." Drew jogged off, to the edge of where the other group was clearing the beach and settling in. The radio next to Red started up with an old Willie Nelson number. He was one of the only country stars I could recognize outright by voice. Willie's plaintive pipes sang of walls and loneliness, drifting off into the gloaming to leave an eerie feeling deep down under my heart. I wanted to change the station, or turn it off completely. Drew was already walking back. It was hard to tell in the light, but he looked pale, and also strangely shaken.

"You okay?" I wondered.

Drew made as if to sit, but then just sort of lingered there, every eye of our group waiting for an answer. "Um, yeah. I...ugh, that was weird."

"What?" Ben wondered. "What did they say?"

Drew shrugged. "Nothing. I mean," he rubbed at his forehead and cast a quick look back at the group, "that's just it. They didn't say *anything*. I went over there, said 'Hi' and invited them over. Told them we had fireworks, everything. Not one of them answered, or even looked at me. It was, God, I don't know, it was...kinda fucked up."

Caleb had paused at the firework station, watching his clearly nervous uncle with rapt fascination.

Drew wrinkled his nose, as if gathering his thoughts for some other distasteful observation, but then chose to remain silent. I held his gaze, reading his posture and body language. Drew was more than just tense. He seemed borderline terrified. I tried to read what else he wasn't telling us in his face, but came up with nothing.

Fiona latched onto my arm, and I could feel her small body trembling. "It's okay, sweetie," I whispered.

"Well that ain't no big deal anyway," Cortland finally said, a big grin peeking out of his white beard.

Drew shook his head sadly. A cold shadow had passed over the group in response to Drew's report. No one seemed really sure what to say or do next at the news, though plenty stole furtive looks at our neighbors.

Joaquin shrugged. "So what? They're rude. They didn't talk to you. Who gives a fuck? They're over there doin' their thing, and we're over here having fun." He took the tongs from Matt and began to fuss with the sizzling burgers. "More food for us, more fun for us, eh?" His sureness at taking control of the situation instantly began to ease the pressure. After all, he was right, we were here to have fun, not to fixate on some strangers we didn't even know. "Caleb, get those fireworks going again, *jefe*. Give me a big red one, eh?"

Caleb delivered, sending up a large mortar that shook the beach with its explosion, shooting out a streaming flower of crimson starfire to hang above us before twirling to nothingness. Applause and nervous laughter. Everyone was still stealing glances at the other group, myself included. One of the older boys came closer with his hatchet, swiftly relieving a tree several yards behind us of its lower branches. The whole time he neither looked in our direction, nor acknowledged us in any way. The boy dragged the branches back to the large pile.

"Shit's not gonna light," Red said into his Pabst can. "Too green."

Cortland riffled through some bluegrass notes with his harmonica, trying to lighten the mood further. Still the group on the other side of the island continued their unceasing industry. Now two had stolen our way to gather driftwood and strip low-hanging limbs. Caleb and Zachery continued with the fireworks, sending them up in answer to like-kind signals from nearby islands. More food and drink was handed around, and soon enough we were ignoring the other group just as effectively as they ignored us.

"Can we do these big ones?" Caleb asked of Ben, grabbing a large, plastic wrapped box from the overflowing crate of fireworks.

"Sure, it's all fair game," Ben said. "You're the maestro!"

"Thirds, anybody? Hotdog, Andrea?" Joaquin said, taking his place behind the grill.

I shook my head, but took great pleasure in watching him stoke the coals to life once again. Joaquin's bright grin shone out of his dark face, catching the last hints of dying sunlight as he shook out a half dozen weenies from the pack. Fiona joined him and he let her use the tongs, watching her carefully, and guiding her hand to turn the sizzling hotdogs. Though he was prone to jealous outbursts, and we fought far more than I preferred, he was a good man, and truly a good father. Suddenly Joaquin was lit up green, yellow, pink, his magic eyes turned skyward, sparkling with the firework dazzle. Behind him one of the men from the other group had ventured close, where he retrieved a long length of driftwood and began to drag it back to their encampment, cleaving a straight, dark furrow in the sand.

Cortland was really feeling the harmonica now, and Red turned the radio down to make space for the reedy little tune. Cortland stomped a foot in the sand, and Matt took up clapping. Things were getting halfway festive again until I looked over at Drew, who stared vacantly into the encroaching darkness. I reached out and grasped the back of his hand, feeling it tense at my touch and grip his armrest harder. "We should go," he whispered.

"Huh?" I wondered, watching his emotionless face light up with the orange fire of the popping spectacle overhead.

Max Dowdle

"Dogs are done," Joaquin said. I turned, intending to tell him I did in fact want one, when my tongue stopped dead in my mouth. The dark form of the man from the other group had returned, striding toward us along the shoreline. His stride was purposeful as he quickly closed the ground behind Joaquin. I watched as he raised the hatchet. It momentarily flashed blue in the twilight, before the man buried it deep in my husband's neck.

Screams.

A flurry of action as the rest of the strangers descended on us. I saw the grill knocked on its side, coals extinguished in the lake water; Cortland trying to crawl away amidst ferocious kicks to his midsection; Matt and Ben, indecisively lurching toward their boat, only to be thrown to the ground and pummeled; Fiona racing inland to the trees, and snatched back by the elastic straps of her bathing suit. My face was pushed into the sand, and I struggled to breath before I was dragged, flailing down the beach. "Drew! Caleb! Fiona!" a familiar voice screamed over and over.

Rough hands forced me down, face still grinding into the sand and a bed of cypress needles. My eyes were filled with grit. I struggled to see what was going on around me. A heavy bulk was then thrown down on top of me. I twisted my neck around to see what it was, and my voice and my breath caught. Joaquin had been heaved across me, unmoving, the magic having completely drained from his eyes. His blood, still freely flowing from a multitude of hatchet wounds, dribbled down onto my face and into my mouth, drowning out my found voice and worthless pleadings.

A blaze of light illuminated the beach as a bonfire of driftwood erupted. Being as close as I was to the fire, I immediately began to sweat, though I could not actually see the flames themselves from my confinement. More screams, but it was impossible to tell from whom. I tried to worm my way out from under Joaquin, but my hands were being held tight, and something or someone was scrabbling at them, pinching, *piercing* the webbing between my thumbs and forefingers. The pain was white-hot, and the more I opened my mouth to scream the more it filled with blood and sand.

There then followed an eternity of tears and shrieks.

Finally the wailing lessened to whimpers, and I once again could hear the popping of the fire, the distant echo of fireworks, and the chorus of cicadas. I cursed myself. I cursed Joaquin. A thousand

124

different places we could have gone on vacation, dozens of different beaches we could have landed on…but we ended up here. Why *here*? The strangers did not speak a word as I was lifted onto my knees and sat next to Drew. He would not meet my eye; instead he stared deep into the dancing bonfire. I could see his hands gathered behind him, pierced through the meaty webbings with a sharpened stick. I tugged at my own hands, realizing that was how they were held fast. To Drew's right Ben and Matt were cowering on their knees as well, held fast by two of our ragged attackers. To the left more strangers squatted over the bodies of Cortland and Red, relieving them of their clothes and shearing their heads close under the snip of scissors. Through stinging tears I watched the children of the group standing on the other side of the fire, holding Caleb, Zachery, Sofi and Fiona on their knees. The children of the strangers, a mongrel collection of filthy spawn, came in all shapes and ages, but the one thing they all had in common was their complete lack of ears. Each wore the massed scar tissue of some old visited violence on either side of their head.

Still not a word was spoken amongst the group as the long lengths of young tree trunk were erected in a circle around the fire. Boughs of cypress were tied to each stick, creating a natural, festooned border to the encampment. When Matt began to protest and try to stand, he was met with a swift pop to his mouth, and forced back to his knees. The sun was gone, and with it the fireworks gained in intensity, lighting our island with a storm of rainbow hues. I shuddered as a glowing stick was withdrawn from the fire by the oldest woman of the group and brought close to Caleb's face. I fell forward and retched when the pulsing, glowing brand was thrust against first one ear and then the other. The stick holding my hands together was yanked, pulling me back upright with a brutal bolt of pain. I could not watch as the operation was repeated on our other young ones.

It was then that I forced my mind elsewhere, floating up, out the top of my head like some astral projection to escape this hellish unreality, where I felt weightless, and a total evaporation of pain. I saw the circle of trees arranged around the fire, so like the little Stickhenge Drew had made. How was that even possible? On the horizon a motorboat slowly inched by, one single light burning atop, and a distant whine waning in the night.

Come closer, I implored. And for a moment it seemed to.

Did the tiny light twinkle ever so larger?

Did the hum of the motor grow ever so louder?

No other sounds encroached on the darkness. Even the cicadas' trill had died to nothingness, as if they too were watching in anticipation of the ministrations that were now coming. The strangers took positions in the circle, adult and child alike. They opened their mouths as one, tilted their heads back to the kaleidoscope sky and let forth a great hum in unison; a call of intoxicated ecstasy that signaled this new beginning.

With magic in my eyes I looked toward Joaquin's still body, counting him among the lucky dead.

Herringbone, The Reflecting Pool

Recorded in grand ledgers are hatches,
Pawns lonely upon a board.

But whither the bronzed King?
This familiar token, his reward.

127

Longing in state for some sign,
Toppled, deposed in the Queen's tomb.

The table is cleared and another begins.
Nature's perfect geometry resumes.

> Excerpt from *To The Empty Sky, Fly*
> Frederick Bilton
> Herringbone Manse
> Drummond Lake, Virginia 1914

Hands closed over Charles's neck, forcing his head below the black water. He struggled against his attacker, and his own legs, tied down with bundles of bricks, kicked ineffectively beneath the dark surface, scattering the blind fish from their cold meals. He managed to surface and gasped a great breath of humid air only to have it immediately wrung from him. The last tremors of life treading through Charles's jugular pulsed and then, simply winked out. His white, slackened face caught the moon's light a final time before sinking beneath the midnight water…

Charles gasped and sat up in bed. He was covered in sweat and still reeling from the feeling of having been submerged. He rolled out of the bed, struggled to right his soaked cotton pajamas, and padded softly to the bathroom, careful not to rouse Allison. Luckily he remembered to close the door fully before switching on the light. His wife was a light sleeper and if even the smallest crack were left in the door he'd hear about it in the morning. Charles's dark, curly hair lay in wet streamers on his forehead, adding a disheveled fringe to the baggy eyes beneath. His reflection was unsettling, given the nature of the dream. It had been six days since he'd drunkenly fallen into their reflecting pool, hitting his head on the way down and waking in the dialysis chair kept in the sewing room. He looked down at his arms. They were free of the scars normally carried by renal patients, save the two most recent scabs just beginning to flake.

"You're lucky you have such nice skin," Allison had said on one of their first dates, staring at his smooth face, marred only by a tiny scar on his temple, the result of a hemangioma birthmark removal when he'd been five. She'd sliced a finger while dicing tomatoes for the salad. This had given Charles the first of only a few opportunities to attend to her, the great Doctor Allison Coleridge. "You see why *I* don't cook," she'd laughed. Ever since then the roles of their relationship had been iron-forged: Allison the breadwinner, and Charles the househusband.

Fifteen years. This summer would be their crystal anniversary. Charles needn't worry about gifts for Allison because she had all she could ever want, a soaring career with the government-funded PER*syst* Lab, a spacious condo in DC with only a partially obscured view of the Mall, the ancient Herringbone Manse, a large, brick cottage built and designed by her personal hero and famous sage, Frederick Bilton, and finally, the dutiful husband, Charles Willis.

Charles Willis, handsome and vibrant for his thirty-eight years, tennis enthusiast and avid rower. He mopped his face with a hand towel and looked at his pores in the magnifying mirror. No sign of crow's feet, no lines on his forehead. It was amazing. Despite the hateful bags under his eyes he didn't appear a day over twenty-five. He looked for the scar on his right temple, but it had faded completely away over time. She had been right, he did have nice skin.

The dream was subsiding but the horrific way in which he saw his own face, as if *he* had been the one forcing his head under the water, haunted him. Charles raised his hands to his reflection, squinting one eye and imagining his fingers closing over his own throat. He shivered. "Relax, Charlie," he whispered.

With a reverberating splash Charles relieved himself in the toilet, trying to aim into the curve of the porcelain to lessen the sound. He finished and then came the familiar dilemma, should he flush and risk waking Allison, or should he leave the waste and hear about it in the morning? He settled on the latter. Why waken the sleeping dragon now when he could instead be its breakfast? He flicked the switch and slid the door open slowly.

"Go back in there and flush it," his wife's flat voice said from the bed.

Charles touched the switch, illuminating his wife. "Sorry, I didn't mean to wake you."

"It's fine. I needed to use the bathroom." She rubbed at her eyes and checked the red glow of the clock. Two fourteen.

"So do you still want me to fl—"

"Yes! If I go after you it will mix. Disgusting." She'd stood and come to the doorway, watching like a vigilant parent as Charles pushed the handle.

"I'm sorry, darling, I just…" Charles let out a long exhale and shrugged. He wanted to argue. He always wanted to argue, but he owed everything to her and he knew it. It wasn't worth the trouble of her temper.

"You *what*?" Allison said with a measure of wary hostility as she flicked her honey colored hair over her shoulder and crossed her arms.

"I'm sorry, that's all." Charles sidled past her. Allison stopped him at the bathroom threshold, her mood shifting instantly. Charles had long ago become accustomed to her fickle temperament. He could ballet on eggshells if he had to.

"My dear Charles." Her hand stroked his smooth jaw line, free of stubble or blemish. "Are you still having those terrible dreams?"

Charles nodded, the flesh of his neck and arms tingling at the touch of Allison's experienced fingers. "Wait a moment and I'll give you something to help you sleep." Her hand lingered at the top button of his pajamas flirtatiously before she left the room. Charles went back to their king-sized bed to wait for her and the door closed, leaving him in darkness.

The outdoor bar was bare as well. Allison had made sure to dump any alcohol after the accident last Sunday, including the bottle of 1990 Barbaresco they'd been saving for their anniversary. Only a half-empty container of flat tonic water remained, the glue of the label flaking free almost as if to mock him. Charles left the tonic there in the cabinet of the faux stone bar and filled his glass at the tap. He unbuttoned the top of his blue linen shirt and slapped at the gnats buzzing around his neck. No matter, she'd be back at the lab on Tuesday and he'd just simply call the package store as he'd done before and order up a bottle of Knob Creek. A tip of twenty dollars was enough to get the manager's brother to pedal it out to him. This time he'd take care to sink it out under the glassy waters of Lake Drummond, unless of course he drowned before he could. And would that really be so bad?

Charles surveyed the land all the way from the two-story brick Federation style cottage overlooking the water to the series of undulating knolls terminating in the forest edge. There were tennis courts, a boathouse, a carriage house that had been converted into an ad hoc laboratory for Allison, and finally that horrid reflecting pool. Why Frederick Bilton had been so dead set on including a reflecting pool in the landscape designs Charles would never know. Wasn't the three thousand plus acres of Lake Drummond enough? He kicked the crumbling remains of a broken brick into the water. Predictably the bloated white fish Allison was intent on keeping there surfaced, no doubt looking for any morsel to prolong their putrid existence. Each of the fish wore a look of dazed acceptance in their milky eyes, their tiny mouths opening and closing like a chorus of silent albino beggars expecting alms. Charles heard the door bang behind him and Allison's stabbing footsteps on the flagstones.

"I was just thinking that the yard would look nicer if we drained this and filled it in. It's such a hassle. So dirty." He knew the suggestion was a futile gambit but the warm summer air made him feel courageous for once.

"It's a reflecting pool. You're not supposed to see the bottom. Besides, what about the fish?"

Charles turned and put on his well-practiced, coy mask for Allison. "I've never liked those fish. They're, I don't know, ghoulish."

"Well, it can't be filled. It would ruin the flow of the landscape. Frederick Bilton specially put it there when he designed this place so he could sit and ponder. That's where he did his best work! We can't tear up a national treasure. He wrote 'The Mausoleum of Praise' right out under that tree by the water's edge."

Allison had been enamored with Bilton since the thesis for her poetry minor as an undergraduate. A playfully petulant streak asserted itself, wrinkling Charles's lip. "Oh, he barely spent time here. He was in Tanzania with a harem of African women for the last twenty years of his life. Why do you think everyone calls him 'Mungu Fred?' That's Swahili for God, isn't it?"

"We'll keep this place just as it is. It's perfect, Charles. You'll come around. Or maybe we should put up a safety fence around the pool?"

There it was. The nails were inching their way out of the tiger's paw. As fearful of her as he was, Charles reveled in pushing her buttons. It was the only real response he could ever get. The only real show of emotion. With this, Charles had no final say in the matter. Allison had bought the land clear out with her own money, she could torch all twenty acres from towering pines to lawns of tall fescue if she desired. The pool would remain if she wanted it to; for it was one of the primary features she imagined tying her to Frederick Bilton. Charles grumbled under his breath.

"What was that?" The coldness was nipping at the edges of her features again. "What did you say?"

"Nothing. Nothing will change, of course."

"See that it doesn't. Oh, Charles, my nearly perfect man, how much easier is life when you see things my way?" Capitulation on his part, that was the only way to win her back. He delighted in pulling the strings, but he knew when to let them lay still.

Charles nodded and sipped from the glass of water, all the while imagining he could taste those ghoulish fish, their leavings traveling through the porous soil, and into the well water. Easier indeed.

Allison shook her wrist, turning her watch around so she could read the face. "Bother. It's nearing time for your treatment now, dear. I'll meet you in the sewing room." The door banged again and she was gone.

The ripples in the pool were subsiding, replaced by the black mirror of the still surface. Charles squinted in the sunlight and finished his water. This was her dream they were living, and had he had any say in how they got here? There was a reason the area around Lake Drummond was called the Great Dismal Swamp. It *was* dismal. No amount of Allison's love for the multi-kneed cypresses or candy-coated sunset views, or even the legendary memory of Frederick Bilton could change that. This was her world he was living in.

The familiar tubes in his arm. The hum of the machine. The blood exited Charles, the impurities were sucked out of it in the process of ultrafiltration and then the heparin infused blood was pumped back in. Fresh blood, new Charles. It only cost four hours a session three times a week. Every time he sat in the chair he was reminded of the diagnosis, internal damnation sent down by a capricious God. Cancer had been ruled out, hepatitis and other infections came back negative as well. A mystery gifted by nature.

Simply a poor serve to an unprepared player. Allison dropped her gloves into the biohazard disposal and gave Charles a kiss on the cheek. "Why don't you get some reading done? I'll be back at two. Buzz if you need me."

Charles felt like a doll in a play set. *My Nearly Perfect Husband* comes complete with Membranous Glomerulonephritis, and a smirking awareness of lost opportunities. Allison left and Charles scanned the shelves. This was called the "sewing room," yet there was nothing in here except his machine and shelves filled with a random assortment of books left by the last owner. Though there had been plenty of needles. He looked down at his arm as if in confirmation of a needle's presence, and then quickly glanced away from the offending steel. His eyes fell upon the books. He had kept meaning to burn the old harlequins and self-help paperbacks, replace them with something palatable, but he never thought about it until he was trapped in the chair and it was too late. His eyes wandered out the window to the yard with the black rectangle staring up at the sky. Allison strode purposefully toward the carriage house, slowing only to gaze into the wavy reflections of the pool. Charles's hand hovered over the buzzer, he wished to simply call her as soon as she entered her lab just so she'd have to walk back. Any small torment could be seen as a victory, but he stopped himself, finding solace in the quiet.

The machine's hum lulled him and he began to drift, waking when the sun was at its apex, reflecting a white ball into the pool outside the window. There was still almost two hours on the pump's timer and Charles cast his sleep-blurred eyes to the bright nature outside. The carriage house doors opened and Allison emerged, her hair pinned up in a workmanlike bun and her features still worrying over calculations. She carried one of the blue containers that dialysate came in. Charles looked over and noted that the one hooked to the machine had just enough to finish out the session. He heard the front door open, Allison's footsteps in the hallway, and then she was standing in front of him. She lugged the heavy jug to the corner and set it down. "Thought you were supposed to be reading. Why don't you pick up 'Gone With the Wind?' That's a good long one. It's your favorite."

"No, it's *your* favorite. And I already read it," Charles said as he watched her adjust the container so that it sat flush against the wall. "You're going back into the city tomorrow?"

133

"Are you trying to get rid of me, Charles?" Allison asked. Her face was unreadable, silhouetted as she was against the bright window. She loomed over him like some great monolith, blotting out the sun.

"No, I was just hoping you might pick up a cake, for our anniversary."

"Oh, my dear, sweet, Charles." Allison moved out of the light and smiled. She strode to the bookshelf and took down a book. "Whatever you wish. I'll be back to unhook you when you're done." She dropped the book on Charles's lap. He stared down with distaste at the cracked paper cover of Gone With The Wind.

"You've outdone yourself, Charles." Allison stabbed a rosemary infused chunk of pink lamb with her fork. Though Charles might be described as lazy and malcontent, he could still cook a good meal. Mostly due to all the classes Allison had sent him to, grooming him for his work at home. He knew that had he been somehow able to carry children then that would have happened long ago as well. As it was, Allison was unwilling to sacrifice the time for childbirth, so they remained locked in their dynamic, Charles the stand-in child for Allison's latent motherhood.

"So that jitterbug Danforth I was telling you about, at PER*syst*. He believes that stem cell treatments can be extended all the way to the human immune system as well, bolstering the cell repertoire to defend against any antigens, even those that adapt quickly. Consistently degradation has been the culprit, usually resulting in fatality at an early age though." On she prattled with the vagaries of her work. Charles had long ago learned to let the information sail by, inserting the correct sounds of interest where necessary. He looked his wife over in the warm light cast by the flame-shaped chandelier bulbs. She was starting to show her age. Long hours were beginning to tell on her face, wearing deep lines into the once silken countenance. With every bite she took he spied the yellowing teeth, and with every twitch of the eye he fixated on the minute burst capillaries in her sclera. "You're staring at me, Charles," Allison said. "Have you even been listening?"

"What? No, I'm sorry, you—um, you look so beautiful tonight," he stammered.

Allison smirked. "You're too kind." She looked her husband over and then added, "We really do have the best life." Her knife scraped the plate as she cut into the lamb and took another bite. "This place, it's marvelous, I never would have imagined I'd own the house that Frederick Bilton built."

Charles nodded.

"You know why I like him so much, Charlie?"

"Yes, 'The Mausoleum of Praise.' Just like everyone else."

"No, it's not just that. Although it *is* brilliant. It's also because he was so unafraid, so singular for his time. One of the first poets to really explore the nonexistence of God."

Charles prodded his broccoli, hating to have cooked it longer than was necessary simply because Allison liked her vegetables soggy. "Allison, you're not an atheist. You've told me many times you believe God set everything in motion."

"That doesn't change how I feel about Bilton. I admire the man. He was raised Catholic, just like us, yet he put all that aside, for reason, for philosophy." Allison's hands were fidgeting, she cracked her knuckles, something she only did when she was unsure.

"So you're saying you don't believe in God anymore?" Charles asked.

"No, don't be stupid. Of course I do, but as a scientist I have to make concessions to the world I see around me, don't I? *We* are the dominant species on this planet. *We* decide what's important and what's not. The plants, the animals, they're all physical objects, materials to be used. And use them we will. You can make sure of it."

Nearly a week of sleepless nights and not even a drink to lessen the edge. Now Allison was going mad on him. The pressure brimming inside Charles burst. "It sounds like you think you're God."

Allison slowly set her knife down and swallowed. Her voice came out in a deliberate monotone. "I see. I'd thought we could have a civil discussion, like we used to. It seems dinner is over. Clear the plates, Charles. I'll be in the lab. Don't wait up."

"Wake up, Charles. I'm leaving," Allison's voice cooed in his ear. Charles opened his eyes to the soft light of dawn. He'd been fast asleep, the first night since the accident that he'd been able to sleep all the way through. Irritation flared up like a splinter driven underneath his nail. He'd gone to bed contrite, sorry for what he'd said to Allison, but now he wanted to rail against her for waking him. The vitriolic words stopped in his throat when he saw the kind expression on her face. Allison smiled. "I hope you have a good day. I'll be back early tomorrow if everything goes well. And don't worry, I'll have your favorite cake in hand. Coconut."

That's your favorite, he wanted to say. Instead he only smiled and shrugged into her embrace.

Allison's hands clenched against him as she pulled away. "What is that?" She was looking down, past the bed and onto the floor.

"What?"

"*That*." She pointed.

Charles leaned forward and saw the black, squished caterpillar of a Marcoliani cashmere sock peeking out from under the bed. "Oh, Allison, I'm sorry, I must have dropped it in the dark…"

She pinched the offending garment with two fingers and raised it up. "I work hard every day, and I only ask one thing, that you keep this house in order. We'll talk about this when I get home, Charles." With a flick she threw the sock at him where it landed in his lap.

"Honey, wait, don't leave me like this. Honey?"

The slam of the front door and the squeal of tires in the driveway were the exclamation points on her anger. Charles stared down at the limp sock. In a fit he grabbed it up and hurled it across the room. Charles leapt from the high mattress and kicked the laundry hamper, spilling the contents on the floor. It felt good. "Keep *this* house in order," he growled, grinning. He took great pleasure in not only not making the bed but also going out of his way to unmake it, peeling the blankets and sheets and throwing them in a wad into the corner. With a slap he spilled the tower of pillows to one side. Charles strode into the bathroom and relieved himself without lifting the seat. He leered at the sight of the yellow dribbles left on the porcelain and then looked in the mirror. On a wild impulse he pulled at the buttons of his pajama top, freeing them from their threads and casting them into the sink. His muscled, hairless torso heaved with excitement. The violence of the act felt good. He stared at himself in the mirror. If Mungu Fred, "God" to the heathens of his harem, had been able to do anything he wanted, then so could Charles. He smiled at his reflection. It was a new day, and he was reborn.

With a saunter in his gait Charles descended into the kitchen. He made himself an artery clogging breakfast, exhausting the freezer of its store of bacon and using a whole stick of butter in the production of his pancakes. What did he care anymore? Allison would have a fit, he'd have his blood filtered and they'd be right back where they started. Normally trained to clean as he cooked, he let the sink pile up with dishes and left them to dry with hardening batter and congealing grease. Charles was full and happy as he placed his feet on the kitchen table and leaned back. If only he had a drink, that would be the perfect start to the day.

It wasn't even nine. There was no way the package store was open at this hour. Charles rubbed at his uncombed mop of curly hair and stared at the exciting ruination around him. He tried to remember actually seeing Allison discard of the alcohol. Had he seen that, or had she simply hidden it? Charles stood up and began his hunt in the kitchen. Despite his newfound nihilism he was still cautious not to break anything. Every bit of chaos he was creating could easily be cleaned. The search found the cupboards free of any hidden alcohol. He searched the rest of the downstairs. Still nothing. The second floor yielded the same results. Deciding Allison really had disposed of the alcohol he went around the side of the house to check the recycling bin, but it only held the jars and plastic containers he'd put there in the course of meal preparations.

The day was growing hot and Charles was sweating. Though he was aware of how silly he must look, standing in his pajama bottoms, flushed with aggravation, he didn't care. He kicked at a small garden pagoda, resulting in a stubbed toe and cursing. As he hobbled back to the front door he checked his watch, realizing it was after ten. He hurried inside, consulted his wallet to make sure he had cash on hand and then called the package store.

"Ah, Mr. Willis," the clerk said with some reticence.

"Yessir, Sam," said Charles, wincing as he put weight on his injured toe. "I wanted to see if I could get a drop-off maybe?"

"Sure would like to, Mr. Willis. Thing is, your wife called, said that we, uh, might better not fill any orders for you right now. Said something 'bout it 'not being prudent.' You there?"

If Charles had been any stronger the receiver might have shattered in his grip. He hung up, discarding the idea of trying any other stores. Allison would have called them all. How dare she. *Prudent?* It was too much. She'd demeaned him for the last time.

He went to the garage and retrieved the crowbar and coil of thick garden hose. The mischief on his mind had now turned to destruction. Charles knelt at the edge of the reflecting pool and gently fed the entire hose into the quiet, dark water. The fish began to come to the surface, made curious by his actions. Charles waited for the last bubble to drift up from the water-filled hose and then he clamped his palm over the end. He dragged the hose back out of the water and down the hill, leaving one end in the water. The grin on his face widened as he let his hand off and watched the water begin to spill forth, a slow siphon on the reflecting pool. "Goodbye, fishies." He stormed past the pool, ignoring the leisurely dropping surface, and headed for the carriage house, Allison's sanctuary.

When Allison had first landed her position at PER*syst* she'd tried to explain it to Charles, but he'd quickly found that most of what they did was beyond him. He knew she was involved in stem cell research, and he knew that she was passionate about it, but he'd been content to leave it there. The carriage house was her domain and Charles had always respected that, until now. The steel Cromlech brand lock flashed in the sun, taunting Charles, a symbol of Allison's control over him. He placed the pry bar in the door and pulled. The lock itself was strong but the wood was old and it began to give. After ten minutes of incremental headway he quit his assault around the lock and began at the hinges of the door. The wood there was even softer, splintering under the claw of the crowbar. The screws in the hinges protested as they were ripped from the wood and the door fell outward at an angle. Charles forced the other hinge and it gave way fully to a dark interior.

With a flick of the switch the fluorescent lights buzzed to life, and Charles began looking about for something to break. There was a low desk with a sleeping computer monitor on it. The old-fashioned chalkboard above was covered in formulae scratched into the erased clouds of previous equations. Rows of his dialysate jugs were arranged against one wall underneath a series of fluid filled vats. Charles inspected the opalescent liquid, trying to discern the purpose of the containers. "What have you been up to, Doctor?" Charles stared for only a moment before rearing back and slamming the crowbar into the glass, spilling forth the sour-smelling contents from each container in turn. The cement floor was awash, drenching his bare feet. Charles stepped back from the mess and inspected the rest of the room. High on a shelf sat the handle of Beefeater Gin that had disappeared from the bar; it was keeping company with the bottle of anniversary wine. "Sneaky, Doctor."

Charles grabbed at the gin and even before settling into the wheeled office chair, he'd twisted the top off and downed a good pull. "Oh yes, that's right!" he sang to the exposed rafters.

The sun rose, beaming through the high window of the carriage house as the bottle of gin reached the half empty mark. Charles poked at it, watching the unsteady bob of his finger with a bleary eye. "You're a good little ginny, aren't you?" The desk and computer had been locked to him but he didn't care, the alcohol was more than enough of a reward for his trespass. He stood on unsteady feet. It was time for wine. He tapped the bottle of Barbaresco and it wobbled, teetering at the edge of the shelf. "Oh no you—" With a smash the bottle shattered, spilling its crimson contents to mix with the still drying vat liquid. Charles hiccupped in surprise. "A shame...yeh, a shame."

With just enough mind to navigate the broken glass, Charles took up the jug of gin again and stumbled from the carriage house. It had been hours since he'd been outside and the full heat of day had set in. He guzzled the gin, far past the point at which he'd complain about the taste. The weeping willow beside the reflecting pool swayed in the lazy wind and Charles stared up at it while he walked forward. "For once shall...see all motion, aghast the world in blaze. A passel of rites for, uh...the ocean, despair the Mausoleum of Praise. Piss." Charles took another swig and canted forward as his foot tipped over the edge of the reflecting pool. This time there was no water to soften his fall. He fell in a jumble on the silted bottom, feeling the dying flop of a blind fish in the small of his back. His breath had been knocked clear and he labored to find it. "Ugh, no," he mouthed as he raised his muck-stained hands before his face. The thin layer of sediment and dying fish had created a slight cushion and it seemed he was unhurt. Charles began to laugh, staring up at the blue skies above, sobered enough by the fall to realize he could have hurt himself badly. "What do you think of your precious reflecting pool now, Doctor? Mungu Chuck strikes again."

Charles struggled forward, finding just enough balance on his hands and knees to catch his breath. The fingers of his right hand closed over something solid underneath the remaining few inches of water. He pulled it forth, shuddering at the sight of what looked to be an old baby doll, tethered with a frayed rope to a large brick. He turned the doll over, splashing filthy water from a leftover puddle on its surface in an attempt to clean it. The mud fell away, revealing pale flesh pickled by its time underwater, and a blaze of reddish stain above the right eye.

A hemangioma birthmark.

The dead face turned up at him on a loose neck as Charles handled the small body.

It was the face of a real infant.

Charles's mind burned hotly, free of any lingering effects of alcohol. Allison. The treatments. The lab. He'd been a prisoner here at Herringbone, the living doll-husband to a woman who…what? What had she done?

The gray body hung limp, accusatorily in Charles's trembling hands. The hotness in his mind turned to anger, as he imagined casting Allison into the drained reflecting pool to encounter this unmentionable sin of hers. His strong fingers flexed, bursting the small, frail torso, and a filthy ichor belched forth from the swollen flesh, painting his hands black.

Charles dropped the abomination in horror, and scrambled back, hands mushing, tearing into more rotting, gelid forms lurking beneath the mud. Beginning to feel sick he searched about for a way out of the stinking pool, fumbling at the algae-slick sides. Failing to gain any purchase he froze as he caught the movement of flies swarming about to land on clusters of pale, round masses glistening in the hot sun; each pallid dome fuzzed lightly with fine, dark hair.

More bodies.

Frantic, Charles threw himself forward and began to inspect what he saw. Mixed in amongst the still convulsing fish were *dozens* of newborns, each in a deep state of decay, and each with the familiar birthmark painting its temple.

From over the lip of the now empty pool there came the familiar sound of a car engine being shut off. Charles Willis fell to his knees and wept.

Repast

Andrew guided his pickup around the curve that led into the dust-choked parking lot outside **Hanlow's** General Store & Deli. He let the wheel slide in his calloused hands, and there was Joe, smoking a cigar and leaning against a shining red jeep beneath a blighted oak tree. The air was warm enough to have the windows down, but downright hot if you stood in the sun. The oak's jagged shadow swallowed Andrew's vehicle, and he gave a little, tentative wave to Joe as he cut the engine. Thirty-five years had snatched most of the hair from Joe's head, mottled and lined his fair skin, and granted a considerable paunch to his midsection, but he still had the wide shoulders of a hammer-thrower, and the sharp smile of a jazz guitarist. Joe spread his manicured hands on the hood of Andrew's truck and winked. Andrew recalled that night so long ago when Joe, knife in hand and face lit devil-red by firelight, had given him that same knowing wink.

As soon as the door opened Joe pounced on Andrew. "A. J.! Look at you. Still a beanpole. I'm glad you came!"

"I almost didn't." Andrew wheezed as Joe let up on the crushing embrace and held him at arm's length. "It's Andrew now. I go by Andrew."

Joe put on a serious face. "*Right, Andrew.* So grown up." He laughed the rattling chuckle that Andrew remembered so well, something akin to a locomotive chugging into a station. "Hope you're hungry, *Mister Andrew Burton Jr.*"

"I could eat." Andrew looked his old pal over, indulging only a moment in the schadenfreude that accompanied the up close realization of just how bad Joe looked, waning under the crush of time's indomitable wheel.

"What do you think?" Joe stubbed the cigar on the sole of his bison leather hiking boot and added, "Hip joint for brunch. Found it last year when I was playing the links out at Occoneechee."

Hanlow's was the kind of place that routinely popped up in this part of the state: a sort of rustic eatery cum high-end grocery that billed itself as a "five-star feed store." This was where trust fund kids from the city returned to the earth to get dirt under their nails and offer a green alternative to the hicks in the sticks. "Farm to table" was the mantra here, and they wore it on their sleeves, from the kitschy beef cut charts on the walls, to the solid maple end-grain butcher block tables with beeswax finishes. "Looks fine," Andrew said, parting the folds of a menu as they settled into a table near the window.

"You gotta try the Rancher Holiday. Lil' bit of everything there. Canadian bacon, three kinds of sausage made on premises, jelly and cream cheese stuffed French toast, eggs any way you like…mmmm, mmmm." Joe nodded to the server, and without consulting Andrew said, "Two sweet teas, and two Rancher Holidays, hon." The pretty blonde, nose rings notwithstanding, turned toward the kitchen to retrieve the drinks and place the orders.

"Wait, no." Andrew adjusted his glasses while his eyes sped across the menu, trying to lock on something, anything. He'd forgotten just how much Joe was wont to take charge. "Just a short stack for me, and two eggs scrambled. No bacon."

The server vanished and Joe raised both bushy eyebrows. "No bacon? You're not one of those veg heads now are you?" He let the question hang for a moment, and then said, "Haw! I'm just ticklin' your ribs, man." The steam engine laugh chuffed by.

"No. I'm watching my cholesterol," Andrew said with a smirk.

Joe was watching *him*. His expression grew earnest, sun-reddened skin warmed by the morning light slanting in the window. "I'm glad we could do this. I mean it, Andrew. Thirty-something years, that's too long. I wasn't even sure I had the right number when I called."

Andrew raised his hands, palms up in a supplicating gesture. "Well, it was. And you have me now. I took the whole weekend. You look good, Joe."

"Aw." Joe shrugged off the compliment for the nicety it was. "Cheryl's driving Jessica up north to visit schools. Princeton and UPenn this time. That kid, I swear, she plots circles around both of us. Studying corporate ethnography, or ethnographic corporations. Social recruiting or some shit." Joe laughed. "Poor daddy-o can never keep it straight. I'll always be just a numbers guy."

More details about Joe's life followed; spluttered out between liberal gulps of his iced tea. Married for eighteen years to a woman who was his junior by a decade, just the one daughter, CFO of Chambling Capital for the last five years, where he could expect to pull down more than 500k with bonuses this year alone. There was a rambling brick manse in Hope Valley, Durham's most posh neighborhood, and a beachfront house on Cape Hatteras where the family Vinson could spend their summer weekends.

"Quite a spread, eh? Don't be jealous now." The food had arrived. A simple plate for Andrew and a long cutting board for Joe stacked high with meats, cheeses, French toast, biscuits, ramekins of herbed butter and a foursome of preserves. He poked his fork in Andrew's direction. "And don't think you can pick at it either."

143

"I'll be okay," Andrew said as he poured the thick syrup. At least it was the real stuff.

Joe tucked into the feast with mendicant focus, chewing through every offering from one end of the board to the other. He talked over bites, describing his ascension at Chambling after Sevine Financial, where he'd snagged a job out of college, went the way of the buffalo. Andrew didn't mind the natter. He well remembered Joe's unwillingness to talk about anything beyond his favorite subject, which was himself. Despite the amount of food, Joe's slab of wood was cleared of all but crumbs and meat juice by the time Andrew was mopping up syrup with his last bite of pancake. Joe waved the server over and handed her two twenties. "Keep the change, hon."

Andrew reached for his wallet, but the waitress had already left. "Joe, let me pay you back."

"Bologna. Fill us up with gas if it makes you feel better. I thought we'd take the jeep. Your truck doesn't exactly look like it could make the trip." Joe winked. "Besides, gives us a chance to talk more."

Andrew glanced out the window at his fifteen year old pickup with the long crack in the windshield parked next to Joe's angular jeep, crouched there like a ruddy bull. "I guess that's fine."

"They won't care if you leave your truck." Joe slurped the last of his tea and swirled the ice. "Here, I brought something I wanted to show you." He reached into the breast pocket of his gingham shirt and withdrew a photograph.

Andrew wiped his hands, took the photo, and beheld a trio of ghosts. Owlwatch Lodge loomed up dark black in the background, silhouette impaled by spike-top sentinels of pine. Caught in the flash, specter pale and still suffering under a layer of late-leaving baby fat, was a twenty-three year old A. J. Burton, hand on the shoulder of Joe Vinson, smiling his jazz guitarist smile. Andrew's heart stuttered as he looked at the third person in the picture, at a face no one had seen in thirty-five years.

Staring back at him was the face of Graham Moss.

December 15th, 1979

A sudden flash blinded A. J.'s twilight-adjusted eyes.

"Keep your hands to yourself, queer," Joe said playfully, knocking A. J.'s arm aside and administering a rowdy punch to his shoulder.

Graham grabbed his Instamatic from the hood of Joe's Suburban and popped the hot flashcube off, blowing at it with a jet of icy breath. "Last of that roll."

"I thought you guys would be here at seven," A. J. said, rubbing at his upper arm, playing it off as a shiver against the cold. A soft-edged ball of color swirled in his vision as he crunched along in the gravel behind Joe.

Graham heaved a leather carryall from the backseat and stuffed his camera into it. "Yeah, Joe had to stop for supplies. And then he got us   lost."

"So says the navigator." Joe shook his head and gave a little *tut-tut*. The rear hatch squealed when he wrenched it open. Inside were five six-packs of Stroh's, kept from rolling around the wayback with a buttress of sleeping bags and blankets. Joe thrust three into A. J.'s empty arms and gathered up the other two. "Cold out here. March, soldier!"

Bottles clinked in A. J.'s grasp as he navigated the steps, looking over his shoulder at his buddies. "Did you get a chance to check the forecast? My dad always said it's not good to go out if it's snowing too much."

"Cool your pipes. I checked, I checked." Joe poked A. J.'s butt with an elbow. "Go, go. I'm freezing my dick off out here. It's just going to be cold, no snow, man. Right, Copernicus?"

Graham mumbled what might have been assent from behind a paper grocery bag.

"Besides, your daddy's not here to stop you one way or the other."

The wind bladed along the outside of the lodge like an ice-scraper on a windshield, raising the hair on A. J.'s bare arms. Then they were inside, back in the close warmth he'd been charming from the squat woodstove for the past two hours while waiting for Joe and Graham to arrive. The interior of the lodge was a single wood-paneled room measuring six hundred square feet, with one small half-bath off to a side. It was spartan but well cared for, and built with earnings from Andrew Senior's booming tractor business. Besides the woodstove, there was a hotplate, refrigerator, handful of built in cabinets, smattering of furniture and a ladder accessible loft for sleeping.

"Owl*snatch*, here we are!" sang Joe, depositing the beer, less one, on the counter and plopping into an overstuffed recliner. He popped the bottle and took a pull. "Sah! Where boys become men, and men become more manly. Got anything to eat?"

"What, here?" A. J. asked. "No, my dad doesn't keep anything." He opened the refrigerator to put the beer away, showing Joe an empty interior. "There's a few old cans in the cupboard, but they don't have labels."

"That's why *we* had to bring the food." Graham spoke slowly as he shook the grocery bag in Joe's direction and waggled his eyebrows. "Do you ever pay attention?"

"*Psh.* Well, let those dogs free. I'm starving."

Free the hotdogs they did, four apiece, along with a bag of potato chips and two cans of baked beans. With full stomachs and beer-fueled stupors, they retired to the loft, sinking into sleep as the wind skidded over the lodge, and the owl chorus began its merrymaking in the trees outside. It was good to be in this heart of heat, amongst friends.

A. J. awoke to the smell of coffee, and the whipsaw drone of Joe's snores. Dizzy-headed he slipped on the way down the ladder and lurched about on heavy feet. With a cup of coffee to warm his hands, and an orange parka over his shoulders he stepped out into the gray morning light. Graham was hunched over a trio of rifles laid out on a blanket on the gravel next to the Suburban. Wild, bed-mashed hair and an oversized brown hunter's jacket made him look like some kind of primitive scientist scrutinizing specimens for dissection. He picked one up as A. J. approached and said, "Savage model one-ten. Detachable box magazine. Tuned-in Bushnell scope. This is a popular one at pop-pop's shop." He grew serious. "Brought two of those, but I swear if they get a single scratch I'm done for."

"Alright, alright," A. J. said, waving his hands and sloshing his coffee. "What's the other?"

"That? That one's mine. Winchester model 64. Hand-checkered stock, and accurate as all get out. You could split a bug's eyelash with this thing." Graham hefted the gun and popped the scope's end cap. He braced himself against the hood of the Suburban and took aim somewhere down the mountain. His finger caressed the trigger. "Joe didn't tell you what happened did he?"

"Huh?" A. J. took a small sip and promptly burned his tongue. Still too hot.

"Sevine Financial. They only have room to bump one of us up to permanent. It's me. Was supposed to be a secret until the New Year, but someone in accounting blabbed to Joe." Graham let off the trigger and looked at A. J. "Boy, he was raging in the car last night. Not about *that*, he didn't even bring it up. Just every other little thing. You know how he is."

A. J. nodded. "He's sleeping fine now." He tried another sip and made the burn worse. "Sh! Oh, I guess he'll get over it."

"Yeah, well, don't expect him to be all peaches today." Graham wrinkled his nose at the cottony clouds piling on the mountain line. "We should get out there. Flip you to see who wakes up His Majesty."

Tails lost for A. J. and he went back inside. Oatmeal and hard-boiled eggs, bundling up, supply checks, and an hour later the threesome were armed and prowling down through the pines, leaving Owlwatch where it crouched on the ridge behind. A. J. stepped lightly on the smooth pine needles, holding the gun gingerly like it was the infant Jesus. "The deer trail is supposed to be just a quarter mile or so, where the grade levels out."

"I'm going to shoot a buck. Eight points minimum, I guarantee it." Joe struck a dramatic, soldierly stance and peered through his scope.

Graham crept between two trees, keeping his head low and eyes alert. "You've never even hunted before."

"How hard could it be? Point and *BLAM!*" Joe's bray of laughter roused a covey of ptarmigans free from the tree above.

Graham frowned beneath his toboggan cap. "Yeah, well we first have to find a deer, and that's not going to happen with you scaring everything away."

"Watch out. Theodore Roosevelt on the trail." Joe snickered.

"Shut up, Joe," Graham whispered.

"Gonna bag us a buffalo, Teddy?"

Graham didn't bother reigning in his irritation. "Shh! Jesus."

"Guys, come on. Leave it alone." A. J. fumbled at his gun strap with his gloved hands.

The ground became flatter here, and the trees parted to reveal a deep chalice of valley cut through the Great Choir Mountain range. It was then that the first great bucket loads of snow dumped fast and thick. A powerful gust of wind blew up the mountain face, setting all the pines to sway. The snow whipped sideways, and A. J.'s voice was drowned out by the harsh swish of pine needles above.

"Huh?" Joe yelled.

"We should go back," A. J. said again.

Joe smirked and shrugged. "It's just a bit of snow, man. Don't be a pussy."

"Graham?"

Graham looked from A. J. to Joe and back. "Go on back if you want. Snow's good for tracking. I'm out here to hunt."

Joe squared his shoulders. "So am I."

"You're both crazy." A. J. turned and stalked back up the hill toward Owlwatch, hunching within his parka against the cold and snow. It took a lot of fighting the wind and bracing himself against the trunks of trees to get back to the cabin. Snow already frosted his father's silver Bronco and Joe's Suburban like cupcakes. A. J. clopped up the stairs in frustration and slammed the door behind him. A reversal of his preparations played out: gun stowed by the door, parka shed, and the coals in the woodstove stoked back to life. The last thing they needed was to be snowed-in. No phone. No neighbors. The closest civilization was Saxon's Forge, thirty-three miles down what would likely become a snow-choked mountain. His dad wasn't even expecting him until next week for Christmas. School break had already started; not that anyone there would miss him anyway. His only two friends had already graduated and were outside, playing Great White Hunter. A. J. felt empty inside, and the coffee was teasing his bowels loose. He headed for the toilet, hoping the pipes outside hadn't frozen.

That was when he heard the gunshot.

BANG!

Andrew jumped at the sudden clank of a mechanic's garage door jolting to life and trundling upward. He opened the package on a mixed-nut bar as he crossed the gas station parking lot.

Joe withdrew the fuel nozzle from the jeep and shook his key ring. "You drive. You know the way better than me."

"Are you sure?"

Joe hopped into the passenger seat. "Go on. See how she handles."

Andrew settled behind the wheel and keyed the jeep to life. The jeep had less than a thousand miles on the odometer, and she drove as smooth as she rode. It was noon, and hot, but with the top down, and the gradual rise in elevation, Andrew remained cool. They passed the signs for Skyhook Mountain and Vulture's Gavel. The latter could be seen, sharp and dark against the sky to the north, deadly to all but the most seasoned climbers. Andrew finished his snack.

"Got you a little granola fix, huh? Should have joined me on the Rancher Holiday. I'll be full 'til dinner." Joe patted his belly. "Speaking of…see the cooler in the back?"

"Yeah." Andrew peeked in the rearview at the large Coleman cooler snugged in behind them. "What's in it?"

Joe clapped him on the shoulder. "A surprise you're going to *love*, I guarantee it." He rubbed at his stubby nose, paprika red with gin blossoms. "Like I said on the phone. I thought we could set things right. I always believed good memories can erase bad ones." He flashed a half-smile when Andrew nodded. "Hah! You're buttoned up tighter than a clam's ass at high tide. You going to tell me about what you've been up to all this time, or what? How's the tractor business treating you? I see the billboards everywhere."

Andrew knew this would come up eventually, but he still didn't know what to say. Should he just admit that his father had passed him over so that his baby sister Ellen could take over Burton Lawn & Tractor? Should he detail how a nervous breakdown after the hunting trip at Owlwatch had knocked him out of college and landed him in a clinic for three years? That Ellen took pity on him and paid a full-time wage even though he only worked two days a week managing warehouse workers, if that? Joe sat grinning in the plush leather of his brand new vehicle. Andrew cleared his throat and simply said, "Still good. Burton's is number two in the state."

The turn for the little community of Saxon's Forge came and went in a blink. Andrew veered left up a slender hairpin curve where the trees towered up over a series of ever-narrowing roads. Thirty-five years had not done much to change this part of the state, and the land was largely as virgin and secret as it had been when this had been Indian Territory. The jeep climbed up the last of the road and suddenly they had arrived. Dark Owlwatch, now three times its original size, commanded this quarter of the mountain face. Joe whistled as he looked up. "Your old daddy made some improvements."

Andrew cut the engine. "No, it was me. Dad's too old, and Ellen hates this place. They haven't been in years. But, I spend a lot of time up here." Andrew reached toward the cooler.

"Nah. Leave that till we get back. I want to get out there while it's still light." Joe pointed to a faint trail leading northward along the mountain face.

"Oh, I didn't realize you wanted to do that first." Andrew shut the jeep door and let himself be led beneath the wooden posts holding Owlwatch up. He gave only the briefest glance to the base of the stairs before following Joe onto the trail.

His heart had already begun to beat faster.

December 16th, 1979

Blood pulsed in A. J.'s ears as he stared down at Graham's body, now lifeless and crumpled at the base of the stairs. A deep drift of snow was already gathering along one side of him. The peppered trail of black blood leading from the forest had been covered hours ago by the insistent blizzard. A claw of icy wind scrabbled at A. J.'s face.

"I told you to close the damn door. There's nothing we can do for him," Joe slurred this from the table in the corner where he mechanically worked through another game of solitaire. "Not till the storm clears."

When Joe had burst through the door after hauling Graham's body back to Owlwatch, it had been all A. J. could do to calm him down enough to get him to speak in whole sentences. "We got separated and he – he just kinda jumped out at me. I don't know. God, the idiot! What was he thinking?" Joe had collapsed into a heap in one of the chairs, mumbling, "He's dead. He's really dead."

Joe had calmed down considerably in the hours since then, due in no small part to the cache of Andrew Senior's moonshine they'd found under the sink while exploring the kitchen for food. Twelve mason jars were squirrelled away down there; each filled to the brim with clear liquid strong enough to eat the paint off a radiator. A. J.'s head was fuzzy from the caustic drink. He kept finding himself wandering to the door, wondering if he should go down there and cover Graham up. Joe was probably right; there wasn't anything they could do for him now. A. J. stumbled through the kitchen area and knocked aside the cans they'd opened earlier while hunting for food. Something had gotten into the tin, rotting whatever had been inside and leaving behind a mess of blackish mold. His hollow stomach balked at the idea of another belt of the moonshine, but it wasn't enough to stop him. A. J. brought the half-empty jar over to Joe.

Joe nodded and tipped the drink down his throat. "Gah! Where your dad get this shtuff anyway?"

A. J. blinked and pointed toward the wall. "Guess down in the Forge. They're known for their…um, criminal w…ways."

Joe began to giggle. He threw his cards down and put his head on the table. "Know what I'd love?"

A. J. answered by taking another gulp of the burning drink. This had more kick than any alcohol he'd ever had, and he was quickly becoming very wasted.

"I'd love a big hunk a meat. Pork roast. Right here, on this peesh a crap table. Mashed potato, lotta butter, gravy, green bean casherole, a mesha bread rolls. That, or to burn this god damn plashe down." He began to laugh again.

The morning brought a headache that felt like a steak knife driven through A. J.'s forehead. He stood from the chair he'd slept in, and staggered around Joe's passed out form on the way to the kitchen. The memory of what happened to Graham struck him suddenly, and he briefly considered opening the door to stare down at the body before he checked the window and saw just how much fun the blizzard was still having with the land outside, blowing about great clumps of snow like dollops of whipped cream.

"Not any better out there is it?" Joe asked, rising to his feet and rubbing his eyes.

A. J. shook his pounding head.

"Santa come in the night and bring a Christmas ham?" Joe stared at the bare counter and table. "Didn't think so." He went to the faucet and turned the knob. "Welp. Pipes are frozen." Joe grabbed a cooking pot, opened the front door and began to gather handfuls of snow. A. J. peered around the doorjamb and saw that Graham had been completely buried in the white, leaving nothing but a nondescript hump. The meager heat inside the lodge was fleeing fast. Joe closed the door, walked to the electric hotplate and twisted the knob. "Well, shit. Electricity's out too." He deposited the pot on top of the woodstove, and then withdrew another jar from beneath the sink.

A. J. frowned. "This early?"

"Nothing else to do. Hair of the dog, man." Joe took a long swig and shuddered.

The lodge was already warming back up, but A. J. still felt a shiver as he thought of Graham lying under all that snow. He approached Joe and put a tentative hand on his shoulder. "So, yesterday. It was an accident?"

Joe must have detected something in A. J.'s voice for he looked up, suddenly indignant. "Yeah. Of course it was an accident."

"What are we going to tell his parents?"

Joe seemed to roll this around. "I don't know. The truth, I guess." He took another swig and offered the jar to A. J.; who licked his lips and took it, ready for another taste of oblivion in the clear liquid.

Cards and moonshine dominated the daylight hours. The electricity stayed off, but the cabin remained warm. The fire in A.J.'s belly was warm too. Moonshine on an empty stomach was playing hell with his insides, and a sort of delirious haze was creeping over his consciousness. A. J.'s gut sounded a loud protestation. "If this lasts much longer we'll be eating boiled pinecones."

Joe raised an eyebrow. "We've got a pile of frozen meat on our doorstep."

This was dark, even for Joe. A. J. didn't laugh.

"Don't be such a wet blanket. Where's your sense of humor?" Then, in a reflective sort of way, he added, "Though, those soccer players did it down in South America when their plane crashed." Joe teetered over to the pile, grabbed a log from the dwindling pile and shoved it into the woodstove. "Just saying."

A. J. had barely been hanging on to consciousness for the last hour. "I'm out." He put his cards down and leaned back in the chair, letting a warm blackout enfold him.

He awoke sometime in the night, still very drunk. A single candle lit the interior of the lodge and there was a loud snapping coming from beside him. Joe had overturned his chair and was stomping it to splinters. His face lit up fiendishly red when he opened the woodstove door and thrust the broken wood inside, all the while muttering to himself. Upon noticing A. J.'s open eyes he said, "I know what to do. We'll shay Graham disappeared. He went for help when the snow started…and…he never came back. Right?" He slammed the woodstove door and put his hands on his hips, towering like some great, dark colossus in the center of the lodge. "Then we can do what we want with the body. Right?"

"I…what are you even talking about." A.J. shook his head; but he still swam in a sea of moonshine. "Do *what*?"

"My ass is going to be on the line here." Joe's face was etched in flame, and as serious as stone.

A. J. rolled in the recliner, burying his face in the cushion. "Go to sleep, Joe." His mind began to shut down, taking his own suggestion, as the crack of breaking wood resumed.

There followed a dream of meat sizzling on the grill, the smell sharp in A.J.'s nose. He began to drool uncontrollably. The smell was right below his nose. Wetness brushed his lips, and he opened his mouth to receive the warm morsel. His tongue buzzed with flavor. The meat melted in his mouth; veal, tender and rich, reminding him most of the cutlets his grandmother used to serve. But this was *so much better*. He opened his eyes, and saw Joe looming over him with a knife in his hand. A frying pan sat on top of the wood stove, crackling with grease.

"What do you think?"

A. J. jerked awake and fell backward out of his chair. He spat and pawed furiously at his tongue. The muzzy veil of moonshine quickly receded. "What did you do?" The lingering aroma of meat filled his nostrils, and still he drooled.

"Made a lil' midnight snack." Joe winked, his red face demonic in the night. He poked unsteadily at the simmering filet with a knife. He was clearly deeply sloshed. "Whassa matter, don't like it?" Joe began to croon. *"Please, Lord, send somethin' good to eat, lots of crispy bacon and fatty meat."*

A. J. flew up the ladder leading to the loft and huddled in the corner, pressing his back against the low, angled ceiling of the lodge. The air was hot up here, and full of the sweet scent of the frying cut. A. J. pulled his t-shirt over his nose, and waited. He couldn't get the taste of the meat out of his mouth.

Joe's drunken singing eventually died down, replaced by the soft, unmistakable sounds of chewing. The candle smoldered to a stub, and the muted beginning of dawn lit the window. A. J. was very sober, and very frightened. He sat watch for many hours, barely daring to breath.

Max Dowdle

Finally, when the window had become a bright white square, he heard commotion from below. Joe lurked about like a giant rodent scrabbling at this and that, and eventually made the noises of donning his winter wear. A. J. heard the door open and then Joe's hoarse voice croaked up at him, "A. J., meet me outside. I need your help."

"I *had* needed your help. I wasn't myself that day." Joe stared at the bulb of rough granite protruding from the ground amidst the copse of pine trees. Here was the unmarked grave of Graham Moss. Joe shook his head. "You'll never know how sorry I am."

"And *you* will never know how scared I was. Right? I mean I wasn't *myself* either that day." Andrew's face hardened. "You broke me, Joe, and that's why I…went away for a while. But I kept the promises you made me make. Every one of them," Andrew said. He removed his glasses and gave them a thoughtful polish. Then he added, as if a recitation from memory, "Yes, officer, Graham disappeared in the storm. He left to get help, and that was the last we ever saw of him. I have no idea what happened." He looked up at Joe. "Verbatim, right? That was what you wanted me to say."

"Yes." Joe knelt and laid a hand on the stone. "Rest well, Graham." He looked around at the mountain panorama. "A nicer view than some get."

"Is that enough?" Andrew shrugged. "Should we go back?"

"Yeah. I'm getting pretty hungry."

They returned to the jeep and retrieved the cooler, which took both of them to lug up the stairs and into the foyer of the remodeled and expanded Owlwatch.

"I'm impressed!" Joe said. "It's unrecognizable."

Andrew smiled. "It took a while. I still see all the old parts though." He pointed at the cooler. "What are we doing with this?"

"That's dinner. Ah, look, you upgraded to an oven." Joe cracked the lid of the cooler and began to remove some foil-covered dishes. "I'll just pop these in there to warm. Shouldn't take long."

Andrew retrieved two plates and table settings from a handsome, handmade hutch next to a stone fireplace that had replaced the rudimentary woodstove.

"That's damn gorgeous," Joe said, looking out the large picture window that had been installed in the west wall. The trees there were cleared to showcase the view of the setting sun kaleidoscoping over the distant Great Choir Mountain range. The timer dinged and Joe set about carrying the dishes to the table.

"I did what I could. I figured if I was going to spend so much time up here I might as well make it more homey." Andrew joined him with serving utensils. "So, what do we have here? Smells good."

"I had the chef at Kobb Kitchen put this together. Great southern cookin' place in Durham. Check it out." Joe began to remove the crimped foil covers from the dishes, revealing bread rolls, a deep bowl of green bean casserole swimming in cream of mushroom, a hill of mashed potatoes with a caldera of gravy and butter, and finally an enormous pork roast butt dripping juices over expertly browned skin. Joe crouched over the banquet and gathered up the long carving knife. He licked his lips, and paused. "Ah, what am I doing? You're the host. You get the honors." Joe handed the carving knife and fork to Andrew and sat down. "There! A feast. Something to right everything, and commemorate our old friend. This one's for you, Graham." He grew solemn, and Andrew thought he could even see a tear forming beneath one of Joe's red-rimmed eyes. "What do you think?"

The sunset dominated the picture window, bathing the interior of Owlwatch in a warm glow, and catching hot on the knife. Andrew almost felt sorry for Joe, for this was a thoughtful gesture. In his autumnal years Joe was seeking to make things right. But, ultimately it was in poor taste. *Almost, Joe. Almost.* He chuckled at the thought.

"What do I think?" In a flash Andrew brought the serving fork down, spearing Joe's hand to the table. Joe immediately screamed and tried to pull his hand away, tearing the holes larger on the tines, and sending out a freshet of blood. With a deft and practiced gesture, Andrew slid the serrated blade below Joe's jowls, relishing the way Joe's body turned rigid with fear under the fine edge. He smiled at the panicked surprise in Joe's wide eyes, and leaned close. "I think you don't know what you've gotten yourself into. You see, when I said before that you 'broke me,' what I should have said was that you broke me *open*. You gave me my first taste of heaven. And I've never stopped eating it. Slice by delicious slice."

Max Dowdle

The Lonesome Shore

"Guys! The day's already getting away from us!" Iris shouted from the driver's seat. She caught a look of herself in the rearview, and rubbed at a missed smear of sunscreen. The back of the car was piled high with the supplies of their beach excursion. Iris watched the partly cracked hotel door, waiting for it to disgorge her family so they could

157

hurry up and get to the place where they were meant to be relaxing. Maybe this year things would finally go right. She leaned out the window. "Chop, chop! Let's go."

"Coming, Mom!" Jason emerged wearing his swimsuit and water shoes. The toy of the moment was Silvertron. He flew the chunky robot figure through the air, attacking invisible enemies.

"Uh-uh, mister." Iris pointed the mom finger. "Where's your swim shirt?"

Jason's features squenched up into what Sean called his "mole rat face." Jason started walking his robot across the hood of the car. "Mo-om! I don't like it. It's stupid."

"Jason Barrett! You're going to scratch the car. Do you want to get burnt like last year in Orlando? Remember how 'stupid' that was? You didn't even have fun at Disney." It wasn't just the sunburn that had ruined the trip, though that was left unsaid.

"Okay." He hung his head and walked toward the room.

"Tell your sister and father to hurry it up!" Iris tapped at the steering wheel, wishing she had a cigarette. Nearly a year and it hardly felt a day. She saw a convenience store just one block over on Scallop Street. Maybe she could slip over later. She looked wistfully in that direction and a miniature schnauzer barked at her from the neighboring vehicle. Iris wrinkled her nose. She hated dogs.

Finally Sean came out of the room, herding Jason in front of him. Jason struggled into the blue swim shirt, trying to fit his arm through while still holding Silvertron. Sean took a knee and untangled Jason. The last to leave the room was Ada. She absentmindedly pulled the door close while she poked at her phone. Iris had to imagine her daughter was wearing a swimsuit somewhere under the layers of tacky thrift store finds that she'd festooned herself with. The girl slid into the seat behind Iris. "Ada, honey, ready for the beach?"

Ada gave the most minute of grunts. It could have been the clearing of a tickle in her throat.

Iris sighed. Her daughter's face was forever downcast behind that veil of dark hair. She was so secretive now. When had her sweet girl turned into such a gloomy little grouch. It wasn't really that long ago that Ada had crossed that most hallowed of thresholds into teen years!

Sean hustled Jason into the backseat and then stuck his great black-haired head in the passenger side. "We good to go?"

Iris gave him an impatient look. "Yeah. I've been waiting on you three." She instantly regretted the sharpness in her voice. That was not conducive to keeping things "level," which she was committed to doing this time no matter what.

Sean stuck out his lower lip and thumped into the passenger seat. "Okay then. Ready, guys?"

Jason shouted in glee. Ada gave a cheer that might have been mocking, or might not. At least she answered her father. Iris engaged the reverse and backed away from the Sand Plover Motel.

So far Iris liked Avinger Island. It wasn't as touristy as Hilton Head or as exclusive as Edisto. As far as South Carolina beaches went she'd only heard good things. If all went well this could be the new yearly tradition. That was fine with Iris, for the whole of Florida had left a permanent sour taste in her mouth. This was a lot closer to their little duplex home in Winston-Salem as well, making the drive that much more tolerable. Already she could see there were less places someone like Sean could get himself into trouble here than in Orlando. Most of the island was composed of residential or rental houses in the low cinderblock bungalow style, each done up in ever more incongruous and competing shades of pastel. The main drag was called Whelk Avenue, and it was a well-kept, tree-lined thoroughfare that stretched the length of the island. On it were a small grocery store, a few eateries (the brick oven pizza place was rumored to be especially good), the normal smattering of gas stations, and a handful of motels, which is where the Sand Plover was located. Streets were named after shells, and on the whole there was a great sense of "just right-ness" to Avinger. Goldilocks wouldn't have batted a single eyelash at this vacation spot.

"What are we doing for dinner?" Sean asked.

"Hamburgers!" Jason screeched.

"Ada-mouse?" Sean reached back and poked at her knee.

"I don't care," she said, as if this was the most invasive question she'd ever been asked.

"Hamburgers it is, buddy," Sean said, rolling down the window and letting in the sweet sea air. Jason hollered in victory from the back.

Iris left Whelk and turned on to Conch Lane, which led to the beach access. "Well, let's just see how we feel after a long day of swimming."

Max Dowdle

A ripple of irritation passed across Sean's face, but the moment quickly slipped away and he pointed out a cylindrical, turquoise-colored house. "That one's cool. Like a short lighthouse-house. See that, Ada?"

She gave the barest glance. "Yeah, Dad. *Cool.*"

Conch Lane terminated in a broad parking lot that was already largely filled with cars. Iris silently cursed not getting out to the beach sooner. Sean's long, pre-beach shower definitely had something to do with their delay. Why he insisted on showering *before* going to the beach was beyond her, but nothing could stand between him and his morning routine. Iris located a parking space a fair distance from the beach, but at least it was in a patch of shade cast by the scrappy beach trees ringing the lot. Iris stepped out of the car and looked toward the expanse of beach. The pageant of chairs, umbrellas and tents stretched in both directions. It would probably be hard to find a decent spot at this point. Well, not much that could be done about that now.

A silver SUV slid into the spot next to them, popping doors and expelling another family of beachgoers. Husband, wife, daughter, son. All grinning. All blonde. They were like a paler iteration of Iris's own dark-haired Barrett clan. Iris smiled at the toned woman getting out of the passenger seat. The woman smiled back. "Great day for the beach."

Iris gave a light-hearted laugh. She had never been a fan of small talk, but she also didn't want to appear rude. "Oh, yeah. Hope the water's warm."

"It was yesterday. We were here around the same time and you'll never believe, we saw a group of porpoises out there!" The woman caught sight of Jason. "Awww, cute little boy. How old are your kids?"

Iris was already trying to go about her business, retrieving her drugstore flip-flops from the floor of the car. "Huh? Oh, my son's six, and my daughter there just turned fourteen."

The woman's face lit up. "What a coincidence! Same ages as ours!" She gave a little bounce in a sleek pair of North Face running trainers. Iris thought she'd seen them in a catalogue earlier in the summer, costing somewhere in the neighborhood three hundred dollars. "Have fun out there!" the woman said as she ran to catch up to her tall, well-built husband, weaving her fingers into his, and catching his cheek with a sweet peck.

160

"You too," Iris said, but the woman and her perfect family were already out of earshot.

Jason was aiming the laser gun on Silvertron's arm to blow away alien invaders in the clouds. "Jason, stay where we can see you, please." Iris popped the car's hatch.

Sean was retying the knot on his bathing suit for the third time. "Ada, I need you to watch after your brother."

"Okay," Ada mumbled as she leaned against the car, lost somewhere deep in her phone's screen. Jason circled the car lot with Silvertron, dogfighting after flitting dragonflies.

Sean and Iris began to unload the contents of the car into a wheeled beach cart: a raggedy multi-colored umbrella; a newly bought blue beach tent; the well-worn cooler, which contained six ham and Swiss sandwiches, and two peanut butter and grape jelly sandwiches (for Jason), carrot sticks, water bottles, a twelve-pack of diet cherry soda, and six bottles of Lamplighter microbrew; two large bags of tortilla chips; towels; two beach chairs that were seeing their last season; a short shovel from the garden, bucket and smattering of other sand toys; and finally, the miscellaneous bag with an assortment of paperbacks, sunscreen and Iris's cell phone. Iris placed each item very careful, and inevitably, Sean would go around behind her and reconfigure. Finally Iris gave up and let Sean finish the load out. She glanced about, looking for her adventurous son, and seeing him nowhere. He'd *just* been beside the car. Her heart began to thud. *Not again!* "Jason! Jason, get back here!" She turned on Ada. "You were supposed to be watching him!"

Ada's eyes widened, surprised by the lightning bolt of her mom's agitation. But before she could say anything they heard, "I'm here, Mom!" Jason waved from the edge of the asphalt, over where the wild foliage verging on the lot was much denser.

A wave of relief snuffed the sparking frenzy that had been building in Iris's mind. She took a deep breath. "I'm sorry, Ada." Then she added, "Can we put the phone away for maybe an hour?"

Ada's eye roll travelled all the way down to her shoulders as she stowed the device. "Fine, whatever, Mom."

"We have to let him have fun sometime," Sean said with a smirk.

That was the last thing Iris wanted to hear. What had happened last year was one hundred percent Sean's fault, and if he thought she'd

Max Dowdle

forget that he had another thing coming, no matter what the esteemed Dr. Lawrence Fabian might suggest about "building a level parenting plan."

"Mom, Dad! Come here. Look!" Jason was still waving excitedly from the far side of the parking lot.

"Not now, buddy. We're going to the beach," Sean called back.

Jason didn't budge. "No, Dad, really! Come here!" he pleaded.

Sean started toward him, dragging the cart on its bubble tires behind.

"Let's go see what your brother found," Iris said to Ada, trying for a note of amity. Ada began walking, but stayed silent, fiddling with rolling up the sleeves of her oversized flannel shirt. *That's right, my little contrarian, it's hot out here.* Iris immediately chastised herself for the acerbic thought, but her daughter could be *so* obstinate. Was it so hard to just wear beach-friendly clothing like everyone else?

"Whatcha got there, J-Man?" Sean stepped into the swath of shade with his son and peered over the top of his sunglasses.

"Me and Silvertron were following the dragonflies, and we came this way, and look." Jason pulled back a branch to reveal a series of interlocking, weathered stones sunk into the ground. It was a trail so well-hidden that you could barely see the weed-choked stones even while standing right next to them. Iris was not surprised. Her son had eagle eyes and a knack for finding the most obscure things.

Sean grabbed the branch and bent it back farther, staring at the tunnel hollowed out between the dense trees. "Oh, yeah, looky what you found. A secret path. That's pretty cool, huh?"

Jason gazed up at his father eagerly, holding Silvertron in both hands. "Where does it go?"

"Don't know, buddy." Sean held out a hand. "Come on. To the beach we go."

Jason's nose and forehead wrinkled. The mole rat face. "No! We have to see. Just real quick, okay?"

Iris stood beside Ada in the parking lot, watching the stream of vacationers clomping up the distant wooden staircase that led over the dunes and down on to the crowded beach. Prime spots to set up were surely dwindling. Sean was giving her a questioning look. "Can't hurt, can it?"

162

Iris shook her head, trying to limit the amount of exasperation that wanted to bubble forth in her voice. "No. Who knows where it goes? I'm sure it's private property."

Sean smirked. "Just a quick trip. Be a sport." Jason was pleading next to his father. Sean put a hand on his son's shoulder and added. "Tell you what, let's take a vote. All those in favor?"

Sean and Jason raised their hands. Iris looked at Ada, who also raised a hand half-heartedly and shrugged.

Iris threw her arms up. "Fine. Fine." Sean always got his way anyway, and now he'd just used this as another opportunity to drag the kids into a "make-mom-the-bad-guy" moment. *Level parent plan, my ass,* she thought.

"Yay!" Jason sang as he pranced down the path. Sean followed, pulling the jouncing cart over the rough stones.

Iris and Ada ducked under the branches and started on the path. Iris could see that Ada wore an irritated expression on her face as she navigated the low-lying limbs. "You didn't really want to go this way," she said, trying to sound playful and not accusatory.

Ada sniffed. "It's just easier if there's not a stalemate."

"Ah, so you're the swing vote." *Fair enough*, Iris thought. If a successful marriage was cut from the fabric of compromise then Ada was already figuring out loopholes for her future relationships. Iris once again thought that parenting was just as much about what you don't teach your kids as what you do, and let the subject die.

The path unspooled through the trees for perhaps a quarter of a mile. Through the broken foliage ahead Iris could see dunes rising up in front of Jason and Sean. The regular crash of ocean waves could be heard beyond the dunes. Broken slashes of sun skittered across Sean's back and Iris found herself thinking about the twelve sessions they'd already had in Dr. Fabian's office. It felt like a tug-of-war in mud, and she was always on the losing end. Of course Dr. Fabian took Sean's side almost every time. She'd not missed the sly, conspiratorial "man looks" they gave each other. All the unaccounted for hours and expenditures, all the lies and hidden emails, that could all just be explained as Sean acting out because he was lacking intimacy at home. *That's right,* Iris mused, *ever my fault.*

This wasn't even touching on the subject of Sean going back to school again for the third time. Failed out of law, tanked at med school, and now he's trying for finance. How many degrees can one man attempt? All while she pulled twelve-hour days, six days a week at their only source of income, Barrett's Flowers. That business was built from the ground up out of her own gumption and elbow grease, no thanks to Sean. Iris felt the fire of frustration stoking up inside her again, and then she glanced ahead in time to see Sean put a hand on their son's shoulder, and Jason looked up at his father with a smile worth the world. The fire sputtered. Maybe a "level parenting plan" really did mean that each parent just worked toward their individual strengths. Iris didn't know, and she stopped wondering once she stepped out into the warm sunlight and crested the dune. That's when she saw that the beach was empty.

A peninsula of pristine sand extended out into the dark blue water. Fantastic landscapes of clouds populated the wheeling sky. A spray of seagulls lazily flapped by in the distance. There was not a single soul on the sand.

Ada's breath caught in her throat. "Oh, what a great beach," she said, and Iris almost swooned to hear a positive statement from her daughter's lips.

Iris nudged Ada. "Glad we came, huh?"

"It's not so bad, I guess," Ada said as she started down the dune. "I can't believe we're the only ones here."

Sean trailed behind Jason who tore down the sandy decline toward the icy-looking breakers. Iris yelled from the top of the hill. "Don't go in that water yet, Jason! Wait for your sister!"

Sean claimed a flat patch in the name of the Barretts by planting the ragged umbrella like a flag. Iris felt the warm sand caress her feet as she removed her flip-flops and strode to the home base. Jason squatted in the surf, giving Silvertron a bath. Ada shucked off her many outer layers to reveal a black bikini Iris had never even seen. While unpacking the cart Iris stole looks at the young lady before her, wondering just *what* this creature was she saw before her. There were the pale green eyes, twins to Iris's own. And there was the distinctive small mole on her jaw, a mark that had been there since birth. But this girl had grown so much! Ada snapped the bikini straps to straighten them and stretched her lithe frame in the sun. When had she started growing breasts? It was hard to admit it, but Iris felt like she no longer knew her little girl. *Give her time,* Iris's mother Kathleen had said last Christmas. *She'll come around. Just like you did.*

"What's that?" Ada said, gathering her long hair into a ponytail and tilting her chin out toward the vast ocean.

Far offshore a great, glistening shape breached the surface and dove beneath. A moment later it surfaced again a little to the left.

Iris squinted. "Porpoise? That woman in the parking lot said she saw them out yesterday."

Sean paused in mid-setup of the tent and shook his head. "No. Too big to be a porpoise. I think it's a whale." The wind gusted, blowing the thin material around and he cursed, wrestling it back down.

"I don't know," Iris said. "Do whales come in this close?" She looked for the shape to pop up again, but it was gone.

"Hell, I don't know. Don't just stand there. Help me with this, would ya?" Sean's face already had a sheen of perspiration. Iris was well aware just how frustrated he could get in the heat. The quicker they set up everything, and got a cold drink in his hand, the better.

Iris looked out at the waves again and saw Jason now up to his knees. "Jason! Dammit. Ada, go out there with him."

"I know, Mom." Ada was already striding toward the ocean, her long legs carrying her across the fine sand.

Sean and Iris fell into a groove setting up the rest of the beach paraphernalia. Finally, in their own spot of shade, they settled into their chairs and Iris popped the tops off two Lamplighters.

"Cheers," Sean said with a clink of his bottleneck against hers. "To a moment of downtime."

Iris wanted to say something snarky. *You get plenty of downtime.* It was on the tip of her tongue, but she bit down, and instead she reached over and grabbed her husband's free hand. He looked surprised for the briefest of moments, and then tightened his fingers through hers. Could they be happy again? According to Dr. Fabian they could if she tried harder, so that's what she would do. "I'm glad we're here," Iris said. And then, as an olive branch, "And I'm glad we took Jason's path."

"See," Sean said, taking a pull of his beer.

She ignored the gloating. Instead she looked to the right where she could see a great jumble of rocks in the distance covering everything from dune to water, effectively blocking off the beach that was next to the public access. To the left the beach continued on for a mile or two before terminating in a great stand of palm trees that also stretched all the way down to the waterline. "I wonder why no one else is out here?"

Sean raised a bushy eyebrow. "Like you said, 'private property.' And today it belongs to the Barretts."

Iris chuckled. She ran her thumb over the tan skin of Sean's hand and watched Ada and Jason bodysurfing. Silvertron served as stationary sentry on dry land. "Have you got the paperwork all turned in to the registrar? So you can start in August, I mean."

Sean made a *tut-tut* with his tongue. "I don't know. Think I might wait until January instead. Just have to wait and see."

Iris suppressed an urge to scream. Instead she let go of his hand and fished in her bag for a book. "Well…just let me know." Before she could explode she let herself get carried away by the bad airplane novel. Some detective in a wheelchair was hunting a rabbit masked killer in a series of escalating, implausible scenarios. It was poorly written and barely engaging, but it was preferable to talking to Sean right now. Despite the novel's shortcomings she found herself engrossed for the better part of two hours, and when she looked up, there stood Ada and Jason dripping and out of breath.

"We're hungry," Jason said.

"Alright. We've got sandwiches, chips. Dig in." Iris opened the top of the cooler and her own stomach began to grumble. "Jason, your 'peebs and jeebs' are marked. Just hunt around. Ada? What do you want, honey?"

Ada was rummaging in her belongings. She stood up with her phone and tapped at the screen. "Oh, shi – I mean *shoot*. There's no service out here." She held the device up like a divining rod looking for a signal.

"Ada-mouse, you don't need that thing to have fun, do you?" Sean said. His voice registered the slightest hint of a slur. Iris saw three empty bottles by his chair and a fourth in his hand.

Ada scoffed and put her phone back. She held out an empty hand to her mom. "Sandwich."

Iris pulled out the ham and cheeses and passed one to Ada and one to Sean. Jason sat contentedly, bouncing on his knees and chomping his food. Silvertron guarded his right flank, shining hot in the sun. Iris took a bite of her own sandwich and looked southward. About half a mile down the beach, toward the great heap of rocks, were three figures. It looked like two parents and a child, and it was hard to tell but they all appeared to be wearing black wetsuits even though it was so warm out. Iris hadn't seen them come on to the beach, but she assumed they had just arrived. She watched as the taller adult threw a red disk down that quickly unfolded into a commodious tent composed of curved lines. Cool. She'd heard about those rapid deploy tents before, but never actually seen one in action.

Ada saw where her mother was looking and said through a mouthful of chips, "Looks like we're not alone anymore."

Sean craned his neck around. "Bah, and just when I was starting to feel at home."

Iris finished her sandwich and licked a dollop of mustard from her finger. She gestured out at the still nearly empty beach. "Ah, plenty of room at least." The shadow of the umbrella had migrated up her thighs, exposing her legs to the sun. She was feeling quite hot. With a quick guzzle of water she stood up and announced, "I am going for a swim."

"No, Mom, don't! You can't swim after you eat." Jason sprung to his feet, cheeks smeared with peanut butter and grape jelly. "You'll get a cramp and not be able to swim!"

Iris laughed. She tousled her son's damp hair. "Oh, that's just an old wives' tale sweetie." With that she stripped off her over shirt and headed toward the water.

"Who's 'old wives'?" Jason asked.

"God, he's so stupid," Ada said.

A screech from Jason. "Am not!"

Sean made an unenthusiastic attempt at being the parent in charge. "Ada-mouse, don't call your brother stuff…"

Iris didn't hear the rest over the crash of the surf. She braced herself for chilly water, but as she stepped into the rolling little waves she felt…just right. She scanned the deeper waters, looking for the porpoises or whales or whatever they were, but there was nothing. Only the occasional sea bird on a mission far out over the blue expanse. The little family at the far end of the beach was splashing in the shallows. Iris dipped low in the water, letting the gentle waves embrace her. The sensation of water, just warm enough to offer relief, but not so cold as to freeze her blood, was heavenly. She powered over the breakers to find herself in a strangely placid part of the ocean. There was barely any current. The perfect spot to float on one's back and relax.

Jason was shouting about something in the distance, but Iris couldn't tell what it was, and at that moment, decided she wasn't going to allow herself to care. She was going to take this moment for herself…for once. Besides, she knew the difference between a rambunctious yell of play and a cry for help. The latter obviously seared into her memory from last year when Jason, ostensibly under the "watchful eye" of Sean, had disappeared on the crowded thoroughfare in Orlando. Those ten minutes of frantic searching had been the scariest moments of Iris's life. That piercing wail when they'd found Jason, terrified and lost by the big fountain, was a sound that Iris never wanted to hear again as long as she lived.

Iris's vision filled with fluffed clouds that sailed by, buffeted along by high-altitude winds. She was aware that she was drifting slightly, feeling the tug of the barely perceptible currents all around her. A flotilla of sea detritus insistently bumped against her leg and she broke it up with her hand. When she raised her foamy digits to her eyes she saw a tiny crab scuttling across her knuckles. She put her hand in the water and the crab returned to his business in the briny depths.

Something grabbed her foot.

Iris yanked her foot away and jolted upright, finding herself in waist-high water. She saw that she'd floated farther down the beach than she'd expected. The Barrett tent was almost a quarter mile back the other way. She planted her feet in the sand to stop any farther drifting. What had latched on to her foot? She looked to her left, and saw a boy.

At least she thought it was a boy. The child stood armpit-deep in the water and was clad in a black wetsuit. Curiously the wetsuit not only covered the child's arms, but continued onto the hands and up over his face as well. His entire body was clad in the black, textured material. The eyeholes were covered in a sort of tinted glass or plastic. On the whole the kid looked like a cross between a bug and one of Jason's ninja action figures.

"Oh, hello!" Iris said, giving a little wave.

The child's posture told Iris that he was confused. He seemed unsure of what to do with his hands. They were reaching forward tentatively to touch her. When the child spoke a series of small lights on the lower half of his face covering lit up in orange and yellow. He did not seem to speak English. In fact, it was hard to tell what language if any he was speaking through the filter of the fabric, but it sounded almost Asian in some way. Chinese? Japanese? It was hard to tell due to a screen of buzzing pops like a radio tuned to static. The boy was still reaching, trying to touch her.

"Hey there. Where are your parents?"

Another series of words underneath buzzes and clicks. The child dropped his hands and turned abruptly, looking toward the beach. Iris followed his gaze and saw his parents waving him in. The parents were similarly clad as their child. Head to toe black, even their hands, feet and heads. They gesticulated frantically, and Iris thought she could hear the same sort of off-station static language floating toward her over the wind. The child gave her one more look and then bolted for the shore. What were they so worried about? She glanced about, half-expecting she'd see a shark fin cutting the water's surface. There wasn't.

Iris started walking toward the beach, thinking she might as well say "hi" to the neighbors if they were going to be sharing the sand today. The little boy ran into one of his parent's arms and was lifted up. The other parent scuttled over to their space-age tent and began collapsing it back up into a disk shape. The parents kept stealing glances at Iris as she emerged from the water. Before she was even halfway toward them they had gathered up their belongings and were sprinting toward the stone path at the top of the dunes. Iris put her hands on her hips. "Well, that was unfriendly." She trudged back to Barrett HQ.

Sean and Jason were crouched near the tent, fussing over the foundations of a sandcastle. "Where's Ada?" Iris wondered.

Sean gestured north with his nearly empty bottle, the fifth and last. "Wen' for a walk down thattaway."

"We're making a base for Silvertron!" Jason proclaimed. He upturned a bucket of sand to create a turret at one corner of the castle.

"That's nice, honey." Iris sat next to her husband and looked northward, seeing Ada walking along the surf in the distance. "Sean, I just had a weird thing happen."

"Whassit, babe?" Sean regrettably swallowed the last sip of his beer and plopped the bottle into the sand next to Silvertron's first turret.

"Those people, down the beach. That other family. I met them. Well, I tried to. They ran away." Iris smoothed the sand near her hand, feeling the sharp edges of tiny broken shells. "Like they were scared or something. Isn't that weird?"

Sean shrugged. "Who knows? All sorts of people come out here, I'm sure."

"Yeah but, they were also wearing these suits, like wetsuits but it covered their faces too." Iris shook her head. "And they spoke…I don't know how they spoke. It was hard to hear them over the wind and waves. Like…Asian, and *crackly.*"

Jason looked up with the spark of excitement in his eyes. "Were they aliens, Mom?"

Iris shook her head. "No, honey. Not aliens."

"Crackly?" Sean gave a short laugh, studied his wife's face and said, "So, Chinese germaphobes or somethin'. Or maybe they were ultra religious. Aren't there people who can't show skin, even on the beach? Who tha hell knows?" He laid back and closed his eyes.

Jason resumed placing buckets of sand down. "I wish they were aliens."

Iris suddenly felt uncomfortable. "Would you go get, Ada?"

Sean cracked an eye. "Why can't *you*?"

"I want to stay here." Iris pushed at Sean's side. "Just do it. Please?"

With a huff Sean stood and began to amble toward the distant figure of their daughter. "Wait, Dad!" Jason called. "You're apposed to be helping me!"

"When I get back, dude," Sean said in an annoyed tone without turning around.

Iris retrieved her book and tried to read, but she could no longer fall under the spell of Detective "Squeakywheels." She ended up sitting with a finger hooked between the pages and just staring out at the great line of horizon where sea met sky. An immense shape crested through the surface and blew a plume of water high in the air. It *was* a whale. Though it looked absolutely enormous, and from what Iris could see, it appeared to have a strangely long neck. This wasn't like any cetacean she'd ever learned about as a kid.

Jason abandoned his architectural project to run to her side. "Mom! Did you see that?"

"I sure did, honey." Iris wished it would show itself again, even just for a moment. She grabbed her phone, readying it to take a picture.

The phone was dead. "Shucks then," she muttered. It hardly mattered anyway, for the creature did not choose to pop above the surface again.

Sean and Ada were returning. Ada had her flannel tied around her waist and two handfuls of shells which she deposited beneath the umbrella, where Jason promptly began to sort through them.

"What time is it?" Iris asked of Sean.

He brought his watch up close and said, "Looks like, almost five."

Six hours had flown by. Indeed the sun was certainly angling toward the horizon. Iris felt hot, sandy, and ready for a shower. The day's heat had zapped her and now she just wanted a margarita and something to eat. "So, everyone still want burgers?"

"Yes!" Jason gave a little twirl and threw Silvertron in the air, catching the robot on the descent.

"Sure," Ada said. She was tapping at her phone again, hoping for a signal and grumbling to herself.

Sean already had the umbrella folded and stowed in the cart. The rest of the supplies were packed, gathered up and placed alongside it. As the Barrett family left the beach the only thing that marked their time there were the cart's tire tracks and the unfinished sandcastle for Silvertron.

Even though she felt weary, Iris also felt very alive. The beach had been a wonderful place to spend the day, despite the bizarre encounter with the other family. Even more exciting was the fact that she and Sean had not had anything even close to a real fight. Maybe there was hope for this family yet.

The stone path cut through the trees, leading them back to the parking lot. Jason was singing "The Hamburger Song," which was something wholly of his invention and different every time. Iris looked at her daughter, who was stroking a delicate shell she kept cupped in her hand. "That's pretty," Iris said. "Can I see it?

Jason skipped back and forth at the head of the group. *"Hamburgers in soup, hamburgers on rice, hamburgers with lettuces, that makes 'em real nice!"*

Ada held up the shell. It very nearly looked like the shell of a small chambered nautilus. "I thought it was like a cool souvenir. I found it –"

"What the hell is this?" Sean's voice cut Ada off.

Max Dowdle

Iris and Ada joined Sean and Jason. Sean was holding the tree limb aside to reveal an empty parking lot. Moreover the asphalt was cracked apart in great fissures. Voluminous beach weeds sprouted from the cracks, reclaiming the ground the lot had once occupied. There was not a car or a person in sight.

"We took a wrong turn," Iris said.

"Must have." Sean made a show of frustration turning the little cart around. "Hey, buddy. Let me lead, 'kay?" He passed Jason and started back down the path.

Iris looked carefully this time, trying to see where the path forked. Before they knew it they were back at the dunes and there was the beach spread out before them.

Sean gave an exasperated moan and turned around again. "Okay. Eyes peeled, *everyone*. Let's find the goddamn parking lot this time. Huh?"

Iris edged up next to him. She made sure to keep her voice low and level when she said, "Don't take it out on them, Sean. *They* didn't get us lost."

Sean answered with a pair of silent, sharp eyes. The sweat stood out in great beads all along his forehead and cheeks. He wiped at his face and pulled the cart faster, leaving Iris behind. It only took a moment for them to arrive back at the cracked apart expanse of worn asphalt. Not a single other branch of path had been seen along the way. Sean flung the handle of the cart down and kicked at one of the path stones. "Dammit!"

"Are we lost?" Jason snuck his hand into Iris's.

"No, honey. We're not." The sun was dropping fast, and a red haze had billowed up over Avinger Island. Distantly Iris heard the long, sustained howl of a dog. It sounded like it was in pain. "What should we do?"

"We obviously made some kind of mistake." Sean pointed to the far end of the ruined lot. "Look. Over there is a road. I'm sure it leads to our parking lot. We can't be that far from it. Let's just go that way, and we can ask directions if we see anyone."

Iris found she was fine with this. It was a sound plan. "Shoes. Everyone got shoes?" She looked to Jason who wore his water shoes and Ada who had on her short boots.

Sean was crouching and shoving the cart under a dense bush. Iris knelt next to him. "What are you doing?"

"I'm not pulling this thing all over the place. We'll leave it here and come back for it with the car. Here, take your bag. Here's the keys." Sean handed Iris her belongings.

"You think that's a good idea? What if someone came and took it?" Iris checked to make sure her wallet and phone where in the bag and then unscrewed the cap on her water bottle to take a sip.

The cart hidden, Sean stood and waved an exasperated hand at the rubble. "There's no one here." His voice was shot-through with anger, and Iris knew when not to push him. This was one of those times. "Come on, kids!" Sean said sharply as he began to navigate the broken chunks of asphalt. The tortured howl of a dog shook the twilight again.

Low, billowing clouds rushed in to darken the sky as the sun squatted fat and orange on the horizon. All the scrubby trees and sand shone a deep, burnished red. The Barrett clan negotiated the last of the rubble-strewn lot and stepped out on the worn street. A single, flaking red line was painted down the center, dividing the narrow lanes. "This way," Sean said decisively, and they turned left, following the curve of road until it ended in a barricade of strewn debris. With a sharp curse Sean turned them around and led them back the other way.

"I don't think we're even in the right area," Ada said.

Sean stomped ahead. "Of course we are." They passed the broken lot and continued down the red-striped road. Sea oats and tangles of brambles ran wild on either side of the untended roadway. Far ahead Iris could see that the road was blocked by a great tumult of splintered and fallen palm trees. To the left another road led inland. As they drew up on the junction they found a four-sided stone pillar with the weathered shape of a conch engraved into one side.

"Conch Lane?" Iris wondered. "I didn't see this before."

Sean stood at the intersection casting his eyes about and fuming. "Strong wind must have come through and felled those trees. Parking lot could be on the other side of them."

Iris didn't think that sounded right. They hadn't felt anything that could do that kind of damage on the beach, but she remained silent.

Jason's fingers tightened over his mother's. He had a panicked look on his face that made Iris's heart twinge. "Mom, what's going on?" He hugged Silvertron tight with his other arm.

"Just looking for the car, J-Man," Sean said with a huff.

"Ada, honey. See if you can pull up information or something on your phone," Iris said.

Ada shook her head. "Still no service." She looked up and pointed down the street leading inland. "There's some people over there though."

Iris looked and indeed there were people on the street. They stood in front of a squat, steel-shuttered house that she hadn't seen on their way to the beach. Was this *really* part of Conch Lane? She didn't remember it looking so…junky. The asphalt here was also cracked and the ditches on either side were filled with trash. The distant trees at the far end of Conch Lane where it t-boned into Whelk Avenue were massive, but barren of leaves, as if it were winter. A faint orange light flickered at their bases. Fires. It looked as if someone had lit campfires every few yards along the tree-lined thoroughfare. Iris didn't know what to make of what she was seeing. Sean had already started quickly toward the small cluster of people a block away. Iris, Ada and Jason struggled to catch up.

A stocky, older man with a potbelly stood on the battered sidewalk. He wore a sort of soiled, short-sleeved jumpsuit, much like painter's coveralls. His wild white hair and thick gray beard were matted down with dirt. When he saw Sean his grimy, leathern face cracked into a wide grin. His companions had backed away and were loitering on the dilapidated steps of the dark, cylindrical house that had been fortified by crude walls of quickly laid cinderblock. Now that they were closer Iris thought that it almost looked like a short lighthouse. *A lighthouse-house.* One of the men idly fingered a rifle slung across his knees. "Excuse me," Sean said. Iris could detect the hint of caution in his voice. "Could you tell me how to get to the beach access parking lot from here? We need to find our car." Sean gave his best I'm-just-a-silly-tourist shrug.

The man raised a bushy eyebrow, cast a sardonic look at the gaggle behind him, and then burst in to a gravelly jag of uncontrollable chuckling. When this subsided he began to speak in a strange accent, "Cannit hepyi, bedo." He winked at his friends. "Be ifyi gavus axis te yilil' lazzies der, maywi canfen somwi te gavyi a oto." The group erupted in laughter.

"I'm sorry, I don't underst–" Sean saw the way the men were looking at Ada and Iris. "Forget it." He signaled to his family. "Come on. This way." Sean led them toward Whelk Avenue and away from the fading brays of laughter coming from the rough little group.

"Wachin fer dagis!" one yelled out.

"Could you tell what he was saying, Dad?" Ada wondered.

"No. It's some sort of derelict house," Sean muttered as he quickened his pace. "Bunch of rednecks."

Now that they were approaching Whelk Avenue Iris could see that the fires were quite large. A cyclone fence had been erected on the other side, strung between the bases of the thick-trunked trees. Shoddily dressed duos walked the length, tending the fires with long iron poles and adding wood when necessary.

"What the hell is going on here?" Sean said to no one in particular. "It's like a festival for the homeless."

"God, something stinks," Ada said, covering her face with the collar of her shirt. The disheveled fire-tenders didn't even give the Barretts a glance as they passed.

Iris wrinkled her nose. "You're right. It's nasty isn't it?" They took a left on Whelk Avenue, crossing close to one of the roaring fires and Iris saw the source of the stench. It was not logs of wood that were being added to the fires. The bloodied, decapitated bodies of dogs were heaped high on the other side of the fire. The fire-tenders used the hooks on the ends of their poles to drag bodies from the piles and into the roaring flames. A smaller separate mound was composed of fly-swarmed dog heads, which appeared to be reserved for something else, for they were not being burned.

Jason buried his face against Iris's shorts and wept. Iris jammed Silvertron into her bag and lifted Jason up to hold him tight.

Ada's eyes widened and tears began to form. "Wha-what are they doing?"

Iris had no words to comfort her children. Sean groped for something to say, but then fell silent. He grabbed the hands of his wife and daughter and led them quickly away from the grisly scene. The Barretts continued down Whelk Avenue in a sort of silent stupor, attempting to reconcile the horrors around them with reality. Many of the buildings on either side of the road were nothing but bombed-out husks. Smoke and haze choked the avenue, and charred bits of unidentifiable substance flaked through the air. Northward a series of towers was silhouetted against the bruise-colored sky. Overhead, through the gaps in the thick clouds, blinking, low-flying objects flashed by on unknown errands. Terror settled deep into Iris's bones.

The Sand Plover should have been ahead on the right. Instead there stood a hulking, soot-covered brick building with boarded-up windows on the second and third floors. Various shops had been located on the first floor, but these were vacated, and every storefront's glass door that was still in place bore a spider web of cracks over roll-down bars.

Sean sank heavily to the curb and placed his head in his hands. Iris felt faint. There was no reasonable explanation for any of this. Her mind was grasping at anything that remotely made the slightest sense. She thought of any number of old Twilight Zone episodes. Fantasy, but based on real science, right? It was obvious that they'd emerged from the beach into some kind of terrifying, nightmare version of their world. It was the only explanation that made any sort of sense.

The pained howl of a dog echoed down the street. Jason sobbed and kept his face firmly pressed to Iris's breast. Ada wore a look of utterly shattered instability. Sean shook his head slowly back and forth and fretted at his shaggy black hair while Iris hugged Jason closer. "Okay. Okay. We need a plan. What are we doing? Sean, think!"

Night fully covered Avinger Island, and though there were no streetlights, Whelk Avenue was still well lit by the hazy red sky above and the bonfires that burned on nearly every street corner. Iris was looking around at the signs on the stores. Oddly there were no written words, only pictographs. A heart. A simplified body. A cross. Sean looked up at his wife. His face was vacant and uncomprehending in the wan light. "We need to leave the island. Get home. So much for vacation," he giggled, and it was a bizarre, unhinged sound.

Iris shook her head. Sean wasn't going to be any help in this state. Though he had a point. Perhaps leaving Avinger Island was the best course. Iris searched the storefront windows, looking for an answer when she saw the pale face of a young woman wearing a white head wrap behind the broken glass and bars in one darkened stop. A hand beckoned, and she heard a harsh whisper saying, "Yi! Yi!"

"Mom, Dad, look," Ada wasn't referring to the woman in the shop. Instead she pointed down Whelk Avenue where a lone dog with bulky shoulders and a low-slung, roving head stalked toward them. Iris could see that the dog's fur had been mostly burned away to leave a wheal of raw, pink flesh. Much of the dog's lips were missing, revealing cruel, overlong fangs. Hunger, and malice tinged its red-rimmed eyes.

"Sean!" Iris said. She swatted at his shoulder and yanked at his arm.

"Yi! Yi!" shouted the woman in the shop. She knelt by the door and began raising the segmented bars. The door opened and she thrust a hand through, waving them in. "Yi. Kuminni. Heri!" She was young, not much older than Ada, and had the same strange accent as the man by the reinforced house.

The dog's jerking gait had increased, turning into a loping, wild run as it closed in on the Barretts. A ferocious, slavering growl issued from its throat, accompanied by long streamers of drool.

"Sean, get up!" Iris screamed as she and Ada struggled to lift him. Jason wailed and clung to his mother, throwing her off-balance. Iris and Ada managed to get Sean on his feet and the four of them bolted for the dark interior of the shop. Once inside, the bars slammed shut. The dog crashed into the bars at full speed, bending them inward. Its jaws snapped between the bars, and then it clamped on to the bars themselves and tried to work them loose. The only sound louder than the dog's savage snarls was Jason's high-pitched screams. The woman removed a hatchet from her belt and buried it in the dog's skull, abruptly ending the awful creature's life. Ada shrieked. The woman wasn't done though. With a practiced action she removed the hatchet and hacked at the dog's neck until the head was severed from the body.

"Fix'n dad dagis!" the woman spat as she wiped the hatchet head clean on a tattered curtain and then returned it to a loop on her belt. With a sniff she gestured to the interior of the shop and said, "Heri. Morwi kum. Grawawi canan kuminni." Iris looked at her surroundings. They were in some kind of pharmacological dispensary. The shelves were largely emptied, but a few silver-wrapped packets of unknown contents were still left.

The woman was saying something else but Iris couldn't make sense of it. Seeing that the Barretts didn't understand her words she grabbed armfuls of goods off the shelves and pressed them at Sean, Iris and Ada. She opened Iris's bag and stuffed it full of the packages. Iris had her hands full with Jason and no way to stop the frantic woman. She was about to complain when howls filled the street outside.

Sean snapped to attention and grabbed a bag off the counter, packing it with the silver containers. He paused at the distant sound of rapid gunfire.

"What are you doing?" Iris said.

Sean shook his head. "This woman saved us once already. Just go with it. Ada, get that bag over there. Fill it up."

Ada followed her father's directions. Seeing that the Barretts were loaded down the woman gestured to the back of the store and said, "Kummini," just as the pack of dogs began to hurl themselves against the bars.

Iris saw that the door looked like it would not hold long against the onslaught as she skirted by. She followed Sean, Ada and the woman into the back. The woman, stiff of posture and strong of limb, looked unafraid but very alert. She pulled on a handle and opened the back door just a crack, enough to peek through. Seeing that it was clear she opened it all the way to reveal a peculiar, goldenrod yellow vehicle waiting in the lot behind the building. Heavy-duty wheels were positioned on exposed, angled axels, so that the whole contraption resembled a sleek, spidery bullet. The cab was large though, nearly the size of a minivan. The woman produced a small yellow fob, and pressed it to slide the side door open.

"Ge, ge." The woman said, pushing at Sean's shoulder. The family hesitated. A horrible crunch of tearing metal could be heard from the front of the shop. The dogs were breaking through. "Ge ifyi wanti lif!" She pushed harder and Sean ran toward the vehicle, trailed by Ada and Iris carrying Jason. The woman exited, slammed the door behind her and bolted for the spider van. She shoved the Barretts in the back and then swung into the cockpit. She set the fob in a receptacle on the dash and the vehicle powered up. The door slid shut and the engine rumbled with a powerful belch. They began to move forward just as the pack of dogs, wise to their movements, careered around the edge of the building. There was a slight bump as one was swallowed under a spinning wheel where it was converted into a chunky red streak, and they were off, tearing down Whelk Avenue in the impossible machine.

Ada gasped. Iris looked to where her daughter sat and saw a man collapsed in the most rearward seat. He was dressed like the woman, in a white head wrap and dusty, loose-fitting clothes. On his belt was an identical hatchet to the one wielded by the driver. He was of similar age, and quite attractive, though his skin was very pale, for he'd clearly lost a lot of blood from a gash in his lower abdomen. He held a rag over his belly with skinny, shaking hands. "Temommi, temommi," he murmured, over and over.

"Who the hell are these people?" Sean whispered.

Ada rooted around in the bag she'd grabbed and pulled out a packet with the symbol of a red cross inside a red diamond emblazoned on one side. She ripped it open to discover a wealth of first aid items.

"What are you doing?" Iris said.

Ada began sorting the gauze, latex gloves, adhesives and various salves. "He needs help." The man gave her a pained, pitiful expression as she joined him on his seat and helped him to sit up.

Sean set about taking inventory of his own grab bag. "Wear those gloves in there. Don't get any of his blood on you."

Iris stared at Ada, hardly believing how her daughter was swinging into action. Jason stirred against her. He had been quiet for several minutes, but he finally looked up and said, "Mommy, are the bad dogs gone?"

"Yes, honey. All gone."

Jason pressed his face against the glass and watched the fires blaze by outside. Screams could be heard in the distance. The driver quietly muttered her strange language to herself as she traversed the broken streets. The man in the back's voice seethed with pain, "Temommi...temommi," as Ada inspected his wound. Ada had learned first aid in girl scouts, but Iris never would have thought this was how she'd put the skill to use, let alone actually remember any of what she had learned. Iris looked out the window, recognizing the layout of roads as being vaguely familiar. It seemed they were heading out of town, which was fine by her.

"Shhh, stay still," Ada said in a soothing voice.

"Bunch of food," Sean said. "Like MREs. That's good, at least—"

"Fix!" the driver shouted and slammed on the brakes. The vehicle slewed right and ground to a halt in a plume of ash. Iris looked out the domed windshield and saw the source of the driver's ire. The bridge leading off of Avinger Island was a smoking ruin. A barricade of junk had been piled high at the onramp egress, preventing anyone from even driving on to it. The driver hammered at the steering wheel

Max Dowdle

and then popped her door, hopping out on to the broken road. "Anyi otho, fix'r? He? WHIDA THES?" she shouted at the top of her lungs.

Howls answered her.

The woman sobbed long and low, and her shoulders drooped. She pulled the hatchet free from her belt, stood with a wide, ready stance and waited.

"What's she doing?" Sean said, leaning toward Iris's side of the vehicle.

Dogs rushed from every angle. Through the piles of junk, from beneath desiccated trees, from out of broken concrete tubes they descended. She swiped at the vile creatures, taking the first three with swift hatchet blows. The dogs kept coming though, and the second wave brought her to her knees. Screams could be heard between the rabid snarls. The man in the back struggled to exit the vehicle but he was so weakened that Ada easily forced him back down. Iris held Jason close, hiding his eyes from the gruesome sight. Sean leapt to the cockpit and pulled on the door handle, sealing the vehicle before the dogs caught their scent. He felt around for the gas pedal.

"Can you drive it?" Iris yelled from the back.

"I think so." Sean twisted at dials and punched at buttons on the wheel. "I watched her."

"Nnnnnn," Jason whined. "The bad doggies are here too!"

"Then move it, Sean!" Iris watched a contingent of dogs break away from the woman's corpse and begin to circle the spider van.

The vehicle lurched forward, back, pulled a wide semi-circle and then started back the way they'd come. "I think I got it now," Sean said.

"Temommi," the man whispered once more, and then grew quiet.

Iris looked back at how her daughter was doing. Ada met her mother's eyes and shook her head. Tears were cascading down her cheeks. "He's dead."

Iris reached out her free arm and Ada fell into her embrace. "You did all you could, honey. You did all you could." They stayed like that for quite some time, clutching her two children to her breast.

Finally Ada pulled away and took a seat next to her. She dried her eyes and stared forward. Her face was ghostly pale in the interior of the vehicle, and the mole on her jaw was as dark as a tiny bullet hole. "Where are you taking us, Dad?"

"I don't know. I don't know," he was making turns seemingly at random. "It's all so different. It's just such a goddamn mess!" He dodged a burning vehicle in the middle of the road and continued on.

"We should go back." Ada was staring at a spot of blood on the cuff of her shirt. "To the beach. It's the last safe place we were."

Though Sean didn't say whether he agreed, it was soon apparent that he was navigating his way back to the beach. Iris saw a concrete pylon bearing a conch shell and Sean took a turn, bringing them back to the beach access road. All of the fire tenders were gone from Whelk Avenue, and the fires had died to coals issuing bilious black smoke. Several dozen dogs had the run of Conch Lane. They tore at the body of a man, who may or may not have been the blustery bearded fellow, in the front yard of the fortified lighthouse-house. Sean ignored the savage canines, and turned down the road with the red stripe. Soon enough they'd found the entrance to the demolished parking lot. Sean drove to the far end and brought the vehicle to a stop. He took the little yellow fob, shutting the spider van's engine off and cutting its lights. "Hurry, hurry," he said as he slid the wide side door open.

Ada gathered up the bags they'd taken from the store. Iris tried to set Jason down on the cracked asphalt. "Can you walk, honey?"

Jason cringed and held tighter. "No, no, no, no, no." He was groggy, but still determined not to walk on his own.

"Okay, okay. I got you," Iris said with a grunt as she repositioned him. "Hold tight."

Angry barks and howls reverberated just beyond the tree line. The legion of wild dogs fought over spoils, and it wouldn't be long before they were looking for fresh kills. Yet Ada lingered by the door of the vehicle. "What about him?" she pointed to the dead man, white as marble sculpture, in the back.

"What about him?" Sean said. "Just leave him." He grabbed one of Ada's bags. Sean made as if to start down the path and then paused. He quickly went into the back of the spider van and came back carrying the young man's hatchet. "Just in case." With that, Sean felt ahead for the low-hanging branches and stepped onto the worn stones of the path. "Ada, get the cart." Sean hacked at the branches, clearing a way in the dim light. Ada hauled the cart free of its hiding place and pulled it along behind her father. Iris brought up the rear with Jason who somehow had fallen asleep in her arms.

As they left the path, exhausted from exertion and terror, and crested the dune the clouds cleared to reveal a fat, gibbous moon holding court for five hundred billion sparkling diamonds. The spread of the Milky Way veered sharply upward, like a great fuzzy plume of magnificent light. The beach was silent except for the regular, unceasing roll of the surf, and a lightly whispering wind. There were no dogs, no gunshots, and no screams. Sean led them down the dune toward the area where they'd left just this afternoon. Iris's mind swam with the past few hours, hardly believing a moment of it. A dark shape lay on the beach causing Iris to slow her step. As they drew closer she saw the humped remains of Silvertron's unfinished castle, and she sighed in relief.

Without a word, Ada and Sean set up the tent. Iris stood and held tightly to her slumbering son. Ada spread the towels inside as makeshift bedding and Iris laid Jason down. He did not stir. Iris pulled Silvertron from her bag and tucked him in next to Jason while Ada reached into the cart and retrieved the chips. After swallowing three big handfuls she turned toward Iris and said, "Mom. I'm...um...do you think you could come to the bathroom with me." She pointed toward the surf.

"Yeah, sweetie," Iris said. Her voice felt alien in her own ears. She was hungry, thirsty, tired, but completely unsure what to do with herself. As she squatted next to her daughter to empty her bladder all she could think to say was, "Are you okay?"

Ada nodded in the starlight. "I think so." Even in the faint light Iris could see the toll this had taken on the young girl's face. She thought of the young girl who had saved them at the store. A girl not much older than Ada but who had likely seen enough horrors for ten lifetimes...and who now warmed the bellies of wild dogs. "I'm tired but I don't think I can sleep."

"Me either," Iris said as they started back toward the tent.

Ada's breath caught in her throat and her step faltered. "I – I tried to save him, Mom." She suddenly leaned toward Iris who caught her and held her fast.

"I know you did, sweetheart. I know. Shhhh." Iris wanted to weep for her daughter, but she also wanted to remain a rock for her. Tears would come later. "Let's just go back and try to sleep. Tomorrow...tomorrow we'll figure things out." Ada nodded against her shoulder and then broke the embrace.

When they returned to the campsite Sean handed each of them one of the leftover ham and cheese sandwiches and a soda. "You both need to eat." He sat next to Iris, finished off the crust of his own sandwich and drained the last of his cherry soda.

Iris was touched. She sat all of a sudden in a heap and tore into the sandwich, realizing just how ravenous she was. When she was finished she put an arm around her husband's shoulders and said, "Thank you, Sean. Thank you for getting us back safe." No matter what else could be said about him, when they needed him the most he had protected his family. Sean nodded and put his arm over Iris's shoulders. Ada finished her food and crawled into the tent, snuggling up next to Jason.

Sean ran a finger over the smooth hatchet head. "What's going on, Iris?"

The tears she'd been holding back came fast now. Iris collapsed against his shoulder. "I don't know. I don't know," she whispered. "It's like a bad dream, the kind where you're running from something and just stuck in one place."

"Yep." Sean let out a long breath. "I don't think the dogs know about the beach though. I don't hear them at all." He held the hatchet up to catch the starlight. "All the same, I'll keep watch. You should get some sleep."

Iris was already on the verge of dozing away against him. "You're right. What about you?"

"Not tired yet."

Iris yawned. "I...okay." She crawled toward the tent. "Wake me if you hear...or if you see anything." She snuggled down next to Ada, spooning her daughter and son.

"Goodnight, Iris," Sean said without turning. "I love you."

Iris wasn't sure she responded, for she was already drifting away into slumber, carried by the perpetual sound of the surf. Her sleep was immediate, deep and black.

When she awoke it was to the soft snores of Ada. Sean still sat to the side of the tent opening, facing the dunes. Iris shifted on the lumpy ground, trying to fall back asleep but finding any more rest elusive. Her mind blazed with what they'd seen that night. Despite all that they'd been through her thoughts kept turning to the things that had rotted her marriage from the inside. It was just like her brain to turn traitor and stubbornly hang on to old wounds just when she was starting to feel some real affection for Sean again. Sean's two infidelities, revealed in sessions with Dr. Fabian, had been gut shots to Iris, who had never even considered cheating on her husband. The fact that they had been fellow students along the path of his storied degree chase only made it worse. She hadn't wanted to know any details at the time, and she didn't want to know now. She wished she'd never even found out about Sharla and Jessica. Kids. Not even really that much older than Ada. Were there more? It was likely. Iris gritted her teeth, willing the negative thoughts away. *A cigarette would do nicely right about now*, she thought ruefully. If they were going to get through this, whatever *this* was, then she needed to remain "level." She needed Sean.

There was the sound of Sean stirring, and then he reached into the tent and jiggled Iris's leg. A harsh whisper, "Iris, wake up. Wake up!"

"I am." Iris sat upright, keeping her voice low. "What is it?"

"Someone's on the beach." Sean pointed toward the top of the dunes with the hatchet. "Come out here with me."

Iris hurried out of the tent and saw a dark splotch shuffling over the dunes. A flashlight beam emanated from it, skating across the sand left, right, left again. Iris grabbed the short shovel from the cart. She stood next to Sean, and waited.

The figure reached the bottom of the dunes, keeping the flashlight low. Besides the bright light there was also a string of small, bluish glowing lights, as if the person wore a necklace of glow sticks. The figure looked to be male, large, round-shouldered, and walked very slowly with a stooped head. With some effort he dragged an object of considerable weight with its left hand. Sean put an arm out protectively in front of Iris and hefted the hatchet. The bulky, dark figure was only a few yards away. "Stop right there," Sean said, his voice surprisingly rough and strong on the quiet beach.

The mammoth figure stopped. Iris could see he had a shaved head, and dark clothes that seemed to have those strange bits of blue light woven into them. The flashlight ticked up, completely illuminating the Barretts' campsite. Iris squinted and held a hand up. Ada and Jason moved about in the tent. "Mom?" Jason's voice said as he poked his head out and rubbed at his eyes. "Who is that?"

"Would you lower the light, please," Sean said, more of a command than a question.

The light tilted downward, creating a great slash across the sand. With a deep groan the man wavered, and promptly fell to his knees. The flashlight tumbled off to his right. The carried object clattered into a heap as the man moaned again and then fell backward with a hard *thump!* Sean ran to his side, keeping the hatchet at the ready. Iris, Ada and Jason joined him. Ada scooped the flashlight up and held it on the man, causing Iris to gasp at the sight.

As Iris had noticed before, the man was large, well over seven feet tall when he'd stood, but she could now see his features were very broad as well. Wide, deeply set eyes peered out from beneath a beetle brow. His thick hands looked as if they wouldn't have any trouble crushing bricks. He was wearing a sort of cobbled-together armor built of heavy metal plates and cobalt blue mesh. A violent gash had rent the armor of his chest, and the flesh beneath. His blood dribbled thick and black as roofing tar. But by far the strangest thing about the man was the way small blue lights traced paths *beneath* his skin. From his temples to the tips of his fingers, the tiny lights skittered about along subcutaneous rails like trained sparks.

"What is he doing here?" Jason wondered, hiding behind his mother's leg.

The man smiled, showing a set of perfect, artificial-looking teeth. He regarded one Barrett and then the next, seeming to take time to fully appreciate each individual face. When he opened his mouth there issued the sound of garbled, grinding gears. These noises coalesced into words finally, and his voice echoed hollow and ragged out of his throat. "We could never have imagined how beautiful you truly are. All of you. It has been forgotten, much like the poems and songs of old. We were wrong. We know that now." He began to laugh, a deep, hitching sound. "Forgive us. Forgive us."

Sean crouched next to the fallen man. "Who are you?"

The man raised his hand slowly. Sean twitched the hatchet, but remained where he was. The man said one word, "We," brought his large index finger up slowly to stroke the skin of Sean's cheek, pointed at his face, and then his hand fell flat against the sand. He whispered, "Penitent A-336…withdrawn." The lights beneath his skin slowed and winked out. He moved no more.

"Did he die?" Jason wondered, peeking out from behind Iris. He didn't seem at all upset. She wasn't sure if she should take this as a good sign. Her son was clearly overloaded with everything that had happened.

Ada moved the flashlight beam slightly behind where the man lay, illuminating the item he'd brought with him. "What about *that*?"

"I…what is that?" Sean wondered, as he knelt by the long, metal object. He put a hand on it. "Some kind of gun. A *big* gun." He began to lift the massive rifle, struggling with its weight.

"Sean, leave it. It doesn't look safe," Iris said, holding Jason's hand tightly and stopping him from joining his father.

"Gah! Must weigh a hundred pounds." Sean let the weapon down gently.

"Ada, give me the flashlight and take your brother back to bed," Iris said.

Ada handed the flashlight over and took Jason's hand. "But I wanna see the robot man," Jason said as he was shepherded back to the tent, rubbing tiredly at his eyes.

Iris's lip trembled. *Robot man?* Why not? It was no stranger than anything else they'd seen that night. What really amazed her was how accepting Jason was of all this. Childhood was not without its safety net for sanity. Iris looked down at the giant "robot man," leaking a patch of black ichor into the sand. "Sean, we can't leave him here."

"Yeah. You're right," he said with a sigh. "We could drag him over to the rocks over there."

Iris shook her head. "Too far." She looked at the shovel in her hand and then waved it at Sean. He nodded.

It took an hour to dig a hole large enough for the man to be heaved at and rolled into. Even then, it was only three feet deep. By the time the grave was filled back in Sean looked ready to pass out. "Why don't you try to sleep," Iris said, smoothing a lock of black hair back from his sweating forehead. "I can take watch now. I think it'll be dawn soon anyway."

Sean didn't protest. He stood, walked stiffly to the tent and crawled inside, collapsing next to Jason.

Iris was alone. She sat by the huge firearm, wrapped her fingers around the bumpy handle of the hatchet, and stared up at the crystal-spangled expanse of the sky.

The call of a seagull woke her sometime later. She must have dozed for some time sitting there, for when she lifted her head her neck was sore, and a pink haze tinged the horizon. Dawn. One by one the rest of the family woke, and they shared a somber breakfast of chips, Jason's last peanut butter and jelly divided into four even sections, and soggy carrot sticks. "Wait," said Sean when they finished. "I almost forgot." He grabbed the bag from the ramshackle store and dumped the contents on his towel. "Yeah, MREs." Twelve of the little silver packs had symbols representing fruit and grain printed on one side. He ripped one open and found something resembling a granola bar inside. With a sniff and a tentative tap of his tongue he took a bite. After rolling it around his mouth for a moment he said, "It's good. Maybe a bit too sugary, but good." Sean passed them around, and the family ate of the bounty. "We should see what else we got."

Jason took up the building of Silvertron's base once again, leaving Iris, Sean and Ada to make sense of what they'd brought back to the beach. It took the better part of an hour to sort the many silver packets into discrete piles. All in all they had 117 of the variously sized packages, and the contents ranged from food to unknown. None were marked with words, but all bore stylized pictographs depicting the contents. The piles that lay on two towels were divided: thirty-one packets of food, including the breakfast granola, packets marked with a chicken and/or egg, and ones marked with the horned head of a cow; sixteen liquid-filled, long packs showing the symbol of what looked like a fizzy drink; four packs containing forks, spoons and knives; three more first aid kits marked with the cross in diamond; nine flat packs with a symbol that looked like a book or pad of paper; five rigid parcels with an orange line on them and a skull; six packs marked with a cat, which could have been kitty litter, cat food or cat meat; eighteen were stamped with a pill symbol; and the remainder were marked with symbols that did not make any sense at all, including an ant, a black circle, a bundle of wires, a leaf with a split in it, and a lightning bolt. Ada carefully opened one of the ones printed with the black circle and poured a cascade of what looked like tiny, black marbles into her hand. They smelled of bitter, perfumed smoke.

"What are they?" Iris said.

Ada shrugged, returning them to the pack and crimping the top shut. "I don't know. I need a break now though." She stood, dusted sand from her shorts and walked toward the surf.

Iris turned her gaze toward Jason, watching as he continued the wall of Silvertron's fortress. Silvertron stood at attention, sharply reflecting the light of the morning sun and aiming his guns up toward the dunes. Jason was making the squenchy mole rat face as he concentrated on building. Iris looked from her son to her husband and said, "We need a plan." She was feeling much more clear-headed now after getting some sleep, and she hoped Sean was too.

"That we do." He bit at the inside of his lip as he mooned over the collection of odd packages. Iris thought the scruff peppering his normally smooth cheeks looked good. He could be quite handsome at the right angle and in the right light. Maybe it wasn't just safety she needed him for. The little embers of love were still alive deep inside, all they needed was stoking.

The large gun had been dragged over by the towels and Sean ran his hands over it now. "This thing…too big, too heavy to be of any use." His fingers stopped at a ring of steel on the top and on the butt. "Looks like it used to have…hmmm." He grabbed the bags from the dispensary and inspected the clasps of their straps. With a couple of pops he quickly had them both untethered from the bags and fastened together. He threaded them through the rings of the rifle, and in no time had fashioned a sturdy shoulder strap. He looped it over his neck and then braced with his legs, lifting the giant gun. With some effort he got it balanced and was able to walk. "That's good," he grunted as he fiddled around with the handle, looking for the trigger and any other controls he might need.

"Cool, Dad!" Jason yelled from his project. "Shoot it!"

Sean went to a knee and shrugged out of the strap. "Not right now, buddy." He looked at Iris and said, "Okay. I have an idea."

"I'm all ears, gunslinger," Iris said with a smile, impressed at his ingenuity.

Sean took the yellow fob out of his pocket and shook it lightly. "It's like this: we rest a bit longer. Eat, drink, get our strength back. Then we pack up. Take everything back to that vehicle. We know the bridge is out, and judging by how that girl reacted, I have to assume it's the only one. Well, forget the bridge. We take the vehicle, which is safe, and drive it till we find a boat. When we get the boat we –"

"Whoa, whoa, whoa," Iris interrupted. "Find a boat? Where will we just 'find a boat'?"

Sean waved away her criticism. "I saw a marina on our way in yesterday. There has to be at least one old junky boat there we can use."

Iris shook her head. "Who's to say that there's any boats at all? You saw how everything was. Everything's *changed!*" Her eye wandered to the hump of sand where the giant robo-man was buried.

Sean threw his hands up. "*I'm trying*, okay. I'm open to any better ideas. We can't just stay here forever."

He was right. Iris knew that, but the idea of finding a boat seemed like a long shot. "No. Fine then. It's fine. A boat it is." She slid her hand into Sean's. "Should we really wait so long though? Why don't we leave now?"

Sean pointed to where Jason continued his industry. Ada sat next to him, pounding sand into a bucket. "Look at them. They're having fun, and…I just, I want to watch this a bit longer."

Iris nodded, seeing what Sean was talking about. The sight of their children playing in the sand made for a beautiful picture, and she too never wanted it to end. "Okay," she said, stifling the wave of tears that wanted to break free.

As both phones were now dead, Sean's watch was the only way they had of telling time. The Barrett's decided to take one last dip. The water was just as warm as it had been the day before, but the joy Iris felt at being with her family was tempered by the knowledge that they would be leaving this place again shortly. When Sean's watch read noon they left the water and sat down for lunch from the silver packs. Dried, full of rationed food and water, they began packing the cart once again. This time Sean suggested they leave the tent, empty cooler, umbrella, chairs and sand toys behind. The only items they loaded on to the cart were the most essential silver packs and the large gun.

Sean took a knee by Jason and said, "Okay, buddy. I need you to be brave for me, just like Silvertron. Okay?"

Jason smiled and raised the robot above his head. "I can do it!" he shouted, and then slapped his father a high-five.

Ada buttoned her shirt up, looked back once at the campsite and said, "We're really going back out there then?"

"We have to." Iris tried to restrain the worry in her voice, but she wasn't sure how successful she was. "Everything will be okay." Seeing how Sean struggled with the laden-down cart she grabbed onto the handle as well and helped him haul it up the steep dune hill. At the top she took a deep breath and said, "Here we go."

The Barretts moved slowly down the now familiar path, keeping alert for stray dogs. When they neared the end, Sean moved the branches aside. Iris expected to lay eyes on the yellow spider van. Nothing could have prepared her for what she saw instead.

A field of wild, *Venusian* plant life had replaced the ruined lot. Towering ferns, taller than any person, dotted the landscape. Flowers two feet across bloomed like great, floral chains of trumpets. Thickly clustered stalks of grass shone in vibrant, emerald green, and thorny vines as thick as pythons rambled about, tethering themselves to any support they could find. The field hummed with the mixed chorus of ten thousand insects. In the distance colossal trees with great serpentine limbs wove into a dense blanket. Iris gazed upward at the towering clouds and there received the greatest shock: a cluster of creatures, large as blimps burst through a bolus of clouds and soared northward on wide, bat-like wings. She pointed.

"I see them," Sean said. He pulled at the handle of the cart. "Let's go."

Iris's knees felt watery but she forced herself to follow. She would go anywhere Sean said to go now, so thoroughly had he proved himself already to this family. The van was gone, the shattered chunks of asphalt were gone, but there was a break in the vines at the far end of the field. Sean led them toward this. Grasshoppers popped by and dragonflies flitted about.

"Oh! Big bugs!" Jason yelled, pointing up into a nearby tree.

Iris followed where his finger indicated and saw a grouping of hideous, fleshy walking stick-like creatures clinging to the upper branches. They *were* big, at least eight feet long. Their whip-like antennae waved, stroking the tree bark as they dug viciously clawed forelimbs into the meat of the tree. A shushed drone came from their mouthparts as the Barrett's passed the base of the tree. Iris frowned. "Keep moving, honey."

As they neared the edge of the field there came a distinct rumble from nearby, though Iris couldn't exactly tell what direction. A crash followed the sound of tearing vegetation. Sprays of exotically colored birds exploded skyward. The Barretts left the field and found themselves in a moss-covered gully. The faintest remnants of cracked stone or cement could be seen between the velvety patches of moss.

The cart moved more easily here as Sean led the family onward. There was another crash, this time much closer, and then they heard something that sounded like a cross between a roar and the high-pitched whine of a buzz saw. Iris plucked the hatchet out of the cart, feeling the balanced weight in her hand.

Sean wasted no time shrugging into the makeshift strap and heaving the heavy gun up to where it could be of use. Iris could see the sweat cascading down his cheeks as he aimed the large rifle into the wild brush toward the cacophonous sounds therein. "Everyone stay behind me."

The day was suddenly still. Only the steady drone of the insects buzzing in the weeds cut the silence. Sean breathed in short, shallow bursts.

"Mom, Dad, we should go back," Ada said quietly.

"We can't," Sean said through gritted teeth. "We have to leave. No way but through."

The tree in front of them trembled, and then split. A gargantuan shape rushed out of the foliage. Scales, spikes and a fringe of brightly colored fur flashed in the sunlight. A fifteen-foot tall bipedal behemoth built from solid slabs of muscle rushed toward them. Sean stepped back quickly, knocking Iris, Ada and Jason aside. The hatchet went flying out of Iris's hand, and amidst all the chaos she wondered what on earth she was seeing. The monster looked stitched together from twenty different animals, and even some plant or fungal life. The one thing she did know was that its abundant array of six-inch fangs meant death. Iris knelt, groping in the weeds for the hatchet, knowing that it would do no good against such a monster.

As the creature closed in on them Sean raised the gun and pulled the trigger. A fireball erupted from the muzzle of the big gun, shearing the side of the creature's sharp, reptilian face away. There was a loud pop as the gun's recoil drove into Sean's shoulder, snapping the bones there like so many twigs. Sean collapsed in pain as the colossal creature fell, screaming and thrashing in pain. The beast twisted, lashing out with every limb, and brought its flailing, thick tail down across Sean's back like a fallen tree. The ground all around them shook. Iris screamed.

Jason and Ada rushed to their father's side, trying to pull him free of the giant creature's twitching flesh. Sean was already receding very quickly. His sweating, pale face looked ghastly in the harsh

191

daylight. Iris crawled to her dying husband and fumbled for his hand. There was no movement left in it. The sparks in Sean's eyes dwindled to tiny points. He whispered his final words, "Go…back to the beach. It's safe…now…" and then he was gone.

Ada backed up, her hands trembling. "I…I…I…what can, hrmmm," she mumbled as she put her hands to her temples and shook her head furiously.

Jason hugged Silvertron close as he put a small hand to his father's unmoving head and petted his hair. "Daddy?"

Iris turned to her children, the sight of them bleary behind full, flowing tears. "Ada, Jason, we have to go." Already there were more sounds moving amongst the surrounding vegetation. "Now, we have to go *now!*"

"What about Daddy?" Jason cried.

Iris grabbed her children's hands and they fled toward the beach path. The green of the field was almost sickly in its vibrancy. Iris ignored the strange, giant creatures in the sky above. She ignored the flies and gnats that stuck to the sweat on her face. She ignored the fleshy walking sticks in the trees near the path, and the clamorous buzz that issued from them.

They were twenty feet from the path when Jason stumbled and Iris lost grip of his hand. In the two seconds it took for her to turn and try to help him back up one of the enormous insects from the tree above descended with a creaking thud, straddling Jason with its segmented legs. Jason didn't even have time to scream before he was neatly sliced in two.

"NO!" Iris shrieked.

The insect twitched its antennae toward her, regarded her with round, unblinking eyes and then plunged a black proboscis into her son's torn body.

Iris sagged. Blood pounded in her ears, and she was born away. Her thoughts swam in a sea of hurt and anger. *Bye-bye, Jason, my sweet little boy. Bye-bye, Sean, my one and only love.* Hands gripped Iris tightly under the arms. Dragged. Her bare feet slid over the rough, weathered stones of the path. She looked up and saw Ada's face, wrinkled in effort, as she heaved Iris's body down the last few feet of the beach path.

They reached the top of the dune and Ada dropped Iris heavily and collapsed beside her, cheeks shining with tears. "They're gone.

Dammit! They're gone!" Ada said, hammering a fist into the dry, uncaring sand. Iris lay on her back for a long time, looking up at the azure dome of the heavens. There were no clouds, and no massive, flying creatures, just the bright, steady sun. Presently she stood and loped stiffly down the decline toward the tent, which gently flapped as a breeze caressed the beach. She could hear Ada behind her, feet scuffing in the powdery sand. Iris ducked into the tent and sat heavily amongst the cast-off silver packets of unknown goods, welcoming the shade.

Ada sat next to her mother. In her hands was the small nautilus shell, which she turned over and over. The spiral twirled, and the tender sound of her skin on the shell echoed the soft roar of the surf. Ada was staring out at the water. After a very long while she sniffed and spoke, "Have you noticed that the tide never changes? We've been in the same spot the whole time, and the waves never get closer, and never go out. That's impossible, isn't it?"

Iris hadn't noticed, but now that Ada said something she was surprised she hadn't. It was true. Silvertron's fortress still stood untouched five feet from the lapping waves, where it should have been swallowed sometime in the last twelve hours. Iris shook her head. "I don't think I understand anything anymore."

Ada sifted through the discarded packets and found the one she'd opened with the black circle on it. She poured out the contents on the tent floor and flicked the fine black spheres around with a finger. "There's no way out is there, Mom?"

"I don't think so, honey." Iris stared at her lap. "I used to think that when Jason got lost last year…that that was the worst feeling I could ever feel. I was so angry at your dad for…well, for a lot of things, but for drinking so much and losing him." She sighed, long and slow. "I was wrong."

"I miss them already," Ada said in a soft, distant voice. With the tip of her finger Ada stirred the hard little spheres and a puff of their acrid smell filled the tent.

"Me too." Iris saw what her daughter was doing and said, "Don't play with those, honey. They could be dangerous."

Ada ignored her mother.

"I think I'll take a swim," Iris said with a quaver in her voice. She abruptly stood, wiped at her eyes and began to peel off her shirt and shorts. "Would you like to come?"

Ada shook her head, her hair a dark veil in front of her face.

"Okay. I'll be back soon," Iris said walking toward the water. "Don't go anywhere." She waded out into the warm, choppy little breakers and dove under the surface. It felt good. Her mind was a broken battleground, and she needed something, *anything* to make her feel alive. The predictable, friendly ocean was there to fill the need. She floated on her back, tasting the salt of the water and attempting to shield herself from intrusive thoughts about the last twenty-four hours. Sean's face hovered in her mind. *Just when you think you've figured someone out they're taken away.* Her tears mingled with the ocean all around her. She felt peace. *This must be insanity,* she thought and laughed to herself.

Iris stood and looked toward the tent. She could see the humped, dark shape of Ada inside and she sighed in relief. At least she wasn't alone here. After floating for a short time, when she felt calmed, or at least calmer, Iris headed back to the tent. "That was nice," she said, shaking droplets from her hair. "You should think about going out, Ada. Ada?" As Iris got closer to the tent she could see that what she'd mistaken for the shape of Ada was actually just the cooler and a pile of towels. Ada was gone.

"Ada!" Iris whipped around, looking up and down the beach. There was no sign of the girl. "Oh my god! Ada?" She stepped back in disbelief and nearly tripped. She looked down and saw she'd stumbled through the wall of Silvertron's fort, crumbling it to bits. "ADA!"

Iris looked toward the dunes, but Ada wasn't there. She bolted southward toward the large ramble of rocks. Maybe she'd gone to find a spot to relieve herself. Iris didn't think that was true, but she had to look. Her heart pounded and the air was hot in her lungs as she arrived at the jagged mass of rocks. "Ada, where are you?" she screamed. No answer. She whirled in panic, looking back toward he tent. Far in the north stretched the stand of palm trees. She took off at a sprint.

The hot sand burnt Iris's feet as she blazed across the width of the beach. A stitch knitted her side and she slowed to a jog. After a few moments she arrived at the cluster of silent, uncaring trees. There was no sign of Ada here as well. Iris trembled in dread. "My baby girl, my baby girl," she mumbled over and over. "God, no, why?!" She looked toward the tent once again and saw a figure had appeared there. Elation soared inside her bosom. "Ada!" she yelled exuberantly as she hurried back to the campsite.

The cooler had been dragged free of the tent into the open, and a lone figure sat upon it. When Iris was midway back she could already see that it wasn't her daughter. It was a very tan woman, perhaps a few years older than Iris. Crimson paint had been applied to the upper concavity of her ears, giving them a rubicund appearance. Her salt and pepper hair was cut short, and she was as hard and toned as an Olympian. One muscular shoulder wore a web work of old scar tissue. She sported a sort of rough leather vest, scuffed jeans and a set of fearsome-looking hunting boots. A curious, spear-like weapon with a gun handle rested on her lap. At Iris's approach the woman stood and stepped quickly toward her. Without a word she produced a coil of rope and pounced on Iris, binding her hands in quick, expert knots. Iris hardly had a moment to protest before a gag was fastened over her mouth. She bucked against the restraints, but the woman was very strong. She marched toward the dunes, dragging Iris with her. Iris kicked furiously. She felt like a tiny piece of detritus bucking about on the surface of the vast ocean. She had no control over anything anymore. With a final burst of effort she went limp, and let herself be dragged down the path and away from the sunny beach.

Iris stared up through the foliage and observed a strange thing occur. As they progressed down the path the sky grew markedly darker, until it was nearly black, and the air grew so cold that Iris began to shiver. It was as if they'd come underneath an enormous, stealthy cloud of winter. They emerged from the path into a scorched field, and full night. Iris looked about, trying to reconcile this with the bright daylight she'd just been in, and bit at her gag. The woman dragged her a little farther into the clearing, and then dropped her heavily on her side. Iris watched as the woman pulled a slim, black device from inside her vest and began to speak into it. The strange language was like nothing Iris had ever heard before. It consisted mostly of a kind of inward, lip-popping noise, punctuated by whistles and occasional glottal ululations of half-formed words. It was harsh, yet musical at the same time. The woman waited, heard a response in the same bizarre language and then put the device away.

Iris trembled where she lay on her side. A cold wind blew over the burned field. This had just been a verdant expanse only an hour or so ago! Where were the rambling vines? Where were the wild flowers? Where was the body of her son? All that was left was ash and the charred, broken chunks of trees intermingled with scabby weeds and spindly beach grass. The tattered clouds above looked to be fed by plumes of smoke rising from beyond a stand of still living trees in the distance.

The woman's hard face wore a look of profound annoyance, and a sliver of fear. Apparently displeased with what she'd heard from the device, she silently gathered splintered sticks and dried brush together into a pile. She produced a small lighter with a very insistent, powerful flame and ignited the kindling, quickly bringing to life a bright, hot fire. The space around the fire warmed considerably, and Iris struggled to sit up. The woman sat for a long moment and stared at Iris. There was something so unsettling about the woman's gaze, so proprietary. Iris wanted to look away but she found she was riveted to the woman's pale green, questing eyes.

The woman stood, walked to Iris's side with the spear in one hand. She plunged the blade into the ground and knelt next to Iris to help her to a sitting position. She removed the gag, but left her hands bound tightly together.

Iris flexed her jaw and spat, "Go ahead and kill me. I don't even care anymore." The woman made no sign that she understood Iris's words as she retrieved her weapon. "Just be done with it." Iris kicked a leg out and hit the edge of a stick protruding from the fire, producing a flight of active sparks.

The woman sat opposite the fire. When she spoke it was in a measured, carefully worded fashion. "I need you to remain calm, and listen to me. Can you do that, Mother?"

The final word hit Iris between the eyes like a bullet.

There was something in the woman's face…Iris searched it, and all at once knew it was the truth. There was the brow shape of Sean, the faint spray of freckles beneath the deep tan, and low on her left jaw, the distinctive dark mole. "Ada? Is it…how?" Iris's heart felt as if it were going to lift right out of her chest. "But, you're," she paused, "so *old*."

"I'm thirty-eight. The same age as you." She came back to her mother's side and began to untie the rope. "You're not going to run away on me now are you?"

"No, of course not," Iris said, rubbing at her wrists. "Did you really have to tie me up like that?"

"I had to get you off that beach as quickly as possible. This seemed like the best way to do it. I'm sorry about that." Ada sat by her mother, stared into her eyes and put a hand to Iris's cheek. "I've missed you. I'd almost forgotten your face."

"Forgotten...how? I just saw you. I went for a swim...and now..." Iris trailed off, taking Ada's hand in hers and looking at the calloused, strong fingers of her daughter. Iris looked around the dark field; her eyes round with dismay, as if she were expecting at any moment another of the walking stick creatures to dive down from the treetops.

Picking up on Iris's fear, Ada said, "It's safe now. Those things, the ones that got Dad and Jason. They're gone. Long gone. Mostly hunted to extinction in these parts."

Iris could barely register anything her daughter was saying. Reality had disappeared in an implosion of grief and surreality, ceasing to make any sense for her. A series of blasts rocked the land beyond the dark trees surrounding the field. Lights lit the distant clouds like a southern visitation of the aurora borealis. "Ada, what's happening?"

"In the nearly two years I was on the beach looking for you the tide turned...we've lost this land." Ada looked up at the sky as if waiting for something. "It had been hard to take it in the first place." She ticked her eyes toward Iris. "But...it was absolutely worth it."

None of this was comprehensible. "Two years? What do you mean 'two years'?"

Ada stabbed the fire with a long stick and gave a soft, pensive smile. "Let me ask you...how long ago was it that you left for a swim?"

Iris frowned. "I – just, probably half an hour, maybe less."

Ada nodded, as if that was the answer she'd expected. "Mmm. That's about what I would have guessed." She sighed. "I have a theory, and given everything I've learned I'm pretty certain of it now." She looked deeply into her mother's eyes. In that moment she appeared every inch a tired warrior who had seen far too much in her lifetime. "Time moves more slowly on the beach. Given what you just told me I think it's pretty accurate to say that for every minute spent on the beach a year goes by out here, in the rest of the world." She stopped and let that sink in.

Iris reeled. She began shaking her head furiously, grabbing at her temples, trying to understand. Of all the possibilities she'd run through her mind over the past twenty-four hours, aliens, alternate realities, nightmare fugues, a time discrepancy had never even occurred to her. "Wait, you don't mean…"

"Yes. I came to the beach to find you. It took almost two minutes, and here I am, two years later, and everything's gone to shit." Ada threaded her hand through Iris's. "For you it was almost half an hour since I left the beach. For me, twenty-five years have passed. I've had a long time to think about the math, and to study what little there is left of recorded history." She grabbed Iris's hand tighter. "Mom, this," she raised her other hand to indicate all that surrounded them, "is more than a thousand years in the future. Entire empires rose and fell while we were on that beach. Mankind destroyed the world and rebuilt it, refashioning the very fabric of living things. Stay on that beach long enough and you might be the last person alive when the sun goes supernova." Ada laughed ruefully.

Iris yanked her hand away from Ada's and buried her face. It wasn't possible. None of it was possible. And yet, creatures that shouldn't even have existed killed her husband and son. Her daughter now stood before her very eyes the same age as her. Iris jumped to her feet, wanting to bolt, to run back down to the safety of the beach and be done with this horrid dream.

Ada put her hands on her hips and looked out into the field. "Just yesterday, one thousand years ago, this was a parking lot. We parked our car right over there." She gave a harsh bark of a laugh. There was a small tone from the device in Ada's pocket and she looked skyward. "We can't stay much longer. My people…they're…the people I'm with now, are at war, and our enemies have grown stronger while I was away."

As if in answer to this there sounded the quick squelch of a low siren from beyond the trees.

"Shit!" Ada said and began to stomp the fire to cinders. "We have to go." She withdrew the small device and spoke into it once again. After hearing the response she gathered up her spear-gun weapon and grabbed her mother's hand. "This way!"

Once again Iris felt helpless in the face of events outside her control. "Who is it, Ada? What are we running from?"

"Ungeta." Ada's voice was a harsh whisper as she led Iris through a patch of trees and onto a wide, scrubby path leading away from the burnt field. "They control this territory now." Ada had positioned the small communication device in a high pocket on her vest where she could hear updates from it without having to constantly take it out. The little black rectangle clicked and popped, seemingly delivering useful information, though Iris could make no better sense of it.

The siren sounded again and Ada froze. "Who are they?" Iris wondered.

"Shhh." Ada pulled Iris between two large trees and stopped again. She pointed.

Through many layers of half-burnt forest Iris saw a curious sight. What looked like a procession of faintly illumined figures stole between the blackened trunks. They were far away, and difficult to make out, but Iris was profoundly unsettled by their wraithlike appearance.

"Ungeta," Ada whispered. "If they find us…then…well, let's not let that happen. There's a place near here. It might be safe while we wait."

Iris spoke in the quietest voice she could muster. "Wait? Wait for what?"

"A miracle." Ada's smirk did not fill Iris with hope.

The train of Ungeta disappeared from view. Ada and Iris stole from their concealed location. Ada walked forward and rested a hand on a pitted nub of stone protruding from the ground. It looked as if it had once time been fashioned into an obelisk-like shape, but now only about three feet remained. "Recognize this?"

Iris shook her head. "No, should I?"

"This was the carved street sign we saw. Back when we left the beach and got chased by all those dogs." Ada gave it a final slap and pointed down a rather unremarkable, overgrown stretch of land. "Welcome back to Conch Lane."

Iris gingerly laid a hand on the rough stone. Conch Lane. She stifled a laugh. Nothing so pleasant sounding could possibly exist in such a wasted-looking world.

"This way," Ada said. She hefted her spear-gun weapon on one shoulder and walked down what was once a bustling little beach access road. Ada escorted Iris through a twist of rusted metal and broken stones, kicking at small lizards that hissed defiantly. "Those are poisonous," Ada said, mashing one of the little reptiles with the butt of her weapon. Ada slowed, looking to the left toward a low stand of trees. "It should be here somewhere…there!"

"I don't see anything," Iris said, peering into the gloom. She was cold, tired and hungry. On top of that she didn't even know what she was looking for.

Ada's hand threaded into Iris's and she jerked her toward a dark hollow in the trees. A moment later they were at an arched entrance cut into a cylindrical building that had been armored with thick plates of iron long ago. It was only a shell now, and the land had done its very best to reclaim the ponderous structure. This time Iris needed no prompting to recognize what she was looking at. She remembered it very well from their flight back to the beach as the pack of dogs had fed on a man mere feet from where she stood now. "The lighthouse-house."

"Yeah. I remember when Dad called it that," Ada said sadly. "Wait a moment. Need to see if it needs clearing." She withdrew a small metal whistle from one of her vest's many pockets and blew into it. There was no sound, but a small orange light shone on the tip. A moment later there came a panicked metallic scraping from inside the building. The sound traveled upward and then Iris saw the source of the noise. She froze, looking at one of the horrible walking stick-like creatures, identical to the one that had ended her son's life. It clutched the top edge of the building and regarded them with cold, multi-part eyes. Ada blew the whistle again and the thing staggered, nearly losing its grip on the building before leaping twenty feet to a nearby tree and scrabbling away into the darkness at a furious pace. "He won't be back." She looked at Iris. "Hurry, get inside."

Iris stepped lightly into what she thought would be a darkened interior, sure she was going to catch an insect claw to the neck at any moment. It turned out that the roof of the structure had been removed and the inside was bathed in the same sick mauve light filtering down from the sky as the rest of the forest. Iris stared at the tumbledown interior, trying to get her bearings. The enclosure was littered from wall to wall with rusting metal furniture and heavy equipment and what looked like the remnants of fences and cages. The place had clearly been converted from a house into a sort of…what…junk yard? Iris flicked a finger against a rust-eaten sheet of metal near the wall, sloughing off layers of ferrous dust. "Ada, what is this place?"

Ada crouched near the warped bars of a cage. "This was my home."

"What? What do you mean? When?"

"Hmmm." She consulted the black rectangle and then said. "We have some time." Ada's eyes flickered, rolling toward the dusky heavens as she summoned distant memories. "When I left the beach…you were swimming. I was playing with those little black spheres, and I stuffed a bunch of them into the nautilus shell I'd found to make a sort of rattle. I just sat there, rattling this shell and watching you float. Sad. Thinking about Dad, thinking about Jason. I thought about how unfair everything was. How this nightmare had found us and claimed us. Destroyed us. I wanted to go back. To bring Jason and Dad's bodies back to the beach to be with us. The longer I sat and listened to the rattle the more I thought that was the only right thing to do. I left you to float, I stuffed the shell into my pocket, I stood, and I walked up the dune. Maybe it was the biggest mistake of my life. I certainly thought that later, though I'm not sure I do anymore. I left you, knowing it was dangerous, knowing there were things, monsters in the field. What I didn't know was that I'd leave and not be able to get back. I didn't know that I'd lose you too." Ada stopped, noticing that her mother had slumped to her knees and was crying softly in the dimness.

Ada crawled to Iris's side and put an arm around her. Iris could feel the warmth of Ada's body through her clothing. She was running very hot despite the cold weather. Iris leaned closer to her daughter, letting herself be held. She'd grown even more tired, and a profound drowsiness was threatening to take hold. "Go on."

"I took the path, but when I got back to the field Dad and Jason were gone. Jason's toy, Silvertron, was there, but it was all tarnished like it had been sitting outside for a long time. I picked it up and looked for Dad. All that was left where he fell was a pile of bleached bone. The gun that he'd used had turned into a rusted, broken thing. I was confused, planning on going back to the beach, when some people who'd been hiding grabbed me. Tied me up, blindfolded me and brought me here. This place was a little village then. They forced me to work as a washerwoman in a stream not far from here.

"Two years I worked. I learned their ways. I learned their language. Occasionally a woman named Veet would take me on hunts to kill *fpoh*. Those insect things, like the one we just saw. This was their main food source." She felt Iris tense at the mention of eating the creatures. "It wasn't so bad. They reminded me of the lobster you made for my thirteenth birthday. Anyway, I tried to escape a number of times, to get back to the beach…then, I probably would have made it back while you were still out there in the water, who knows? Veet had a sharp eye though, and she never let me far from her side. She was…not averse to punishment." Ada swallowed and continued. "More time passed and we had to move along, for food began to run low, and before I knew it we were very far from here. Other tribes moved into this space and claimed it as their own. During this time many of us perished, and Veet become our leader. She was a fierce warrior, and within five years she'd expanded our new territory far beyond its original borders. I became her second-in-command, training every day to learn all that she knew."

"*Was* a fierce warrior…what happened to her?" Iris said.

Ada shook her head. "We were–" the return of the siren cut her off. Ada snapped to attention. The siren was much closer than it had been before. "Get low," she mouthed and pressed Iris down to a prone position. Ada spoke a few quick words into the small communicator. There was no answer.

Where the siren had only been short blips before, it now trilled unceasingly as it grew closer. A static-filled scrape of a noise, like a saw through bone. A sharp spotlight flipped on, bathing the face of the lighthouse-house to create a burning crescent along the unroofed rim, and filling the doorway with a shaft of illumination. Ada remained still, her hand pressed firmly down on her mother's back. Voices speaking a strain of the whistling lip-pop language conversed nearby. Suddenly the voices were silent, and three figures stepped into the enclosure.

Iris watched them from the divot of ruined flooring she hid in with her daughter. The men faintly glowed a pale blue-green in the darkness. Iris now saw this emanated mostly from their long cloaks, which swished over the debris-strewn ground. The cloaks continued up over their heads in a sort of hood that completely enclosed their heads, only leaving eyeholes for small, puffy eyes to peer through. Beneath the shimmering cloaks the men wore impressive-looking armor. Each also held something that looked like a cross between a truncheon and a handgun. They fanned out, and Iris stopped breathing as one drew closer. With every step the man's personal illumination threatened to reveal the two hidden women.

Iris felt Ada's hand slowly release from her back. Ada whispered a simple phrase, barely audible. "No way but through." The woman's powerful body tensed beside Iris, and before she could hold her back Ada had sprung from their hiding place, twirling the spear point of her weapon up into the jaw of the closest man. He fell in a heap, instantly dead. A spray of dark blood painted a constellation of violence across the pure expanse of his still glowing cloak. Ada had already moved on to the others. Iris could only helplessly watch as her daughter deftly avoided contact from the other two men's weapons. Bangs erupted from one man's firearm, flashing the curve of wall, but missing Ada. Ada's fluid movement transformed her into a machine of slaughter before her mother's eyes. The men, large with muscle and slow, were helpless under the spinning blade of Ada. The second fell with an arm sheared off at the elbow and a deep gash unzipping his midsection. The third's life was ended with a savage kick to the temple and conclusive stab to the heart after falling unconscious to the ground. Ada was not done yet. Her tour of savagery had ended near the arched entrance to the structure. She immediately dropped to one knee, aimed the spear point toward the light and pulled the trigger on the gun handle. A muffled *pop* and a projectile whizzed free from a barrel beneath the blade. The answered crack of glass and the sudden darkness told Iris that the bullet had found its mark.

Whistled shouts and the trilling siren echoed beyond the curved wall of the building. Ada scurried back toward Iris, a sheen of sweat coating her veined arms. She pressed a moist palm to her mother's cheek and said, "Are you okay?"

Iris, dumbstruck, tried to form some kind of response. "I – I – yes, I think so." Was this really her daughter?

"Get down!" Ada yelled over the increasing scream of the siren. "There are still more out there."

No sooner had Ada forced Iris back into the hollow in the floor than the wall next to them became riddled with holes. Great booms of concussive force sounded and huge, fist-sized chunks of iron were punched out of the barrier, pelting Iris and Ada with chips of rubble. Ada was whistling shrilly into the little communicator, but there was still no answer. Iris looked into Ada's pale eyes, seeing an endless well of strength and determination there. The harvest of something she'd seen glimmering in Sean's eyes when they'd first met, and in the few hours leading up to his death.

A new sound echoed in the forest. A great thunderclap reverberated the quickly deteriorating walls of the enclosure and Iris cowered. "What *now*?"

Ada smiled. "Our miracle."

Iris saw a bright flash of orange and heard screams from beyond the walls. The siren warbled and cut off in mid-shriek. Flickering light danced in the doorway, accompanied by the cast shadows of figures writhing in pain. The sounds of men burning filtered into where Iris and Ada were holed up. Suddenly the forest was quiet, all except for a low, soft hum.

A crackle of twittering clicks on Ada's communicator and she stood. "Safe now."

Iris and Ada emerged from the lighthouse-house to find a ruined stretch of ground. Weeds and Ungeta alike were reduced to black ash. The siege equipment was torn to shreds and smoldering in the patch of destruction. Before Iris could even say anything, a shape, something akin to an enormous, battered piece of driftwood, floated into view above them. An eldritch orange light glowed from within recessed crevices all along the length, pulsing with power. A steady hum originated from deep within the vessel. Iris felt unsteady on her feet. Ada quickly hopped to her side, bracing Iris as the craft came down in the center of the charred patch. The asymmetrical shape, forty feet at its longest dimension, looked nearly organic in almost every way, as if it had been grown instead of built. Ada hefted her spear and grabbed Iris's hand. "Our chariot has arrived, Mom."

Despite a current of trepidation Iris allowed herself to be led into the craft. The interior had much of the same cultivated look as the outside, though it had been refined into a space inhabitable by humans. Some surfaces almost appeared shell-like in the sparkling orange light that suffused the space. Windows looked out on the dark field. Iris was brought to a low bench that had been grown out of a wall. Ada sat her mother down and ticked a finger against the wall's surface. A small spotlight fell on them. Iris felt like she was in the whirled heart of some enormous, shaped nautilus. Speech did not come easily. "This…what is this thing, Ada?" She ran a hand over the bench, feeling the surface that was at once smooth but also had enough give to provide a comfortable seat.

Ada tapped at some recessed tabs on the wall, and the powerful hum of some deeply ensconced engine changed pitch. "A little of the ancient technology still exists. This is known as a *stirrit*. There aren't many like it, but Arksel and I have engineers who know how to service them."

"Arksel?" Iris asked, running her fingers over the smooth surface of the bench.

"Him." Ada pointed toward a compartment at the front of the vessel where a large, dark-skinned man wearing an impressively fearsome outfit of burnt orange rough fabric and black leather leaned against a curved doorframe. The inner cups of his ears were painted red like Ada's, and he had a magnificent head of jet-black hair and beard to match, like a lion carved of midnight. "This is Arksel. He's my, well I guess the word would be 'husband'." Ada moved to his side and the tall man gave her a kiss on the cheek.

They had a long exchange in the popping whistling language while staring into each other's eyes longingly. Iris realized then that if what Ada had said was true then those few minutes for Ada on the beach really had been almost two years for Arksel. She watched the way her daughter's face lit up when she looked at the man, and it reminded her all over again what love really felt like. Arksel stroked Ada's arm and then, to Iris's surprise, he turned to her and with some difficulty said, "Please to meet, Mother." He looked to Ada to see if he'd gotten the words right and she gave him a patronizing pat on his muscled shoulder.

"I've been teaching him English," Ada said with a smile. Outside the *stirrit* the sky flashed with dangerous light, and new, portentous rumbles grew steadily closer. A phalanx of sirens caterwauled in the distance. Ada looked out a window and said, "We've overstayed our welcome." Ada whistle-popped some things to Arksel in his native language that sounded quite harsh and Arksel ducked back into the front room. Iris was pressed against the wall as the *stirrit* began to move. Ada joined her and pushed another key on the wall. "I'm going to need to help get us out of here. You can stay here for now."

Iris briefly lost her balance as the bench extruded outward from the wall, extending to bed length. The surface softened considerably, and Iris gave a little bounce. It was nearly like a mattress. "Where are we going?"

Ada smiled. "Home." She walked to the front of the *stirrit*, and turned. "Are you okay?"

Iris gave a resigned little laugh. "I could use a cigarette."

"Sorry to tell you things like that don't exist anymore." Ada gave a playful little shake of her head. "I'm glad you're here, Mom. I missed you."

"I...thank you, sweetie. Me too," Iris said, turning away before more tears could come tumbling out. There'd been enough tears for one day. Enough tears for a lifetime. Iris rolled on one side and stared out the oddly shaped window. Dusty clouds skimmed by quite fast as they picked up speed. Iris thought about the years floating by faster and faster. Iris thought about numbers. One year for every minute. How long had they spent on the beach that first day? The other family that she'd tried to talk to. It made sense now. Two hours must have passed before she'd seen them. A hundred and twenty years? Was that possible? Environmental protective suits? Perhaps. And when had the Barretts left the beach, five, six hours after arriving? The dogs. Was that really what...the year 2500? What about when the giant robo-man had wandered on to the beach? How many hours, and how many years had passed? Sean's death? That feeling of being bucked about on a vast ocean returned to Iris. Minutes, years, millennia. All understanding of time blipped by like the blurring, frayed length of an unraveling rope slipping through her hands. There would be no life preserver at the end of it. Iris began to doze, hoping to wake up in her king-size bed in Winston-Salem, surrounded by periwinkle-colored walls and under a four-bladed white fan from Crate and Barrel.

A dream of flower petals. Bouquets in **Barrett's Flowers**. The store was full. Fuller than it ever could really be. Flowers of all colors covered every surface. Amidst the thorny stalks were piles of bleached bones. Wisteria vines wrapped around giant vertebrae, and blood red roses twining through the arch of ribs. Hundreds of skulls, weathered and cracked, sprouted wildflowers from violent splits and empty eyeholes. Iris reached, tearing petals and leaves from stalks, trying to find one certain skull. She yanked handfuls of flowers out by the roots. The dying, cast-off petals fell to the ground. The sharp sounds of an argument woke her. Ada and Arksel's voices, full of quick whistles and staccato lip-pops, carried back to the hold of the vessel.

Iris sat up and rubbed her eyes. She looked out the window and was surprised to see that it was dawn and they were well above the cloud layer. A wan patch of sunlight drifted over her legs as the craft banked right. Ada stormed into the room and hammered a palm against one wall. The doorway irised shut with a series of shell flaps. She gave a little scream and then sat heavily on the shining, spark-flecked floor of the *stirrit*.

Iris joined Ada on the warm floor, caressing her scarred shoulder with a tentative hand. "What is it?"

"Arksel. He's…oh, he's, hmmm. I don't know if I should talk to you about this."

Iris's lip twitched. She knew almost nothing about Ada and Arksel's relationship, and didn't want to jump in, dictating how anyone should behave. "Well, I'm here if you want to talk."

Ada smiled and looked into her mother's eyes and groaned. "I just feel guilty for coming to get you. Our…people suffered while I was gone, and maybe it was selfish, going to fetch you like that. Arksel says it wasn't, but I guess I was just venting."

"I trust you to know what's right for you, Ada. You certainly seem to have grown into a capable woman." Iris wasn't sure what else to say. "You…I may be biased, but I'm glad you came to get me."

Ada nodded and reached up, wrapping her fingers over her mother's. "Me too."

Iris stood and walked to the irregular window. She watched the ground speed by through rips in the blanket of clouds. Large swathes of land were scorched in great, dark furrows. Black shapes moved along the ground in herds, but they were too far away for Iris to see what they were. Buildings, what were left of any, were slapped together out of found materials, and any waterways they flew over were choked with brown effluence. Iris began to ache deeply while looking at the destruction that had been wrought on the face of the earth. "How bad is it?"

Ada leaned on the curved edge of the window. "Before…I didn't understand the extent of it. Arksel filled me in more this morning. Two years ago our people numbered ten thousand. Now we are half that. Our land is less than a fifth what it was. Our resources are being hijacked, bled daily by the Ungeta." She moved away from the window and walked toward the front cabin.

Iris turned. "You shouldn't beat yourself up, Ada. Do you think it would have made any difference if you were here instead of coming to find me?"

Ada stopped but did not face her mother. "Yes. *I* am the one who protected them for so long. *I* am their *kizec*. Their queen." She tapped a tab on the wall and the doorway flapped open. "I have to help Arksel pilot into Tanannet."

"What's 'Tanannet'?"

"Our last refuge." With that, Ada vanished into the front of the vessel.

Iris regarded the wasteland below with sorrow for a long while, and then a surprising thing happened. Green appeared. Actual living vegetation spread its lush fingers wide and enfolded the battered land. They dipped down below the clouds now and Iris gasped when she saw where they were headed. A broad, fecund valley stretched out before her below the *stirrit*. Snaking waterways punctuated by waterfalls cut the land into a jigsaw of thick jungle. Flocks of white birds flapped along, idly surveying the land. Here was truly a land of plenty. The *stirrit* shot low, skimming over healthy treetops. They dipped even lower into a wide gorge and Iris saw their true destination. A city, carved out of the rock face of the gorge walls itself, hove into view. She could see people, dark of skin like Arksel, on balconies or traversing rope walkways. A large river of fresh water cascaded between the two domesticated walls of Tanannet, hosting a gathering of swimmers and fishers. The *stirrit* turned abruptly and slid into a cave midway down a wall, swallowing them in darkness. The hum from its internal workings slowed, then died completely, though the orange glow inside intensified, lighting the interior surfaces with a saturated shine.

"Mom," Ada said. "We're here."

Iris followed Ada and Arksel into the cool cave, marveling once again at the organic hull of the strange vessel she'd just traveled in. Ada led her through a maze of stone passageways spiraling upward until they emerged onto a veranda fashioned from an outcropping of rock. Muslin shades were drawn against the sun, which was just beginning to peak over the opposing rock wall. Iris watched the people of Tanannet bustling about their daily duties. "It's beautiful, Ada."

With a smile and small bow Arksel continued on without them, leaving Ada beside her mother. "I know, Mom. Now you see why we can't lose this. It's peaceful here." She tapped a palm against the stone rail and said, "I have to leave you for a moment and check on something. Do you mind?"

"No, that's…fine, Ada," Iris said, relishing the feel of the warm sun still creeping higher. Ada left down another passageway and

Iris was alone. A trio of boys splashed in the water sixty feet below. Iris smiled. They could have been children from any time, from anywhere. No matter that someone who was technically more than a thousand years old was observing them without their knowledge. Iris watched the balconies across from her for a long while, forgetting about everything that had happened in the past two days, and letting herself finally feel at rest for a moment.

Iris heard a throat clear behind her. "Mom. I hope you won't mind one more surprise." Iris turned and saw Ada in the doorway. In her arms was a small boy, no more than four years old. His bronze-colored limbs were long and lean, and he had an arresting set of large, green eyes under a tumble of black hair. In his hands he held a familiar, yet very tarnished, toy robot. "This is our son. We named him Jason." Ada set the boy down and click-whistled a few words to him. He ran toward Iris and leapt into her arms, planting a big kiss on her cheek.

Iris shook with a lightning bolt of emotion. Her son, Jason, had been ripped from her arms not twenty-four hours ago, but here was a grandson, every bit as beautiful and intrepid as his namesake. The little boy hugged his grandmother tightly and made sweet, trilling little whistles. A second bolt struck Iris as she realized that Ada had sacrificed time with her son to come and find her, missing two years of the little boy's short life. Tears cascaded freely down Iris's cheeks and the little boy raised a hand to touch them. He smiled and wrinkled his nose. The mole rat face!

Iris looked to her daughter and saw not joy, but dismay. Ada's expression had grown dour. "The Ungeta are four days away from Tanannet, maybe less."

The look of helplessness in Ada's eyes tore at Iris. So much happiness had just been placed in her arms, only to have it threatened. She set the boy down and wiped at her eyes. "What will you do? What will *we* do?"

Ada shook her head. "There's nothing. No time to prepare. This is not a defensive position. It was always meant as a sort of retreat, not a stronghold." She hammered a fist against the stone. "How could I have been so stupid?"

Jason looked up at her in curiosity, perplexed by the strange language coming from his mother's mouth. He slipped his tiny hand into hers.

Max Dowdle

Iris frowned and tapped at her forehead. "Do you have more ships, like the *stirrit*? Can you evacuate?"

"Not just like the *stirrit*. But, yes. We can move the people if we need to, but this is it. We don't have anywhere *else* to go. All our buffer zones and fortified retreats have been burned or taken." Ada ground her teeth together. A vein of fury pulsed in her forehead, and her face grew nearly as red as the paint adorning her ears.

Iris looked from her furious, powerful daughter to the small boy at her side, so innocent and perfectly formed. *Walls, safety, and security...everything crumbles away eventually*, she thought. Silvertron, held tight in the small boys hands, sparkled wanly up at her in the orange light of the morning sun. She thought about the vast impenetrability of time itself, and how it was the greatest wall that could be erected around anything beloved.

Time was a fortress that would never wash away.

Iris took a deep breath and spoke very calmly, "Ada, there is only one truly safe place for us to go."

DARKER
IN THE SUN

This first edition printing of
Darker In The Sun: Stories Of Daytime Horror
could not have been possible without
the generous help of these individuals.

THANKS

Christopher Norwood
Michael Harvey
Mike Barry
Nick Hemsing
Ty & Crystal Hudson
Jennica Greco
Kendall Jones
Marcos Garza
Jeffrey & Lisa Vaca
Carlton M. Brown IV
Kinslayer Webcomic
Hector R. Ramos
Lewis Evans
Bekah
Kelley Spence
Derek Devereaux Smith
Brian Groh
Albert Rackenberg
Boris Undorf
Holger & Sasha Trinks
James Miron
Kristen A. Rismiller
Jenny & Rick Menzi
hello@glencarlson.com
Merriman Dowdle
Isaac & Leigh Miller
Daniel Miller
The Salcido Family
Jordan Beiter
Reamer Bushardt
Justin Burbage
Matt Conner
Harrison Schlewing
Kristie Sexton
Lorenzo Martinez
Virginia Tormey Friedman
Kevin Mooseles
And the rest of all our Kickstarter Backers!

MAX DOWDLE is the creator behind the mind-bending graphic novel *Shattered With Curve Of Horn,* as well as co-author and artist of *An Unlikely Refugee,* a non-fiction graphic novel held in the collection of the Smithsonian Institute. Painter, writer, teacher, Max Dowdle lives in North Carolina, the state of his birth, where he continues to seek illumination of life through ever-expanding expressions of art.

ARTAGEM
GRAPHIC
LIBRARY